D1193905

ANNA INCOGNITO

anna incognito

LAURA PREBLE

www.mascotbooks.com

Anna Incognito

For more information, please contact:
Mascot Books
620 Herndon Parkway #320
Herndon, VA 20170
info@mascotbooks.com

Library of Congress Control Number: 2018912810

CPSIA Code: PRFRE1019A
ISBN-13: 978-1-64307-136-7

Printed in Canada

For all the broken, bruised, battered, and abandoned people:

"I do not understand the mystery of grace—only that it meets us where we are and does not leave us where it found us."
—Anne Lamott

1

BLIND SPOTS

On this germ-infested dirtball called Earth, creatures called humans eat, drink, shit, and otherwise play elaborate games of hide-and-seek. All of these things carry with them enormous risks. Foodborne illnesses account for a significant number of deaths each year, and those don't even include water. Heard of cholera? Typhoid? Flint, Michigan? Water. Can't live with it, can't live without it. And don't get me started on shit. Hence, the game. Hiding, seeking, hiding again…on and on, an endless cycle.

All of that hiding and seeking eventually kills you. Because whatever you *do* find, even if it's incredibly precious, will be washed away, buried, tucked into a forgotten shoebox and hidden again, and you'll never, ever find it. And this will break your heart.

I am currently hiding from a small, cream-colored envelope printed on high-end paper stock, the kind you find in a quaint stationery store in a quaint neighborhood that became unaffordable two years ago.

It's lying on the counter next to the kitchen sink. It's an invitation, actually; I haven't opened it. I haven't opened it for 46 days, six hours, three minutes, two seconds. It catches the corner of my eye every morning, taunting me. If I don't open it, I don't have to answer, and if I don't answer, I am not committed to attending anything. I hate crowds.

The fancy cream-and-gold envelope bears a stamp in the corner, with one edge partially folded up, that has a drawing of a duck on it. Why would anyone design postage stamps? Why do we need art on postage stamps in the first place? With the economy in such dismal shape, it certainly seems that we could do away with something as unnecessary as waterfowl on our government documents. Stupid duck.

"Anna?" I hear the nasal whine from below my kitchen window. My downstairs neighbor, Petra, is waving to me from the alley where the trash cans sit, ready to assault me with bacteria. I know that sounds paranoid, but seriously...they are full of dog hair and flea detritus and God knows how much fecal matter. Petra owns a grooming salon for pets, and the stuff she throws out in those garbage bins should be categorized as hazardous waste. I am probably breathing a toxic mixture of dog doo and cat dander every time I open the window, which I don't. Unless she yells at me, in which case I can't avoid it.

I slide the aluminum frame up, and hold my breath, waving.

"Anna!" she yells again, motioning for me to open the window wider. I shake my head, and she sighs loudly, exasperated. "I'm coming up."

Petra comes to my apartment about twice a week, usually to complain about a client or a boyfriend. We're not exactly friends; I'd say that it's more a kidnapper-kidnappee relationship. I cannot escape. When she decides to bluster into my place it's like a parade cartoon balloon escaped from its moorings and I just duck, hoping not to get run over.

I hear the inevitable *galumph* of her broad ass thundering up the stairs, the click of the tiny patent flats she somehow wedges onto her hippopotamus feet.

"Anna?" she says in a sing-song voice. I know I won't escape, so I open the door and she hurricanes in with a sweep of spicy perfume, yards of red crepe flowing like a pirate flag from her massive chest. Tiny purple bows dot the neckline, nicely framing her turkey wattle. She tries to hug me. I dodge it.

"My God, this day!" She throws herself onto my sofa, and tiny motes of anti-bacterial talcum powder rise up like dust devils from an arid polyester desert. "I think it's going to get up to 95, easy."

"It's summer and it's inland California," I mutter, backing into the corner by the fireplace. Petra's orange, straw-like hair could ignite at any moment.

"Of course, it's summer, but at least it's not humid!" she says, nodding, using the ends of her red shirt to mop the fat lady sweat from her forehead. I imagine salty drops embedding themselves into the fabric of my couch cushions and I shudder. "That's why I love California. Where I grew up, Flatbush, oh my goodness! The humidity! But here, everybody wants their poodles clipped, their cats declawed and such. I'm so busy I can't even take the time to eat." I see her notice the fancy envelope. She pulls herself up and grabs it, ripping open the corner before I can stop her. "Oooooo...what's *this*?"

"I'm calling the police," I warn.

That stops her. "Why?"

"You opened my mail. That's a federal offense."

She rolls her eyes at me and continues serrating the edge of the envelope with her blood-red nail. "Please. As if you'd let a bunch of smelly policemen bust in and root around your place." She slips the invitation out of the envelope. Her face goes pale. "Oh."

"What is it?" Now *I* want to know.

"Nothing." She hides it behind her back. "Nothing. Just junk mail."

I frown at her. "Nobody sends junk mail in that kind of envelope."

"Oh sure." She's edging toward the door, envelope in tow. "Nigerian princes, you know, all the scammers. That's how they get you to open it."

I cut her off from her exit, brace my body against the door.

She panics. "There might be anthrax in it?"

I'm too fast and she's too big. I snatch the invitation from her. I read it.

Sound is sucked into the vacuum of crisis, crumbs of birdsong and motorcycle engines and ice cream truck jingle-jangle mixed together into a heady cocktail of nothing. A rush of thunder hits my ears, and the next thing I know, I'm flat on my back, looking up into the untended fields of Petra's nose hairs. "Oh my God, Anna, are you with us? Darling, come on! What happened?" She's fanning me with the sweat-stained pirate flag shirt. Jesus! I'll be fully engulfed in infectious disease before lunch.

"I'm fine," I mutter, waving away her swollen sausage fingers.

"You don't look fine. You look like you passed out."

"I did pass out."

"It might be the heat," she offers, motioning toward the window, the sun, the conspiracy of God and the Weather Channel. "Summer, and all."

"It's not the heat." I struggle to stand, and I still feel woozy. My wig is askew, I can feel it, so I try to tug at it without her seeing. "Excuse me for a minute." I weave a path to the bathroom, close the door, turn on the bare bulb above the sink, and in the mirror, there is a pale woman staring back at me. She's 42, with a dark, straight bob of a wig perched on her head sideways. Bad, bad, really bad. Dr. Denture's *wedding.* That's what the goddamned invitation was. I'd tell myself I never would have guessed, but I would be lying. Of all the things it could have been, an invitation to the inaugural ball of Howdy Doody would've been more predictable. But Dr. Denture's *wedding?*

Tap, tap, tap. "Anna?" From the other side of the door, Petra's whine fills my hallway. "Honey, are you okay?"

I dab a cloth at my eyes which are round dark spheres, root beer jawbreakers rolling around in the gumball machine of a head attached to my narrow shoulders. "Dr. Denture. Married." The statement rings through the bathroom, echoes off the scrubbed white tile, swipes silver off the mirror, and lands in the back of my throat, where it swells and threatens to choke me.

My translucent skin stretches over my skull like a balloon, moon-white and thin to the point of splitting. That skin, that balloon, tethers my soul to the Earth, the germy dirtball full of disease and disappointment. I guess this is why I pick at my skin incessantly, trying to breach the membrane that holds me in. I bite at my fingers until I turn the geography of my hands into a bloody map of my sins and transgressions. I'm hoping for release.

That doesn't mean I want to…leave. I think I resent my balloon. I don't like being so committed to something physical. And yet, I am.

"Anna?" Petra stands sentinel on the other side of the door. A frightened *tap-tap*, a jiggle of the door handle.

"I'm washing my face," I call, violently turning the tap on so the water gushes into the porcelain bowl and onto my pants. I splash some water to support the story and pump some soap into my palm, but the soap stings and finds all the ragged crevices in my fingers, the cracks and fissures I break open anew every day. I am my own Prometheus. It heals, I bite it, it heals, I bite. Rinse and repeat.

Soap stings like a bitch. I try putting bandages on my thumbs, but they get wet, and then the skin underneath looks like a fish belly, bloated and white and dead. But if I don't put on the bandages I constantly pick at the ragged edges, trying to smooth them down with the imperfect instrument of my teeth, which are, ironically, full of germs.

Whoever designed this life had a wicked sense of humor.

"I'll come back later," Petra says as she clip-clops away. "I hear my client's cockapoo having a panic attack. Hang on, Sugarbucket!" She's yelling support to the dog, not to me. At least, I *assume* I'm not "Sugarbucket." Plus, a dog panic attack is a much bigger deal to Petra than a neighbor panic attack as I'm unlikely to crap on her carpet. Then again, this has been an unusual day.

I don't go very many places due to the unusual demands of my trichotillomania. That's the uncontrollable urge to systematically yank every hair from your body. It's a very high-maintenance disability, actually, and when you combine it with obsessive compulsive disorder, things can often become downright unmanageable. My problem with mental illness is that most people see it as something of a choice. Just think about the context of comments like "that's crazy!" or "that's nuts!" You just don't hear people saying things like "that's diabetes!" or "that's epileptic!" when something is cuckoo and considered weird.

Somatic psychologists like Dr. Denture believe that mental illness is absolutely the equal of physical illness, that they are simply twins born of the same womb (the womb, of course, is the frailty of the human condition, otherwise known as that germ-ridden meat bubble, the body). Dr. Denture preaches that the body and its engine, the brain, are the physical manifestations of all of our flaws: psychic, spiritual, and dermatological. If there were some efficient way to Botox your brain the same way you can your wrinkles, probably everybody would feel better, and our collective cerebellums (cerebelli?) would look and feel younger.

That would be great, but so far, it's much easier to fix the paint job than the computer navigation system in the ol' soul sedan. Minds are a terrible thing to waste, but in order to make sure they work we have to pump them full of pills and potions, and wear wigs, and stop biting our fingers, and cry about our mommies, and analyze our collective penises (Peni? Penne?) for obvious signs of cigar burn.

So my point is, I don't go out much. You can probably understand why. My version of small talk tends to frighten people, men especially.

Edward Denture was an exception. He was exceptional.

Counting the rough tan and gray stones that make up the wall of the building opposite my apartment, I think of the time six months ago when Edward and I first met. It was at the laundromat. I know that's an unusual place to meet someone who would change the course of your life, but we both had run out of underwear. And so, our meeting seemed very practical, and Edward was nothing if not practical.

The Fluffitorium was the closest washing place to my apartment, and, through special arrangement with the management, I had thoroughly cleaned the facility after hours with a potent mixture of Lysol and volcanic pumice. Some people with more sensitive noses complained that they lost consciousness, but in general I think that had more to do with the proximity of the Whistle Stop bar and a certain absinthe Happy Hour special than with my cleaning solution.

Although I had cleaned thoroughly until two in the morning (the kind owner who lived above the shop had locked me in so I could stay as late as I wanted), I had slept later than I intended, and since it took me nearly three hours to sort my clothes, I didn't get to the Fluffitorium until nearly one in the afternoon. Luckily, I had the forethought to stripe yellow caution tape across the best washer and the best dryer before I left in the early hours, just in case I wasn't the first one in. Having a sparkling-clean washer and dryer took a lot of stress out of my day, I have to tell you. Washing at a laundromat is one of the·most frightening things a germophobe can do. You'd think it would be fine, with all the soap and hot water…but you have to account for the fact that your fellow launderers are strangers, and that they could have poor hygiene habits. I could be facing full-on poopy pants spinning about, under-soaped, on delicate. With cold water. It's all just a wild card, and I'm not willing to gamble with my life.

So, I walked into the shop carrying my hypoallergenic Egyptian cotton washbag with super micro-HEPA filtration, and there was Edward Denture, wantonly using the machines I had cordoned off with caution tape.

"Excuse me," I whispered, a nearly-inaudible croak, to this tall, ridiculously handsome man who hovered like a folded praying mantis over my washer. He didn't hear me at first.

A rage familiar only to those with a hair-trigger temper and an acquaintance with psychotropic drugs mixed with premenstrual hormones overtook me, and I closed in on him, coming within two feet of his massive shoulder. Stretched over it was one strap of a pair of suspenders patterned with a black-and-white negative print of Sigmund Freud's face.

The praying mantis man turned to me, and I stared up into a ferret face, a weasel idol carved of alabaster, studded with greenish sapphire eyes, wild-white at the edges. His eyes reminded me of the horses I frightened at my father's stables when I was a child. They expressed just a hint of panic edged with the desire to run like hell. "Yes?" he asked expectantly.

"These are my machines." I said it sub-audibly. With my mind. He just stared at me.

"Did you say something?" He asked in a deep velvet voice, British, cultured.

I nodded. He noticed that I had made a mental comment. *He noticed!* I felt flattered.

Again he said, "Did you say something? I thought I saw your mouth move." He was looking *at my mouth*. That put me in such a state of excited fear that I nearly bolted out of the place despite the fact that my underwear was in desperate need of washing. Underwear. *He would see my underwear.* And that's when he touched my arm.

I felt like someone had lit a rocket under my wig.

I stared at his hand. You can tell a lot about a person from their hands, actually; whether they work outside, whether they're married, whether they wash properly. This man had the most perfectly manicured fingers of anyone I'd ever met. It made my heart leap with joy. No nasty germs under those fingernails, certainly. Curved on top, perfectly spatulate nails (a sign of intuitive insight), crowning long, slender pianist fingers.

"Could we sit for a moment?" His voice snapped me out of the hand examination. When I focused on his face again, the wild look was gone. His eyes were calm and slightly crinkled at the edges like the crust of an unbaked apple tart. I felt hungry suddenly. "Could we sit?" he repeated in that lovely baritone. I nodded.

He gently steered me by the elbow to a wooden bench near the detergent dispenser. Before I could sit, he took a package of wet wipes from his pocket, efficiently plucked one from the pack, and cleaned the seat and back before gesturing toward it. I sat, ecstatic.

He didn't clean his side of the bench, but he did sit down next to me, keeping an appropriate distance. I clutched my bag of underwear nervously.

"My name is Edward," he said, smiling. He waited, and I guess I was supposed to introduce myself, which I did, sub-audibly. "Could you say your name aloud?"

"Could you tell that I said it in my head?" In my amazement, I forgot to remain paralyzed by my fear of strangers.

He grinned, those beautiful blue-green eyes crinkling again. "I sort of thought you might have. But it would help if you said it out loud."

An awkward pause. So many thoughts were swirling around in my head...but I couldn't say any of them. So, Edward spoke again. "Listen. I'm sorry about the machines. I came in and all the others were being used, and I was in kind of a hurry. I just started a wash cycle, though, if you'd like to put your things in with mine. As long as they're permanent press, of course."

He grinned congenially as my insides melted. The thought of my underwear co-mingling with his clothing nearly caused me to have a syncopal episode (that's fainting. I prefer the term 'syncopal episode' because fainting sounds like something a Victorian lady does on a fancy couch. I am far from Victorian, and even farther from being a lady.)

"Could you look at me?" he asked. I turned to face him. He smiled again. "You have very lovely eyes." I felt a hot blush rising from my neck to my face, and I stared down at the floor again. "You do. Well, anyway, I can see this is making you uncomfortable, so I'll just take my things and get out of your way." He rose and stretched, and when he did, my face was parallel with the snap of his khaki pants. I felt my blush intensify.

He was going to disappear if I didn't say something. I watched him walk to the washing machine, open the door, and scoop out a pile of wet oxford shirts in a rainbow of colors. He piled them into a white plastic basket, turned, and tossed me a casual wave before he scoped the laundromat for another open washer. There weren't any. The place was packed. He shrugged, turned to me again, and waved as he snugged the basket against his hip and started to walk toward the door.

"Wait!" I heard myself yell as I bolted straight up from the bench.

Edward turned and, standing in the doorway, he was framed with a golden corona of pollution-filtered sunlight from behind. It was as if we were alone, as if everyone else faded into the dark shadow of a movie scene. Just as I took a step toward him, an immense woman trailing a cloud of children muscled through the door, knocking Edward inward and to the floor with the force of a flesh tsunami.

And then she made a beeline for our washer and dryer.

This is how I knew it was love: I went right to his side. I paid no mind to the underwear, or other people and their various germs. I knelt next to his prostrate form, fanned him with a circular from Pests-R-Us, and saw nothing but his injured body. "Are you alright?" I whispered. I nearly took his hand.

He sat up, shook his head, and blinked twice. "What happened?"

I gestured toward the flip-flop-wearing family loading the washer with the efficiency of a surgical strike team. "I guess they needed to do their laundry."

And then he smiled at me. He looked into my eyes. "What's your name?"

I tried to tell him, but I couldn't. My own name stuck in my throat, a boulder of insecurity.

"Okay," he said, a slight grin tugging at the side of his mouth. "Want me to guess? How about Matilda?"

I shook my head. I felt my wig slip slightly. I couldn't do too many more of those shakes or I'd lose it all together.

"Cleo?"

"Anna." My voice sounded like a distant recording of a weak, wispy spirit trying to communicate from beyond. Plus, it squeaked. I cleared my throat slightly and tried again. "My name is Anna." Better that time. Clearer.

"Anna. Nice name." He pointed to his suspenders. "That was the name of Freud's daughter, you know."

"Hmm."

"Anna." When he said my name, it sounded like music. I felt something stir, somewhere below my belly button, and the feeling disturbed me.

"I have to go," I muttered, gathering up my things and making a dash for the door, dirty underwear be damned.

"Wait." He blocked the exit. With his height, it was easy to do. "Listen, if you ever want to talk, give me a call." He fished his business card from his wallet and handed it to me. My fingers brushed the skin of his hand; an invisible zing of electricity traveled up the length of my arm as if I'd been hit by lightning. I couldn't even look at the card. I clutched it in my damp hand and scampered out of the Fluffitorium, watching the dirty ground with every pace, monitoring the hurried steps of my immaculate canvas shoes.

"Phone me if you'd like to," he called after me.

I didn't look back. My heart pounded, oxygen intake lessened, and colors ran in party-bright streaks as I followed my shoes back home. Not until my door—my good solid door—was shut behind me and my laundry was safely stowed in the antibacterial hamper did I pause for breath, pause to really look at his business card.

My pulse beating in my ears, I traced the edges of the card and examined every molecule. Ivory, thick stock, with a sage trim (a wonderful color for mental illness: it connotes a non-threatening atmosphere as well as suggests growth, as in plants.) His name was embossed in sans serif letters (very non-pretentious): *Dr. Edward Denture*. Beneath his name, in smaller type, it read *Somatic Psychologist/Life Coach*.

· · ·

The invitation, crumpled in my hand, mocks me.

Married. Dr. Denture. Edward. Married.

The same words keep pinging through a dark field of emptiness, neon streaks that you pass on a freeway when your bus drives really fast through barren nighttime desert. I try to ignore them, close my eyes, hum, curl up on the sofa, but I still see the words streaking by, speeding toward the inevitable end of the world.

Petra clomps up the stairs again; presumably Sugarbucket is either subdued or deceased. "Anna?" she calls as she raps her knuckles on the door.

If I don't answer, she will not go away as most people would. Petra and I share a bond, despite our polar-opposite habits regarding hygiene and wild animals. She somehow pries my secrets out of me. I am unable to keep information from her, as if she's my confessor. This, I believe, is one of God's roguish jokes: pair an obese, codependent woman blithely unaware of infectious disease with a thin, reclusive germophobe cursed with an obsessive-compulsive desire to be left alone. God probably works for cable television.

"Anna, I know you're still in there," she wheezes. "It's hot as blazes out here. Don't make me go downstairs and come back up. I might have a stroke." She's also a hypochondriac.

Might as well unlock the door and let her in. In my careless freak out I only locked one of the three bolts on my door, so it's a snap to open. I retreat to the sofa.

She sits next to me. "Honey," she says gently, as she attempts to pat my hand. I bury my hand between couch cushions. "Let's talk about this."

I shake my head.

"Here." She pries the wrinkled invitation from my left hand. "Now. I know this must be a bit of a shock, hmm?"

I nod.

"When was the last time you talked to him?"

When was it? Suddenly, I feel hot and dry, scratchy and unbearably dirty. "I need to take a shower."

Petra, who is somewhat used to my idiosyncrasies, sighs heavily and pulls a fashion magazine from the ponderous, pet-hair festooned bag she carries everywhere, which is now shedding on my clean floor. "I'll wait."

In the bathroom mirror, my reflection seems older than I am. Ah, the wig. It's so wonderful when it comes off and I can pass it off to Annabella, my wig head. Her skin is perfectly matte, the shade of a Georgia peach. Her closed eyes, lids touched with smoke-gray shadows, float above garnet geisha lips pursed in the perpetual hint of a smile. He bought it for me, as a present. He named her, too, I remember, when we were sitting at a picnic in Collier Park.

. . .

"Open it." He shoved a big box wrapped in blue, green, and gold striped paper toward me. The gold satin bow fluttered in the breeze. Some small voice inside struggled like a firefly trapped in a glass jar, sending signals that this was unusual, not the way therapists and clients behaved.

Spring. I had been his client for a year, nearly, and he knew how much I hated being outdoors, even in sunny California. Too unpredictable and full of contagion, but he had made me do it because it was my birthday.

"Could we just go inside?" I squeaked, eyeing the nearby homeless man scratching at the living creatures in his beard-condo. Ants crawled in the dirt at my feet, and despite the fact that I had worn a black hypoallergenic leotard, leggings, and neoprene boots (germs do not like neoprene, just so you know), I felt uneasy.

"Just relax and breathe," Edward said, leaning against the rotted bark and probable termite detritus of an old oak tree. "Come sit by me."

Shuddering inside but excited about sitting next to him, I moved incrementally closer, scanning our plastic picnic blanket for dirt or, more importantly, rogue animal feces. That firefly voice, small and indistinct, disapproving, nagged at me. I banished it back to its glass jar prison. *Oh, what the hell,* I thought to myself. *It's worth it.*

I snuggled close, and his long, dampish arm draped across my shoulder, releasing an invisible scent cloud of Acqua di Gio, glycerin soap, and burnt matches. The scratch of the pink oxford broadcloth of his shirt, the feel of his chin resting on my wig, our hips nearly touching. It was as if a bubble of wonderful enveloped me, and I was blissfully able to just forget. To forget the world, the germs, the tree, the ants, the homeless beard-condo and its residents. Well, I couldn't totally forget, but enough that I could simply feel…something.

Was it pleasure? As I thought about it, it rolled through my mind, down to my tongue like a delicious cold fruit, a frozen cherry, foreign and exotic. I felt good.

"Open your present," he insisted.

"I don't want to move."

I heard him laugh, I felt it, a wave of sound from his chest to my body. "I'll do it, then."

He very slowly and carefully slipped his finger through the shining lines of tape that held the wrapping together, careful not to rip it.

When it was done, there was a large, sage-colored box with a square lid.

"There. Now open it," he said.

I lifted the lid. A beatific face, eyes closed in blissful rest, caused me to exhale with joy. "What is it?"

He lifted it from the box and turned it so I could see the delicate deco features. "It's a head. For your wig."

I didn't know what to say. I rarely took the wig off, except to shower and sleep, and he knew that. "Why would you get me that?"

He smiled gently, put the head back in the box. "This is Annabella," he said. "She's your relief pitcher."

"Hmm?"

"You know baseball?"

"I've heard of it." I unconsciously stroked her cheek. Smooth.

"In baseball, when the pitcher gets tired, he gets a reliever. So, Annabella is your reliever."

I lifted Annabella from the box. Now that I really looked at her, I saw who she really was: me. A perfect version of me. No pits, no rifts, whole and unbroken.

"Do you like it?" He grinned expectantly at me. I turned to look into his eyes, those bright eyes I could never really look into for any length of time.

"She's perfect."

He sighed, content. I felt something. I just stroked Annabella's head until the feeling went away.

. . .

"Anna!" Petra pounds on the bathroom door as I sit on the toilet, staring at my wig perched on Annabella.

"What?"

"You've got to come out of there." She shifts her weight; my floorboards groan. "It's not that bad. Can we talk about it? Anna?"

I open the door.

Petra hovers like a fish, gasping for air. "Your hair." A statement, fact, said with astonished admiration. "*Your hair.*"

Mmmm. The fuzzy baby duck near-baldness of my ravaged scalp catches the breeze from the hall fan. "You've seen it before."

"I have not," Petra says, shaking her head, still staring as if she expects to see a clandestine message spelled out in dying follicles. "Can I touch it?"

"No." I brush past her, into the hall and to the kitchen, my scalp still breathing delicious freedom. "I need to eat something."

"Oh." Petra's latent Jewish mother tendencies roll right over her need to feel my hair. "Sure, honey, if you need to eat. Got anything chocolate?"

She follows me into the kitchen, which is, as usual, immaculate. As if she's my personal Martha Stewart, she opens the fridge and starts rooting around for yummies, which makes my stomach roil. "Got any of the Nutella? I love that stuff." All I see is her massive haunches sticking out of my refrigerator, as if an unlucky beast had collided head-on with a shiny white semi. Removing herself and closing the door she says, "What are you having?"

"I think I'll have this." I pull a large tin of Belgian chocolate-covered cookies from my alphabetized pantry (the cookies are between baking powder and Bisquick) and pry off the green-gold lid to reveal a pristine landscape of un-nibbled butter cookies drizzled with milk chocolate. Petra hums in delight, picks out a striped delicacy, and, extending one red-nailed pinkie, takes a chomp before spitting it into her hand.

"How old are these?" She discreetly takes the piece of cookie to my trashcan and shoves it in.

Looking at the bottom of the tin, it appears that they are a bit past the best-by date. "They were made in 2000."

"Well, sweeties, those aren't edible." She grabs the tin and purposefully sets in on the counter. "You could get some kind of disease from that!"

"Like what?"

"I don't know!" she says. "Botulism, or something."

"You can't get sick from cookies." I grab the tin and pitch it neatly into the trash receptacle, and Petra gasps like I've committed a heinous sin even though she refused to eat the ancient sweets.

"Well, what else have you got? Want a drink?" She opens the cupboard over my stove as if she's hunting. "You must have some cognac."

"I don't drink."

"Why not, for god's sake?"

"I don't know." I spot a box of water crackers on the bottom shelf. I think if they're sealed they're still okay. I hand them to her.

"Sweeties, listen." She pulls my arm until the rest of me follows, and she plants me in one of my kitchen chairs. She sits in the other, and it sags in protest. "This just can't derail all your progress."

"What progress?" I take the box of crackers from her, rip the end off of the package savagely, and extricate the wafers from their coffin. Ripping the inner wrapping with my teeth, I ease a handful of crisps from the sleeve.

"Don't use your teeth!" Petra screeches.

"Why not?"

"You could break them!" She grabs two crackers and starts to munch noisily, dropping crumbs like snow onto my clean floor.

"What progress?" I ask again.

Her large brown eyes (one with a severely drooping eyelid) focus on me sadly. "You were just getting over him."

"No." I shake my head. My bald head.

"Yes, you were." Petra touches my hand and I instinctively jerk it away. "After he left...I was kind of worried, to be honest." She leans forward, the parasail shirt flapping open to reveal the upper slope of her Alpine breasts. She's still talking. "Now, maybe you should just forget all about this. Forget about the wedding. I don't even know why on Earth he sent you an invitation."

"Because we were friends." I'm still staring at the wrinkles and fine lines traversing Petra's chest. It's almost like photos of Mars I've seen, the dusty red soil crisscrossed with desiccated river valleys, the ancient memories of liquid and the flow of life. "We *were* friends." I'm trying to convince myself.

She pats my hand. "Sure you were, honey. But why torture your-self? Even people who aren't crazy don't do that."

Crazy. I really hate when people use that word.

. . .

I kept Edward's business card for a long time after we met at the laundromat, before I mustered up the courage to actually call. I set it on my counter, and each day I would have a staring match with it. I sat on my sofa and tried to watch some inane television program, but the card kept calling me like an unwanted telemarketer. (By the way, if you really want to get rid of unwanted telemarketers, two strategies have worked for me. The first: tell them you are deceased and cry hysterical-ly about how much you miss yourself. The second: tell the person on the other end of the line the truth, the absolute truth, about how crazy you are. If some people were honest about this, it would scare the living scat out of most people.) And still that business card stared at me, no matter how many times I cried or told it I was crazy.

So, in the end I called him.

"Golden Hill Associates," a smooth female voice greeted me. I hung up.

Who was this woman answering his phone? What kind of a whore-monger was this man, Edward Denture? Why did he have wanton women with smooth voices answering his phones? And what else were they doing for him? Rage. Rage bubbled up inside of me.

Petra came to visit that day. "Everybody has a secretary, sweeties," she said. "That's nothing. Call back."

The next day, I went through the same routine with the sofa, the inane television shows, and the business card, which taunted me from the counter. I ate nothing; I didn't even put on my wig.

At exactly 2 p.m., I called again. "Golden Hill Associates," the same voice answered, in the same sweet, smooth, soothing tone as yesterday.

"I'm calling for Dr. Edward Denture." My face felt hot, flushed.

"Are you a client?"

Was I a client? Or something more? "I have a disability advocate," I blurted.

Ms. Smooth Voice paused. The open space over the phone line filled with disapproving frowns, wry arching of eyebrows, internal chuckles. I knew she was laughing at me, probably making that stupid cuckoo sign to some other secretary sitting next to her. "Oh. I meant, are you a client of Dr. Denture's?"

"No."

Another pause full of hilarious contempt. "Would you like to make an appointment?"

"Well, I certainly didn't call to order a pizza."

"No, of course not." Ms. Smooth Voice chuckled. "He makes lousy pizza anyway. Don't tell him I told you."

She'd eaten pizza with him. The skin on my face grew hotter.

"So, you'd like an appointment," she said smoothly. "When would you like to come in?"

"Whenever he wants to see me."

Now Ms. Smooth Voice sounded confused. "So, you have been in before, or no?"

"No. Are you deaf in addition to being condescending?"

A choking sound. Ms. Smooth Voice apparently gagged on her own superiority. "No, no. I apologize if you...if I didn't answer your questions. Could I have your name?"

"Anna."

Pause again. "Anna. Last name?"

"Beck."

"Alright Ms. Beck. What about coming in...tomorrow? We have a cancellation at 10:30 in the morning. Would that work for you?"

"Yes." A date! I had a date with him! My heart raced, and my face started to pulse as if my blood was rushing in rivers all around my body at hyper speed.

"Alright, Ms. Beck. We'll see you tomorrow. Could you come a bit early to fill out some paperwork?"

"Of course." The phone call ended with a click, and Ms. Smooth Voice was snuffed out, with just the touch of a button. I imagined that it was attached to a tiny nuclear device that exploded in the confined area around her desk, vaporizing her and the other good-looking secretary next to her. My nuclear bomb, unlike conventional weapons, would have no fallout. It would be untraceable.

As I replaced the phone on its cradle, something snapped in my chest, something small and intangible but real nonetheless. I had to tell *somebody.*

Since the only person I actually spoke to in whole sentences was Petra, it was the pet grooming salon or nothing. Ugh. The smell of the place nauseated me. Old wet dog mingled with cat pee and cabbage to create an unforgettable scent sensation.

I carefully settled my wig on my head, adjusted it, and picked my way down the creaking stairs to the first-floor landing. The wooden boards were full of pockmarks, pits in the dirty grain of the dark wood. Sunlight emphasized the tapestry of stains and footprints and food spills and who knows what else, an archaeological record of all of the nasty flotsam, both human and animal, that had landed and bounced on that floor over the years. I flinched, even with shoes on.

I had to walk outside to get to Petra's salon. I hated going outside and avoided it whenever possible. It smelled of people and gasoline and garbage, and I always felt that when I left the house, especially in the daylight, all the smells and stains were waiting to pounce on me, a passel of bloodshot-eyed corruption perched, vulture-like, on the edges of trashcans and fire hydrants. Light made them stronger.

The blue and green sign read Petra's Pet sPot. I had told her when she first put it up that is sounded as if she were cooking poodles and Pekingese in a big cauldron, but she thought it was unbearably clever, so she ignored what I said. The screeching of a devil cat emanated from the salon. I grimaced and grabbed the door handle with my sleeve, pushed it open as wide as I could, and dodged inside before I had contact with the door.

Petra wore a navy-blue sailor suit with what had been a pertly tied red bow around the collar. Unfortunately, some beast at some point in the day had smeared a yellowish substance along one sleeve, and the current feline client had clawed through the red bow, leaving it shredded like the fringy scrubbing strips inside an automatic car wash.

When Petra saw me, she gasped. "Anna?" She dropped the evil cat, then dropped a lid over its bathing area so it couldn't get out. "What happened? You're all flushed."

I was unable to speak. I just stared at her, words sticking in my throat.

"Anna? Did something happen?" She came to the door, ignoring the screeching cat.

She stared into my eyes as if I was inanimate. "Can you hear me?"

"Of course I can hear you."

"Oh, good." She backed up. "I thought maybe you were having one of those, you know, one of those spells. What are they called? Dish disorders?"

"Dissociative disorder?"

"Yes, that's the one." Petra went back and peeked into the cat bath, frowning at the yowling of the detained feline. "You remember, we talked about it the last time, when you were sitting on the curb not moving? After I came back from the dermatologist who burned off that mole? That was terrible. I hurt for days after." Since the fact that I answered her implied that I was not having an episode, Petra started moving bottles and brushes around, pulling a huge pair of yellow rubber gloves from a drawer so she could wrangle the wet cat.

"No. I'm not dissociative. I just…I just made an appointment."

"Hmm." She tipped the lid of the cat bath, and a large drippy paw swiped at her. "Bad tempered little darling. I should drown him and help out the owner." Her brain caught up with what I just said. "You made an appointment? With who?"

"Whom. With whom." I had almost reached my exposure limit and felt the tug of my apartment, but I had to tell her. "I made an appointment with a doctor I met."

"A doctor." She said it slowly, as if it were a magic spell. Her eyes widened. "You mean, like, a therapist? But that's wonderful, sweeties!" She grinned and bounded over to me. She threatened to hug me, but I stopped her with one very firm hand placed in the space between us. "Oh, yes. Sorry. I'm just so happy for you. You're going to see a therapist? How did that happen? I've been telling you to see one for as long as I've known you!"

"We met in the Fluffitorium," I began. But then I realized I didn't want to share all the details. I wanted to keep this secret, private joy to myself, to be sure it stayed fresh and pure. "I'm going tomorrow."

"Oh, Anna. That is excellent news. Do you need a ride or anything?" She went back to the cat bath, ready to extricate the understandably miffed feline.

Did I need a ride? I had no idea. "I might."

"Well, you let me know. I'll be glad to close up and give you a ride. What time?"

"10:30." I really didn't want a ride, but I had no idea where the office was. I must have been excited. I never leave such things to chance. But obviously, the universe planned for this to happen, so all the details would be worked out.

Dr. Edward Denture. He would save me.

. . .

I have to save him.

I realize this in the middle of the night. I'd spent the afternoon avoiding the invitation, but it stares me down. No matter where I go in the apartment its eyes are on me, but when I confront it, it lays there innocently on my kitchen counter. I realize that the cardstock isn't *really* looking at me. I'm not crazy. Not in that way, at least.

But it has been on my mind all day. I couldn't think of anything else. And now, at 4:40 in the morning, I'm unbearably jittery and anxious, my legs won't stay still, and I have the sense that I'm out of phase with my body, vibrating at a frequency that isn't within the realm of the normal world.

I go to the kitchen for some water and take the opportunity to open the kitchen window. The only time I can safely do this is in the middle of the night when Petra has sealed up the day's pet poop in bags and closed the can lids. There's still a bit of a smell, but it's manageable. And the night air feels so good, so unlike the day. I'm really a creature of the night, and except for my dreadful eyesight and fear of flying, I'd most likely be a vampire.

Back to obsessing. He's getting married, and it's clear that I have to go. I've never had more clarity on anything in my life, other than the fact that I loved him—I still love him—and know that we are meant to be together. How to get there, that's the question.

How could I have let this invitation sit there for more than a month? I pick up the gold-trimmed card. I have to switch a light on, of course. And get my glasses. I'm so tired of everything being a three-step process, no matter how simple the thing is. I can't read pill bottles, directions, invitations, anything, without light and glasses. *Doctor Edward Patterson Denture and Doctor April Fennimore-Klein*—couldn't she at least have the good grace to have an ugly name?—*cordially invite you to witness their marriage on Saturday, the twenty-second of June, at two o'clock in the afternoon.* June. How original, April Fennimore-Klein, you bitch. You are obviously a bride who never conforms to convention. *Ceremony and Reception to follow at The Broadmore.* Inside the card is printed the address, somewhere in Colorado. It's happening in ten days. Ten days to strategize, plan, execute, and complete the most important mission of my life. In another state.

How thoughtful of Edward.

He knows I don't travel. I *can't* travel. Planes...just watching the news is enough to make me stay put. I could never take my shoes off in front of strangers, and the idea of getting patted down by one or more over-zealous pornstached men with latex gloves makes my upper lip sweat. Not to mention the planes themselves. A system of ventilation that would kill people if they had the poor sense to breathe deeply. Germs just re-circulate on a plane, so whatever hideous diseases your plane-mates have, you are likely to contract them as well. Oh, and the bathrooms. Well, I can't even discuss that without feeling absolutely vertiginous.

Colorado. Why would he get married in Colorado? Maybe she's from there. April. Dr. Fennimore-Klein. Perhaps a train? No. It would take so long, and it's almost as germ-ridden as an aircraft. Driving. I would have to drive to Colorado to attend the wedding of Dr. Edward Denture and his lovely fiancée, Dr. April Fennimore-Klein.

I do have a driver's license, oddly enough. Edward helped me get it reinstated. I suppose in a more literate world that might be considered irony, but Petra would just say it was a sign from God. Either way, with the blessings of God or fate, I would have to find a way to drive to the accursed state of Colorado, and I would have to do it soon, because time waits for no woman.

I have to stop that wedding.

2

ADJUST SEAT AND MIRRORS

The next day, Petra makes it sound as if I plan to circumnavigate the globe on the back of a white whale. "Sweeties, you simply cannot drive to Colorado from California. How in the world would you do it? You barely leave this apartment!" I've formally invited her to come up (or as formally as a phone call permits) because I need help.

Once I make a decision about something, it is final, and I have decided that I must go to Colorado. I must stop this wedding. Clearly, Edward has forgotten that I am the love of his life, and I have to remind him before it's too late. Like in that movie, *The Graduate*. I'm no Dustin Hoffman, but he's no Mrs. Robinson, so I guess that makes us even. However, for many reasons, I cannot do this on my own. And although Petra annoys me, and constantly intrudes on my personal space, she is, in fact, my only friend other than perhaps the owner of the Fluffitorium, but he speaks so little English it would be impossible to ask him for help.

Petra follows me around the apartment, resplendent in a harvest-gold suit made of shantung silk. Why anyone would wear silk to groom dogs is beyond me, but I don't want to broach that subject, because I'll be in for an hour-long lecture on the feng shui of fabrics.

"This is why you called me? Because of this *fakakta* plan of yours?"

I can't expect her to truly understand. I don't think she's ever been in love. However, I need her on my side. "I know it sounds unconventional—"

"No, it sounds crazy."

"You know I hate that word."

She realizes her mistake and regroups. "I'm sorry, Anna. I just meant…it's not very practical. Do you know how long it takes to drive from California to Colorado? How will you survive?"

"I'm not incompetent." I grab my step stool from the kitchen. "Come on. Help me get the suitcase down from the closet."

"I can't go with you, you know, if that's what you were going to ask." She follows me into the dimly lit hall.

"I don't want you to go with me." Since I rarely use it, my suitcase is stowed in the very back, top shelf of my closet, along with my box of Unwanteds. I suppose I'll have to take that too, if I go. Another complication…but I'll push on. I have to.

Petra grabs my hand as I unsteadily mount the step stool to access the top shelf. Thankfully I dust frequently, so there is little debris, but it is difficult to reach. I stretch and Petra puts a hand on my hip to steady me—which is extremely uncomfortable—but I don't react. "Careful, dear. You don't want anything to fall on your head."

The suitcase comes crashing down, along with the box of Unwanteds. I stay on the stool, thankfully.

"Oh, dear," Petra mutters, prancing heavily out of the way of the falling objects.

The lid on the box has flown off, and its contents have spilled onto the floor. We both just stare at it for a moment, but then I remember myself and scurry down the step stool to try and sweep everything up before she has a chance to stick her nose in it.

"What's all this?" she asks, squinting at my Unwanteds.

"Nothing," I mutter, madly scooping.

"Oh." She picks up a photo with curling edges. "Who's this?"

I snatch it from her hand. "Thank you."

"Anna, who was that in the picture?"

"No one," I answer, shoving the lid back on the box. I obviously need to buy some packing tape before I leave.

Petra is not content with this answer, of course. Honestly, I don't know why I even let her into the apartment. She's a terrible friend, always so nosy. "Was that a family member there, in that picture?"

I have the box firmly under my arm. It's an old, sage-colored, Naturalizers shoebox, and still in very good shape. I appreciate a well-made shoebox. With my other hand, I grab the black suitcase and drag it into my bedroom, throw it onto the bed, and unzip it.

"Fine, Anna. If you don't want to talk about it, just say so."

"I don't want to talk about it." I have to do laundry before I leave, of course. I wonder if I can get into the Fluffitorium after hours? That would mean calling the Chinese man, probably bribing him with something. Maybe those expired Belgian chocolates? No, I threw those out. Petra prattles on, but I hear her voice as a buzzing fly.

"Anna, let me talk you out of this foolishness." She grabs my hand, which makes me stop my frantic running around. Best talk to her, then maybe she'll leave.

"Fine." I perch on the edge of the bed next to the open suitcase.

Petra lowers herself onto a too-small slipper chair. It has no sides, so her gold-upholstered bounty gloops down the edges of the cushion like molten caramel sauce. "You going to Colorado—what good is it going to do? You think you're going to stop the wedding?" I don't answer, but she can see it in my face. "Oh, Anna. That's just—you can't do it. It's setting yourself up for disappointment."

"Why is that?" I still clutch the shoebox, and for a moment I consider throwing it at her head. For some reason, her jabbering makes me angry. "You don't think I can win him back?"

Petra rolls her eyes. "You never had him in the first place! He was your doctor!"

"Patients and doctors fall in love all the time."

"Not in real life. In real life, those doctors go to jail. Is that what you want? You want him to go to jail?" Petra crosses her fat arms and taps her crimson talons along her sleeve.

"He's not going to jail," I mutter, springing up from the bed. "And I have things to do. Now, can you get me a car or not?"

"Can I get you a car?" Her voice rises an octave when she's agitated. It sounds like a leaky teakettle on boil. "Where on earth would I get you a car?"

"What about yours?"

"I need mine!"

"You know people." I yank my drawers open and begin to carefully select items I might need for the trip: a bundle of newspapers from thirteen years ago; nail polish remover; unopened Hanes Silk Effects stockings, nude, size B; an unopened package of cotton briefs; tarot cards with Alice in Wonderland characters on them (a gift from Edward); a little green faux-alligator cosmetic bag that was a gift with purchase, chock-full of makeup I never have worn. I might need that if I am to compete with Dr. April Fennimore what's-her-name. I should make a list, really. Too many things could be left behind without a list.

"Anna, listen to me." Petra's voice reminds me of my mother's. I tune her out, but she keeps rambling as she follows me to the phone table. "You need to think this through. How would you live on the road? You can't stand going outside and you *know* this neighborhood. What would you do in a strange place, where you don't know anyone? Where you don't know the laundromats?"

She has a point, but I can't think about that right now. "I have to go," I whisper. It stops her rambling. "Can you help me get a car?"

Petra breathes behind me, wheezing in the silence. I feel her walk to me, stand at my back, and put a chubby hand on my shoulder. "Anna. If you've decided, I'll help you. But look at me first. Tell me why."

I turn to face her. I feel a blush rising from my neck, through my cheeks, and into the stubbly scalp under my wig. "He's the only man I've ever loved since—" I whisper, hot tears welling at the corners of my eyes. "I can't just let him go. Not like this. This might be my only chance. Ever."

Her mud-brown eyes lined with smudgy charcoal blink rapidly. She steps forward into the bubble of my personal space, but I say nothing. "If it means that much to you…if he means that much, I'll make some inquiries."

I blink too, matching her blink for blink. A hot tear trails down my cheek, a renegade. I don't cry. "I have to leave tomorrow."

"Tomorrow? Anna, you can't just make a car appear and leave on a cross-country trip in one day."

"Dammit—" Oh. That is one mistake too many. Get a grip. I clutch the shoebox more tightly. Get a grip. Nothing will happen unless I get Petra on my side. "Let me explain." I lick my lips, focus. "Time is of the essence, Petra. You saw the date on the invitation. I am already behind because I stubbornly didn't open it when it arrived. I need to plan. I need to make a plan. And I need a car." I look into her eyes. "I desperately need a car, Petra. It's life or death."

Petra runs her plump pink tongue around the edge of her cartoon lips. "I have a cousin. I'll make a call." She reaches out as if to touch me but thinks better of it. "I'll make a call."

I know she leaves the room because her weight causes the floorboards to creak in protest. I'm frozen, willing tears to disappear. My tears will not be tolerated.

The shoebox sits on the bed. I haven't looked at its contents for… seven years? That doesn't seem possible, but I guess it could be. It was convenient, hiding it in the closet. I can't look at it now, though. I have to make my list.

I veer toward the phone table, where I always keep a neat stack of color-coordinated post-it notes that I use to make my lists. Blue is for survival, yellow is for bathroom supplies, pink is for clothing, orange is for food (although, in general, I object to orange. It is far too loud. However, there are many orange foods.) I have a small stack of pristine white post-its specifically for longer, more complex lists. The last time I needed the long list post-it was two Christmases ago, when I was taking an anti-anxiety medication and was considering actually doing holiday shopping.

I ease into the spindly chair. My special pen, tucked into the front drawer, waits for me where it always does. I can only write with a specific kind of pen: it must have black ink, it must have a solid metal body, and it must have ink that rolls rather than scratches. The dollar store often has them, although they tend to run dry more quickly than pens from other places. But when you're on a fixed income, you have to survive. Pen supply goes on blue post-its, i.e., survival. Writing is critical for my recovery, Edward always told me.

To my list. I write meticulously at the top of the paper "Travel Necessities." I underline it to give it special emphasis. Then I write the following items in cursive and flush to the left margin:

Automobile
Annabella/wig
Sanitized wipes
Hand sanitizer
Suitcase (packed)
Unwanteds
Cash
Toiletries
Plastic bags
Credit card (must obtain)

I'm sure there will be more things added to the list, but at the moment, I obviously have some work to do. Petra may be right. I may not be able to do all this in one day.

I do not own a computer or any other electronic device that the modern world deems necessary—except a television, of course. But I rarely watch that. And a very cheap cell phone, the kind the government gives you, like the government-funded cheese they give to hungry people. This hinders me severely when contemplating doing anything outside my home. I do realize the benefit of being able to research things on the computer; for someone with my specific qualities it would be a blessing, really, but I have no way to obtain one. Fixed incomes suck.

Petra has a computer. I sigh and resign myself to descending into the abyss of flea leavings and dog piss.

I pull on my fuzzy black boots in preparation for the trek downstairs. I also have a red vinyl raincoat that I pull on over my clothes; this way, if any errant fluids are strewn about, I will be shielded and can wash it easily when I return home. I move as quickly as I can down through the layers of filth that constitute the hallway and stairwell. I open the street door and am slammed with a smell tsunami of steaming dog, soap, burnt coffee, diesel, rubber tires, perfume (cheap), and shoe polish. As fate would have it, a bald male client wrangling a tiny brown dog with the teeth of a great white shark struggles to push open Petra's door.

I stand, mute, waiting for this obstacle to clear. "Could you get the door?" the man asks, words muffled by snarling and the undulating dog.

Panic.

I do not want to go near that beast or that man. But if I don't, I won't be able to get in, so I snug my raincoat tighter, hitch my shoulder/elbow up so it covers my face, and use the hem of the raincoat to cover the doorknob as I twist it and push the door open.

"Uh...thanks." The man frowns at me as he dashes in with his devil dog.

Petra's Pet sPot is hopping. The crowd of three humans, three animals, and Petra (who counts for at least two and a half more people) stuffs the room with breath, and noise, and unidentifiable odors. Damp, shampoo-scented air swirls around me, demonic clouds of germ-laced moisture. I resist the urge to gag and/or run. My mission is too important.

"Anna!" Petra waves from her station behind the shampoo sink, where some bedraggled hunk of brown fur shivers miserably beneath a stream of steaming water. "You came downstairs! Come in!"

Steeling myself, I brush past the clients, who stare at me as if I'm a leper. I get as close as I dare to Petra and the tub of dirty water. "I need to borrow your computer," I rasp.

"I can't hear you, Sweeties," Petra yelps as she dunks the brown dog under the soapy water. "Oh, Remy, stop squirming! You'd think we've never done this before! Nice dog!" She pushes a strand of red hair from her face with one sudsy mitt. "Now, what did you need, Anna? Speak up."

"I need your computer!" From the looks of the other people in the room, I'm yelling. Even the dogs stop barking, just for a second.

Petra pastes a frozen grin onto her cartoon mouth, wipes her hand on a towel, and tethers the dog known as Remy to a post with a little flexible leash. "Follow me, dear," Petra says soothingly, as if I am a rabid poodle. "One moment, folks, be right back," she reassures the clients, some of whom shake their heads in disbelief, probably because of her lack of professionalism.

She ushers me into a dim, cramped room, flicks on a fluorescent light (they rob you of essential vitamins), and frowns at me. "Why do you need a computer?"

"I need to get a credit card, apparently." I gingerly step around anything that might harbor microbes (everything) and inspect the task chair behind the desk. It looks clean enough. Best if I don't think too much about it. "I need to know how to get onto the internet."

"Anna." Petra positions herself in front of me so I'm looking at her over the computer screen. "Haven't you reconsidered this road trip idea?"

I poke buttons. "How do you turn it on?"

"Anna." Petra uses the voice I hear her use when she's trying to tame a Rottweiler. "I really am not at all sure this is a good idea. I know I said I'd help you, but how are you going to be able to do this?"

"I can." Simple. Two words. *Jesus wept. No exit. Got milk?* All great observations can be summed up in two words.

Petra scrapes a wooden chair over and lowers herself into it. "Please forget this."

"Did you get me a car yet?"

"You just asked me fifteen minutes ago!" Barking explodes from the salon. "Just a minute. I have to go deal with this. I'll be back." She marches out of the room and her voice echoes off the walls, soothing.

The button that turns this thing on is right in front, so I press it right away. The machine whirs and lights up, and after some strange numeric choreography, I am rewarded with a screen emblazoned with Google across the top in jaunty-colored letters. I know about Google.

I type into the little window "credit cards," and the screen fills instantly. It's overwhelming. I must stare at the screen for a long time, because the next thing I know, Petra leans down over my shoulder and squints at her computer. "Credit cards? Anna. You've never had a credit card, have you?"

"I think I did, once." I'm sure I did, in my other life, before. Petra parks in her squeaky wooden chair again. "Anna, please reconsider. I'm worried about you. "

"Why?" I pull at my wig. It feels too tight, too constricting.

"Driving? All the way to Colorado? Alone?" She licks her lips. "I'll get someone to go with you."

"No!" I don't mean to shout. The thought of being in a small, enclosed, mobile space with someone over several days makes me hyperventilate. "No. I have to do this alone."

"Why?"

Yes, why?

"I…need to. I need to be able to do it alone, and I need to see him alone, and I need to—"

Petra shakes her head, resigned to my crazy scheme. "Maybe you could just fly there?"

"No." Small spaces with recirculated air? TSA pat downs? Airborne Ebola? She has no idea. "Don't you have dogs to wash?"

"Everyone's gone." She gestures toward the other room. "It's after five. You've been in here for hours. I was starting to worry about you."

"Hours?" Suddenly I notice two things; I desperately need to use the bathroom, and I am hungry as hell. "I'll…can you come up?" I dash away from the screen.

"Sure, Anna." Petra's voice follows me out the door as I frantically unlock the door to the apartment foyer and bolt upstairs.

Once I'm home, I feel better. I pee, forage for peanut butter (stored between packets of sugar and pretzels), and sit at the kitchen table with an armload of sticky notes in various colors.

By the time Petra has conquered the stairs, I'm already deep into my planning. She clomps into the kitchen and gasps. "Anna, what are you doing with all these notes?" She carelessly picks up an orange sticky labeled NONPERISHABLES.

"Please put that back." I don't look up from my writing, because I don't want to lose focus. "Could you please pull that butcher block away from the wall? I need a clear space."

Puzzled, she does as I ask, rolling the small portable counter to the other side of the kitchen. Ah, a blank wall. Perfect. I gather my few post-its and carefully position them in perfectly straight lines across the top of an imaginary square.

"Are you making a picture?" She tilts her head and studies what I've done.

"No, I'm planning the trip." Under the NONPERISHABLES sticky I add several other orange stickies that read PEANUT BUTTER, CRACKERS, BOTTLED WATER.

"About that." Petra pulls out a chair and plops into it as I study the wall. "I don't think I can get you the car after all."

"What?" I whirl on her, skewing my wig. "Why not?"

Petra stares down at the linoleum. "My cousin...he doesn't have... it's not really workable." She exhales as if the lying takes a lot out of her.

"You're afraid to lend me a car. You're afraid I don't know how to drive."

"No, it's not just that." Her eyes dart to the side. "Do you know how to drive, though? Do you have a license?"

I carefully align a blue post-it labeled HAND SANITIZER under the NECESSARY column. "Of course, I have a license," I lie. "I did know how to drive. I doubt I'd forget it. Mentally retarded people can drive. Monkeys can drive, for God's sake. I think I can handle it."

· · ·

Edward had taught me to drive—well, re-taught me. It had been two months into our relationship, and I was terrified. "You'll be fine," he said softly as he drove a battered blue Range Rover to an empty gravel lot. "Driving is a lot like living. You just point yourself in the direction you want to go, step on the gas, and go there."

"Except living can't leave you in a mangled heap outside a dirty public rest stop near Fresno."

He paused. "Actually, sometimes it does."

As he slowed the car, I felt panic fluttering in my stomach. "I don't think you can teach me to drive."

"Why is that?" The car came to a full stop, but the engine kept rumbling beneath us, a tiger ready to pounce if he let go of the leash. "Why do you think I can't teach you to drive?"

"You're British."

"That is true." He unwrapped his long legs from beneath the wheel and opened his door. "I promise I won't make you drive on the left side of the road."

Madness. Why had I ever agreed to this? I hadn't driven a car in so long, not since—but that was past. I was moving forward. You have to keep moving forward, that's what Edward says all the time.

He opened the door for me and gestured for me to exit. "Your turn." I sat, frozen. "Oh, come on, Anna. You can do this. I promise." I couldn't look at him. If I looked into his eyes, he'd know me for the coward I was. I sat rigid, staring ahead. "Fine. I'll help you."

As if I weighed nothing, he scooped me out of the passenger seat, carried me around the back of the car, and tucked me into the driver's side, neat as you please. He even clicked in my safety belt. I had no time to register what he was doing, no time to protest or even enjoy it, not that I should have enjoyed it. That was a wicked thought. "There. Now we're not going anywhere unless you drive us there." He crossed his arms and smiled.

I watched in the rearview mirror as he once again circled the car and eased into the passenger seat where I had been sitting. That thought alone made me blush. Hot. *So hot*. Why was it so hot here? Perhaps I was ill, or perhaps there was some neurotoxin in the air or water—not common, no, but they do rear up when you least expect them, like monsters. Not common. That's what they'd told me, those years ago.

My hands gripped the leather-wrapped wheel like a life preserver as I stared straight ahead. "I don't think I can do this."

"Of course you can." He covered one of my white-knuckled hands with his own, large and soft. A thrill of electricity coursed through me, terminating in my panties. This happened whenever he touched me, even if it was an accidental touch (which it had been, always, except for this most recent moving of me from one side of the car to the other). I stared at his hand covering mine; our skin seemed mingled, liquefied into one magnificent sculpture of human flesh, and I couldn't feel the difference between my hand and his. I realized: this is what love is. Being unable to tell where you stop and the other person begins.

I stared into his eyes but saw only gentle concern. He withdrew his hand, scratched his ear, and said, "Now, look straight ahead, put your right foot on the gas, gently push the pedal, and go forward. Pretend like the car is part of you."

I pressed gingerly on the pedal, and the car lurched forward, jerky, like a puppet whose strings had been loosened. I looked to him for approval, and he nodded and smiled. "Is that right?" I asked.

"Yes." He placed my hand on the stick shift and covered it with his own. I nearly melted. "Now, we're going to go a bit faster and shift into the second gear."

"Why?"

He blinked at me, his hand still damp on mine. "If you don't go faster, you can't go anywhere."

"I don't want to go anywhere." *Kiss him*, a voice said. *Kiss him*. I was shocked at my own intensity, a bit dismayed about the feelings washing over me like a storm tide. And was he…encouraging this? Was that alright? Was it wrong? My breathing felt labored, I was in a fever. Driving was really not on my mind at all. It was the first time I'd felt—felt anything, really, since—

"Right." He leaned back into the leather upholstery, then reached over me and turned the key. The engine stopped, and all I heard was my own ragged breathing and the song of birds in the trees.

"What are you doing?" I asked.

"Waiting for you."

"To do what?"

"Drive, of course. Look, we talked about this, Anna. If you're to move on, you have to relearn some of the things you've forgotten."

"But not everything." I glanced at him to be sure he understood my meaning.

"No, not everything." He looked down at his hand on mine, and quickly withdrew it. "Do you want to talk about it? Right now?"

"No." Sweat beaded on my forehead. "Let's drive."

I didn't look at him. I could sense that he was deciding something, whether or not to push me to talk...something fine was weighing in the balance, some idea that if I talked, perhaps, we would become too close, or that it would ruin his fantasy of me. Finally, he sighed, and put his hand on mine again. "Alright then. Let's drive."

I wasn't good at it. But I did remember, a bit. Oh, the ecstasy of feeling free, feeling mobile. Even though we were only driving slowly, slowly across an open expanse of gravel and scrub, I was soaring to heaven, borne on the wings of my guardian angel. My savior. My lover.

. . .

"Anna." Petra pokes me with a crimson fingernail. "You can't go on this trip. Not alone. What are you going to do when you...when you have to go to the bathroom? I cannot see you stopping at a rest stop on the interstate. How are you going to survive? Not to mention driving. You get nervous walking to the laundromat, for goodness sakes. What's going to happen when you're dodging traffic on the freeway?"

I realize now that I have to convince her. I have to convince her, or there is no way I can go to Edward. And I *must* go to Edward.

Think carefully. Choose your words carefully. Find a way.

I lick my lips, put a hand on Petra's arm, and ease her into a chair. I sit opposite her, leaning in to show interest and intensity (Edward always said body language is the most powerful way of communicating.) I stare into her watery eyes. I imagine myself exuding sanity. "Petra," I say softly, as if I'm calming a rabid dog. With love. "Petra, believe me. I can drive a car. I can drive a car across the country. I used to function in this world, Petra. It was a few years ago, but I did it. I had a job. Did you know that?"

"No," she whispers, her mouth frozen in a cartoon 'O'. "What kind of job?"

"It's not important." She's staring at me expectantly. Maybe it would help if I told her. "Data entry. I spent my days typing useless information into useless documents for useless people."

"Data entry." She says it in a hushed tone, as if she's praying. "I did not know that."

I nod. "Would you like some tea?" I smile, hoping it's engaging.

"Well, yes." Petra smiles, surprised. "That would be lovely."

I make my way to the kitchen, put the kettle on, turn on the gas, and choose two sky-blue teacups from the cupboard. I wash them out as I continue talking. "I'm afraid I don't have any cream, though."

"Well, this is just wonderful," she calls from the living room. "I don't think we've ever had tea together, have we?"

"You know, I don't think so." This is how people talk to each other. Edward practiced this with me, after we put all the Unwanteds in that shoebox. He had said I needed to reconnect with the "real" world. Even then he was looking out for me. It's like a great puzzle, where all the pieces are falling together, finally. When I started the puzzle, I had no idea what it would become, but now…now I see my past spread behind me, a great detailed map of the world, and I see all that came before and all that came after, even Edward's leaving, as vital pieces in that puzzle. Petra is a piece, too, but she doesn't know it.

"What did you say, Anna?"

"Oh, I don't have any cream. I do have sugar, though."

"Honey?"

I shudder. "No. Sorry, no honey." Honey is ridiculously sticky. I don't know how anyone can stand to pour it, eat it, or touch the disgusting teddy bear bottles it comes in.

"Sugar it is, then. I'd like three teaspoons."

Jesus, no wonder she's fat. Three teaspoons. But I say, "Of course. Just have to wait for the water to boil."

3
RIGHT-OF-WAY

Tea goes well. I pretend to be normal. Unfortunately, Petra is unmoved.

"Anna, I'm so sorry. I can't help you."

A teaspoon clatters to the floor. Traitor. But I don't lose my composure. "Petra, I absolutely understand. It was an unreasonable request." I think I might smash the kettle against her face. No. That would not help me achieve my goal.

She leans against the doorjamb. "Just curious, though…if you were to get a car, what would you do once you got there? I mean, are you going to talk to Edward? Confront him?"

Oh, I can feel her on the hook. She wants to believe in love, she wants to believe in the power of a movie star journey across the interstate, she wants to believe we can change our fate.

So do I.

"Of course not. That was all just…fantasy. I know there's no real possibility of a relationship with him. I really just want to wish him well. In person." I unwind the string from an Earl Grey teabag and gently arrange it at the bottom of the blue china cup. I don't look at her. "In fact, I think it would really help me heal. Spiritually."

Petra believes in the power of love, but above all, she believes in the power of spiritual healing. She is as damaged as the mangy mutts she grooms, and although she has recounted (endlessly) the many ways she's tried locating her higher power, she's no further along than I am, spirit-wise. I know this is a cause she can't resist.

The kettle whistles. Before it can reach a hysterical pitch, I fetch it from the stove and pour the steaming water into the two cups. Breathe. Breathe in the steam from the tea, imagine the power of the tea flowing through my nose and into my brain where it will warm my mind and make me say just the right thing to make Petra help me.

"Here we are." I imitate one of those perky women on TV, the ones who entertain, and buy prophylactics. I set the two cups on the table, two teaspoons, and a Delft sugar bowl with a chip where the Dutch girl's wooden shoe should be. What happened to her foot? When did she lose that shoe? I don't remember dropping it. The bowl belonged to my mother.

"Lovely," she murmurs, reaching for the Dutch girl's mangled foot. That foot really bothers me. I'm not sure I like having a gimpy sugar bowl. But I have to stay focused. Yammering on about the footless girl from Delft will just distract her.

Perky, prophylactic buyer, pretty. "I'm thinking I might go back to work," I offer. Am I? No. Absolutely not. But it might convince her that I'm more normal than I am. Goddamned Dutch girl. Her other foot, milky white, sports a smooth porcelain shoe, recklessly sticking out near a wheelbarrow. Maybe the boy ran over her other foot with the wheelbarrow. Men always hurt women. I wonder if they're lovers? Or if he's her brother? Or both?

"Why are you smiling?" Petra frowns over the steam from her tea.

"Just glad to be here," I say perkily.

"So, you're going to work again?" Petra nods and her cartoon lips stretch into a smile. There's a smudge of lipstick on her teeth, like blood on the fangs of a shark. Do sharks have fangs? Or is that only snakes? I think sharks have teeth. Multiple rows of teeth. I wonder if they live near dikes? Could they swim that far inland? Tulip sharks. Two lip sharks. "Anna? Do you have a lead on a job?"

"Yes." I sip my tea. Normally. "I've been talking to the Chinese."

"The Chinese?"

"The Chinese man. At the Fluffitorium."

"Oh!" Petra stretches that one syllable into five, varying in pitches of excitement and surprise. "What would you do for him?"

"I...I believe it would be some form of accounting."

Petra nods again and sips the Earl Grey. "Well, that's a whole different story then."

"What do you mean?" I sip again.

"If you're going to be working, then I might be able to get you the car."

I try not to squeal, either with joy or anger. So, if I'm working, she can get me a car, but if I'm not, then she can't. Or won't. But I might get the car. Play it cool. "Oh?"

She sets her cup on the table. "Obviously, you won't start working until after the trip, correct?"

"Correct. Of course, the details are still being worked out. We have to agree on a wage, and on my duties, and what the Chinese man needs."

"What's his name?" Petra frowns slightly.

"Oolong. Mr. Oolong."

"Like the tea?"

"Exactly."

She rises from the chair and smiles. "Let me make some calls, Sweeties." She downs the rest of her tea and sets the cup neatly on the table next to the one-shoed Dutch girl.

"I do appreciate it," I say as she waves and walks toward the door. "Do it now."

She shoots me a disapproving look. Obviously, that wasn't a normal thing to say. Dammit. "I'll do what I can," she says, her smile a bit less sure than before. Dammit.

I hear her clomp down the stairs. The door to the street creaks open and slams closed. I stand, take the crippled Dutch girl and her sugar bowl, walk calmly to the kitchen, and hurl them both into the sink where they shatter into hundreds of milky shards.

Thankfully, Petra does not check my Mr. Oolong story. She comes up the next day, raps on my door, and dangles a set of keys attached to a purple rabbit's foot. "I got your car!"

"Come in!" I sweep my hand in a grand gesture, although in reality I'm trying to avoid touching the purple rabbit's foot. Disgusting. I wonder how she would feel if someone sawed her porky foot off at the cankle, trussed it up with metal, and hung some keys from it? Do fleas or mites live on dead bunny flesh? I will find a way to dispose of it as soon as she's gone.

"My cousin Raoul...I told him your situation and he didn't want to help, but then his wife, Marietta, she heard it too and thought it was romantic, so she begged him to let you use the car, I mean, it was just sitting in their driveway anyway. Their teenage son is in jail, so he can't drive it." She finally comes up for air, a whale breaching a sea of syllables. "You have to get your own insurance."

"That's no problem." It's not a problem. I won't have any. I don't tell her this. "When will I have access to this car?"

"Access?" She laughs, her bounteous chest jiggling. "It's downstairs, Anna! That's why I have the keys! Do you want to see it?"

"Of course!" I follow her down the dark stairway, willing my heart to stop beating so fast.

Perched at the curb is a marvel of a vehicle. Impossibly long, sleek, and aquamarine blue, the color of the Caribbean, the color of freedom. Panic sparks in my chest, a tiny flame at first, welling up into an explosion of full-blown anxiety.

"Anna?" Petra's wide smile fades as I slump to the curb. Dirty, dirty curb. I'm going to have to shower. Dammit! This is going to blow the whole thing. I have to get a grip. Petra crouches as best she can next to me. "Sweeties, what is it?"

"Something I ate." I half-heartedly clutch at my stomach while trying to lift my butt from the contaminated cement.

"What did you eat?" Petra feels my forehead, which makes me shudder. I wave her hand away and breathe.

"Not sure. But it must have been bad." I breathe, breathe, breathe. Edward always said that breathing is the key to everything: conception, birth, death. Life. Breathe. Breathe. I feel the anxiety monster shrinking, roaring its way backward into the small, contained space it rents near the back of my mind.

I count to ten. Edward taught me this too. Ten is a magical number somehow, enough time to slow the heart, ten fingers, ten toes, ten little Indians, everything is based in tens, unless you're American. Americans insist on adding two more, making it twelve, which makes no sense at all unless we used to be six-fingered men. I am able to stand. I smooth my wig and smile at Petra, a confident, winning smile, the kind perky people give without thought. "See? All fine." I amaze myself.

Petra's not so sure. She zooms in closer, so close I can see the cavernous pores in her skin. "Anna, listen. If I am going to lend you Raoul's car, you have to promise me that you will be able to drive it. You have to show me right now, or I'm going to have him come and pick it up."

"Fine. No problem." That's what people always say. No problem. I will let it be my magic mantra, my prophecy of things to come. "Let me just go and get my scarf. I'll be right back."

I get to the bathroom, stare at my pale face in the mirror. I should take off the wig. The thought of it flying off into the street terrifies me, so I place it gently on Annabella and grab a dark blue scarf from a drawer, tie it around my fuzzy head, and see a crazy lady staring back at me. "You need to get your shit together," I tell her. She nods as if she understands.

I slide into the driver's seat. Smooth, aquamarine leather interior, a couple of rips in the passenger seat, a cigarette burn on the darker blue floor mat. Within the steering wheel is the tri-pointed shape of a Neolithic goddess, arms outstretched to take me in. A few breaths, and I recall how to start it, which is especially tough since I'm trying not to touch the disgusting rabbit's foot. I manage to turn the engine over, though, and the familiar rumble calms me. No problem.

Petra opens the passenger door and climbs in. "Let's go!" she yelps, putting on oversized sunglasses.

I reach for the...what is it called? Shift? I pull it down and the car lurches forward just a bit. I put my foot on the brake pedal, grip the wheel, ask that dashboard goddess for some help, and turn the wheel toward the street.

"Check your mirrors!" Petra shrieks.

No traffic, so I coach the behemoth into the asphalt sea, press gingerly on the accelerator, and we're cruising down Sheppard Street, just like two normal people.

The trip around the block is a challenge; I have to work very, very hard to keep the anxiety monster at bay. Luckily, there is a curious lack of pedestrians or grandmothers, so I don't have to worry about hitting them. An eternity passes, but I finally arrive back in front of my building, my good solid building with the dirty curb. I park the car and turn it off. The purple rabbit's foot bounces a bit after the engine dies, nodding its approval.

Petra beams. "You did so well. I'm sure it will be fine." She opens her door, scrapes the sidewalk. "Oh, I forget how low these doors are. You better watch that. Of course, you won't probably be opening the passenger side door anyway. Just be careful." She peers in through the open door. "When are you leaving?"

When am I leaving? Leaving has been such a dream, such a wild impossibility, that I realize I haven't done half the things I need to do to actually leave. My mind races, but I calm it, trying not to freak out in front of Petra. "I still need to get a few things together, but I'd like to leave by Saturday."

"That's in two days," she says dubiously, her red lips pursing, eyebrows dipping as she fixes me with one doubtful eye.

"I know," I say. Perky, perky, perky. "I've been preparing. I knew you'd come through with the car." I force a smile. "You're a good friend."

. . .

"I'll always be your friend," Edward said to me the day he told me he was leaving. It was the kind of thing someone would say when they didn't want to upset the other, crazier, person.

We were in the Café Savage, a coffee spot for hipsters plastered floor to ceiling with photographs the owner had taken. The place was full of overstuffed tapestried couches, pillows that oozed dust and skin cells from previous patrons, and a cool glass case displaying tiny dollhouse cakes painted with hard, artistic icing.

Above Edward's head, a huge alligator captured on film crawled toward me, teeth sharp, eyes glinting. The photographer placed this alligator against a background of polar white nothing, so the lizard looked like it was approaching from the clouds, from the nexus, from the Great White Way. No context. It just hovered there, in its white cocoon of nothing, frozen like an artifact.

"Anna, drink your tea," Edward said as I stared above his head. It looked like the alligator was going to scalp him. I could imagine it, all his strong, lovely hair ripped from his head with those serrated-blade teeth, blood spattering all over that crisp white background, oozing down onto the crimson upholstery of the dusty sofa, Edward screaming for mercy as I sat there, sipping as instructed.

"Please say something."

I focused on his face, twisted slightly and appropriately with regret. Sapphire eyes…not real. I wondered if he had the real ones replaced with precious stones. That would explain why he didn't see the important things. "What should I say?" I sipped.

Edward rubbed a thumb around the rim of his Café Savage coffee mug, also polar white like the alligator's lair. Is white the absence of color, or all color absorbed into one? I could never remember that. "Anna," (why did he say my name so often?) "I've explained it for weeks. I know it upsets you, and I'm really, really sorry about that, but I have a personal life also. You can understand that, can't you?" Unblinking precious gem eyes. He was probably not even a real person. If I stabbed his hand with a fork, I'd know for sure.

"I thought this *was* your personal life." My fingers curled, unbidden, around the slightly worn edge of the fork.

He cleared his throat, cracked his knuckles, and started again. "All I wanted to do was take some time outside of our sessions to speak with you about my moving. I know it's a tough thing to lose a therapist." He blinked, rapidly.

"But who is this person? Who is she?"

He looked down at the table. "She's...a doctor also. Someone I've known since university. We—she and I are very compatible, and her family knows my family."

"Is she British?"

He frowns and looks at me as if I'm psychic. "It so happens she is, yes. Why?"

"Edward," I began, but my head started to itch so terribly that I couldn't ignore it. "Excuse me," I muttered, jumping up so I was eye-to-beady-eye with the cold-hearted alligator photo.

The bathroom, a tiny violet water closet festooned with graphic nude photos of ladies from the 1920s, smelled of Glade air freshener and pee. It was a unisex bathroom; these were the worst. Men squirted germs like fire hoses squirted flame retardant. Happily, I didn't need to use the toilet, because I was sure it was crawling with the microscopic hitchhikers of past bathroom attendees.

I took my wig off, gave my head a blessed scratch, then put it back on my head, adjusting the clipped black bangs, smoothing the sleek, dark sides. I was Mata Hari, lady spy. Hmm. He was being forced into this, it was obvious. A British doctor, family friend? His family was pressuring him. The English never quite got over their snobbishness about class. Suddenly, it was so obvious to me. He couldn't be with me because his family would not approve.

Close to the mirror, eyelashes nearly touching glass, I blinked rapidly, as he had done. The effect was photographic and dizzying; I could hypnotize him. But I had to get closer. "Breathe," I told my reflection self. She flipped me off.

Edward was hunched over the table, a folded stork in a brown tweed jacket. I touched his shoulder, and he jumped. "You're back."

"Yes." I sat down next to him on the wine-red couch. He tensed, but I stayed. From somewhere deep inside, my Mata Hari burst forth, and I stared into his eyes—into his flat, wild sapphire eyes. "I understand, about the woman. But you don't have to do what they want you to do. You're a free spirit. Don't go."

"What? No one is—I have to," he whispered, beads of sweat sprouting on his upper lip. I could smell him: damp silk linen, soap, sweat, vanilla. I tried to mesmerize him with my eyes. He tried to pull away. "I'm afraid I've done something— I don't think I meant to do it, but—I've encouraged you. I've tried things, unconventional things, and I think I might have been—wrong."

Bravery came from desperation, I suppose. I knew he was leaving, I knew it in my heart, so I touched his hand. "Edward," I whispered, never losing eye contact. "I love you. You love me. You can't go."

"Anna," he whispered, but it was strangled, as if someone had a choking hand around his throat. He bowed his head, breaking my femme fatale gaze. "I don't want to hurt you."

"You could never hurt me," I said, touching his cheek with a finger. Stubble, sharkskin, wheat fields dried in winter. I willed my finger to memorize it.

He grabbed my wrist, not gently, and moored it to the table. "I don't want to have to say this," he said in that choking, controlled voice.

"Don't say it," I urged, pressing closer so he could kiss me. I knew he wanted to.

He backed away, took a deep breath, and looked deeply into my eyes. "Anna. I've been trying to tell you this, but you don't hear me. I have great affection for you, I do, but I'm not in love with you. I can't be, I'm your therapist, it would be totally unethical, and wrong, and—"

"Love is never wrong," I said, quoting some awful novel I once read.

A grin tugged at one side of his mouth. I could always make him laugh. "I know I must have encouraged this. You're quite—remarkable.

You've been through a lot," he said, rubbing his left temple, massaging unconsciously. He did that when he was nervous. "Your family—"

"Edward," I said his name like a prayer. I leaned in, pressed my ruby lips against his, smooth and cool, and smothered him with all the passion I had saved up inside. Lightning struck my body, from lips to fingers to feet to belly to...other parts. Soft, soft lips, warm rose petal comfort cotton puzzle piece fit right—then he jerked backward as if I'd hit him.

"Anna!" he shouted. His eyes, wide with panic, searched the room for help, for witnesses, for escape. "Stop it." He scuttled to the opposite side of the table, sat in a chair with a distance between us.

The pressure of this moment pushed on him, dense gravity on a delicate poppy, ground him into the unhappiness I wanted to save him from. "Edward, I understand. It's not what society thinks is proper, I know that. But we can't deny our hearts."

Edward pursed his lips and smiled a tortured smile. "Anna. Listen to me." He took one of my hands in his, then hastily let go as if it were scalding. "Of course, I admire you. I've never met anyone like you, and that's the truth. You're intelligent, and funny, and—" He looked into my eyes, and I saw there what I knew to be true. "I'm so sorry," he whispered. "You're terribly damaged, and I so want to fix that—but I can't be what you want. I cannot love you."

Sounds were sucked into a vacuum. Espresso machine whines, clattering cups, spoons clanging, a man coughing, insect-buzz music coming from a tiny fuchsia music player belonging to the teen next to us—all were sucked into a silence that swallowed my world. My heartbeat. Steady, rhythmic, a drum in a desperate jungle. The roaring absence of sound.

When I looked up, he was gone. And there was a twenty-dollar bill on the table.

A lovely parting gift.

4
DRIVER'S HANDBOOK

So, the trip is happening.

Petra has given me the keys. The first thing I do is take off the disgusting rabbit's foot (using thick yellow kitchen gloves) and tuck it carefully in an empty kitchen drawer.

Now alone in my apartment, I watch the dark orange sunset slide inevitably toward the unseeable horizon. I will be leaving soon; it's liberating and overwhelming.

First things first. I need to organize. Perched on my chair, glancing out the window, I begin to plot my journey on an innocent white legal pad (this is critical, since the colored highlighting I use shows up best on white paper, not on yellow.) Here is my list of the lists I must make: things I need for the trip, things I must do before the trip, plans to make for the trip itself, car issues, apartment issues. I will most likely add more later.

Each list will then be color coded so that I can see at a glance where I stand on any given issue. Blue checkmarks will tell me I've taken care of an item. Red checkmarks will tell me that I have a priority item to deal with. But what happens when a red item turns into a blue item? I can't very well just color over the blue item…then I would have a purple item. This is just not going to work.

I will my brain to solve this problem as I linger over a cup of tea. I can't go until I figure it out, and I have to go soon. What do I need? A large white board with colored markers, so I can make changes without coloring over something. Oh…Petra had a whiteboard in that store room, where her laptop hides. I supposed she has colored markers as well. This will necessitate another trip downstairs, I guess. I finish the tea, sigh, and resign myself to more exposure.

Wig on, I pat Annabella on her plaster head, slip on some shoes, and head downstairs. I will have to take Annabella, of course; there are several items I cannot leave behind, actually. What if he decides we should marry there, in Colorado? I have to be prepared for that.

The pet wash is technically closed, so things are relatively quiet at Petra's. She's sitting behind her cash register eating a cinnamon roll the size of her head. "Anna!" she squeals. "Come in!"

I close the door behind me, careful to grab the knob with the edge of my sleeve to minimize contamination. "Good evening," I say cheerily.

"Twice in one day, you come down here," she remarks, gesturing to me with the steroidal pastry. "Want half?"

Ugh. I try to hide my revulsion at the idea of eating something her lips have touched. "No, thank you." I smile endearingly.

She wipes her hands on an oversized striped towel bearing mysterious stains, and stands, teetering a bit. "I was just thinking of you. Your trip. I really want to help you get ready."

"That is excellent. I need some help."

She looks stunned. "You do?"

"Yes." I imagine my face glowing with sisterly love. "I believe you have a large whiteboard in the backroom, and colored dry erase markers. I need to borrow them. And I need to borrow your laptop."

The 'no' is already blooming on her face, so I have to stop it before it fully forms. "Oh, not for the trip," I assure her, laughing. "I just need to borrow them for an hour or so."

"Ah." She tilts her head to the side, squints, studies me like a tarot card for a hint of the future. "Come on, then. I'll help you take the things upstairs."

The back room is still a chaotic mess. I try not to breathe. Petra grabs the laptop, closes it, and hands it to me. "Be careful with that," she cautions as she wraps up the power cord and mouse. She shoves aside a couple of cardboard boxes that exude clouds of particulated dust before finding the whiteboard and a gallon baggie of colored markers. "Here we go. Sorry, it's a little dirty. I haven't used it in a while. You can clean it with rubbing alcohol and a good rag." It's about half as large as my doorway. I don't know if I have enough rubbing alcohol.

"Do you think you could maybe hose it off in your big sink?" She sighs as if she's inconvenienced. I don't want to anger her; she's my one connection to getting what I need at the moment, and she has been very helpful. "Never mind, I've imposed enough. I'll find a way to clean it upstairs."

"Oh, Sweeties, don't be silly." She smiles and drags the board to the pet washing area, muscles it into the deep tub, and hoses it off with the long, flexible sprayer. Rivers of brown flow merrily down the drain. I breathe a deep sigh of relief and thank the goddess of hygiene that I don't have to expose my living space to whatever was in those brown rivers.

As she pats it dry with the stained towel, Petra says, "So, when you see him, what are you going to say?"

"Hmm?"

She keeps spraying the board but looks at me. "What are you going to say to him? Have you figured out what you'll do when you get there?"

"No." I realize this is a definite flaw in my plan. I've been so busy getting ready to go that I haven't even considered what I'll do when I get there. "That's a very good point, though. I definitely need to think about it."

"Well, I guess you'll have lots of time to think on the road." After handing me the laptop, she embraces the white board and grabs the baggie of markers in her teeth. "Let's go," she mumbles through her mouthful of plastic, gesturing toward the door.

As we walk, clutching the computer to my chest, I think: what *am* I going to say or do? Panic wells up from below my breast, swelling slightly—a bubble of anxiety. I will stand there, dumb, staring at him and Doctor April Fennimore-what's-her-name. I'll stand in the back of the church gawking, hair askew, personal hygiene in question. I can see it now.

In my apartment, Petra sets the board down near the door and spits the baggie of markers out. I make a mental note to use the rubbing alcohol on that, too. I gently find a home for the laptop on my dining table, placing the foreign object gingerly on a placemat so it doesn't scratch the wood. I've never been a huge fan of technology, to be honest. It never seems to work for me. Edward thought I avoided it because I wanted to avoid connection, but I find it confusing and annoying, even dangerous. You expose yourself to all kinds of viruses and predations when you use the computer. It's like opening your door and inviting in every manner of sleazy, mud-spattered low life that crawls. I can barely stand the thought of using it, although I see the utility, of course. I'm not unrealistic.

Petra is sweating from the exertion of hauling the big board up the steps. "Could I trouble you for a glass of water, Anna?"

"Of course. No trouble at all." I swallow my intense desire to get started on organizing my trip (beginning with the rubbing alcohol). "Here you go," I say, smiling, as I hand her a pristine glass filled with cool tap water.

"Thank you." As she sips, she frowns at the laptop sitting on my table. "So, you know how to use that, yes?"

"I think so. Don't I just turn it on and then it…works?"

She chuckles, sets the glass down on the wooden table (no coaster, of course not) and proceeds to open the laptop. It's aluminum and covered with fingerprints. I have no idea how to clean it. Maybe I can wear some latex gloves. I think I could still type that way. "Here you go," she says, opening the thing and tapping some keys. "I've set you up on my wireless network. Want me to write down the password for you?"

"Password for what?"

"If you want to get on later and it's not signed on, you need a password." She blinks at me. "You have been on the computer before?"

"Well, of course. I was on it downstairs, remember?"

She nods knowingly. "Ah. Yes. Well, down there, it automatically logs on. Here, you have to sign in, at least the first time. I'll tell you what…if you have problems, come find me."

My head is spinning. I don't know how people work on these monstrous things every single day. From what I hear, some people are on them from morning to night. A small, intense headache starts to sprout behind my eyes.

"Feeling alright?" Petra zooms in and stares into my eyes, which makes it worse. I have to make sure she believes I am totally capable and normal—she might take away the car if she thinks I'm going to freak out.

"Fine." I smile and nod. "Just a lot to do, you know. Planning a trip is a lot of work."

She nods. "When do you think you're leaving?"

"Sunday." I have the date firmly set in my mind, a diamond glowing in the distance.

"That's soon. Three days! How can you get all the supplies you need?" She glances around the apartment and frowns. "Honestly, Anna, I think you should reconsider. You hate leaving your apartment. I hate to think of you alone on the road."

She's right. But I have to go. This is my destiny. So, when your destiny calls, you have to answer. "I won't be alone. I'll have Annabella."

She blinks. "Hmm? Is someone going with you?"

"My wig head?"

It takes a full five seconds for her to understand, and when she does, she explodes with a belly laugh that shakes dust out of the rafters. "Oh! Your wig head!" She pats me on the shoulder. "That's good. I bet you can drive in the carpool lanes! You should fix her up so she has a body, though, so the cops don't get suspicious." She wipes a drip of moisture from the corner of her eye. "Oh, Anna, you are precious. I wish you well. I do need to go…my shows are coming on. But call if you need me."

She waves as she sails out the door, shutting it blessedly behind her.

. . .

"Call if you need me." Edward walked me home from the park the day he gave me Annabella. "I know this has been a difficult day for you. Just call. The service will tell me it's you, and I can come over if you need me to."

The twilight washed the world with gold as we strolled toward home. I was Alice, wandering through Wonderland, kissed with magic and possibility. None of it made sense, and yet, it did.

"Will you come up for tea?" We were at my door.

He glanced up at the second floor. He'd never been where I live, but knew I lived on the second floor. That was a good sign, wasn't it? He'd been thinking of me. "I probably shouldn't."

"I promise, the apartment is clean." I smiled at him.

"Oh, I have no doubt of that." He flashed me that broad, lopsided grin that I'd come to love. "But I don't want to overstep." So British. So proper.

"Tea is a civil right," I replied boldly. "It's good manners. Nothing more."

"Hmm." He looked down at me, frowning. "It's just—well, you're right, of course. But since I'm your therapist, I shouldn't be crossing that boundary, you know. Into your home life."

"You know so much about me, more than anyone has ever known." I stared shyly at the sidewalk. "We really have no secrets. I don't see how coming into my home is any different from sitting in the park."

He can't argue with *that* logic. And he is a man of the mind.

He sighed. "Right, I suppose. I shouldn't have taken you to the park either."

"No, I'm glad you did!" I gazed up into his jewel-like eyes, polished translucent blue jade. "It made me feel…human."

He laughed then, shook his head. "In for a penny, in for a pound." He gestured toward the door. "Lead the way."

I gleefully opened the door, seeing the place with new eyes. It was drab, the hallway, the stairs, depressing. Perhaps this was a bad idea.

"Here we are," I said as cheerfully as I could. I opened my door, balancing his gift, my Annabella, and walked in, turned, waited for him to follow. He hesitated.

"Ah, Anna," he stumbled on his words, then stood silent.

"What is it?"

He stared past me into the apartment but wouldn't meet my eyes. "Happy birthday, but…I think I should go."

"No!" I think the force of my words stopped him. He blinked rapidly, surprised. "I mean, you can't stop now. You're…here. Do you know how long it's been since someone…anyone…walked into this apartment besides me?" Oh yes. I would stoop to using guilt. I was not too proud to beg.

"That may be true, but—"

"Fine." I tried to appear resigned but strong. "If you want to make this weird, that's fine. I just wanted to offer you some tea, nothing more. If your code of honor is more important than being a decent person and accepting some harmless hospitality, then—"

"Oh, bloody fine then." He stepped ceremoniously over the threshold. "There."

I tilted my head to the side, beamed at him, and said, "There now. Not so hard, eh? Come in, come in!" I carefully placed Annabella on the sofa.

I kept my distance. I knew he would frighten easily. I don't think he knew yet, as I did, that we were much more than a patient and a doctor.

He stood awkwardly just inside the door, leaving it open so as to have an escape route in case I jumped him, I guess. I bustled into the kitchen, calling breezily over my shoulder, "Could you close that door? The hall is always dusty." I didn't look back.

I busied myself with making tea. My hands were shaking. I heard him moving in the next room, his weight on the boards of my floor, the rustle of his clothing moving over his body. It was as if my senses were heightened; as if a kaleidoscope of dusty, murky colors had shifted suddenly, brilliantly, illuminating a silver-white swath of clarity. How right it felt. How unmistakably right.

"Sit anywhere," I sang as I stared with malice at the teakettle, willing it to boil. That never works. It took its time. Nothing for it but to pretend to be normal. I stopped myself from sprinting to his side, and instead mimicked the casual, devil-may-care gait of the uninterested. I leaned against the wall, studying his silhouette, his fidgety right leg, his long, elegant hands as they traced nervous patterns on his thighs. "Do you take cream and sugar?"

He nearly jumped, as if he'd half expected me to have disappeared down a rabbit hole. "Ah." He smiled, only with his mouth. His eyes darted nervously from me to the wig head next to him and then back to me. "Cream, if you have it. Thanks."

I took a tentative step toward him, and he inched ever so slightly away. "It'll just be a minute while the water's heating," I said. "She's so lovely."

"Hmm?" His arched eyebrows and tensed thighs told me I had misspoken, almost fatally.

"I mean Annabella," I sputtered. "She's lovely. I just can't get over how wonderful she is." I gingerly picked her up from the sofa and took a step back so he could relax, focusing on her clear, smooth surface and inquisitive eyebrows.

He knotted his fingers in and out, cracked knuckles, stared straight ahead. It was unbearable. The silence fell between us, a thicket of awkwardness. I was determined to prune it even if I couldn't trim it all the way back. "Please relax."

"Hmm?" Again, he looked at me as if I were about to pounce.

"You're a doctor. You're a professional man. What are you afraid of?" I couldn't believe how bold I was, and I had no idea where the ability to communicate was coming from—divine intervention, I supposed.

He blinked, surprised. "I'm not—afraid? Why do you think I'm afraid?" He turned toward me. A good sign.

"You think I'm going to try to seduce you." I imagined that Annabella blushed at my boldness. Edward certainly did.

"I think no such thing." His blinking had gone rapid-fire, and the twisting of fingers had become almost comical.

"You do. I don't blame you." Where was this confidence coming from? Was Annabella shuttling invisible waves of encouragement across the apartment? Was it the cosmic good? I had no idea. I didn't really care. "I promise you, Edward, I will do no such thing."

The blinking slowed. The hands rested. He laughed, first a small chuckle, then more from the chest as he shook his head. "Of course, you won't. God. I'm so sorry." He jumped up and scrunched his chin into that sheepish down-turned grin I loved so much. "I've just—I need to tell you something, and I don't know how to do it." The words halted, as if they dreaded coming out of his mouth.

The teakettle wailed, giving me an excuse to scurry to the kitchen. What did he have to tell me? My heart beat faster. As I poured water over two tea bags (I know, it's not really proper, it should be loose tea leaves, strained, ready for fortune telling...at least it was an English brand, not Lipton's or some other nasty American brew.) I realized I had no cream. No cream! Why didn't I think of that ahead of time? Stupid.

I balanced the two cups of tea on little saucers. It was all ruined now, though, because of the cream. That was a bad omen. I dreaded suddenly what he would say. I briefly thought that I should run out of the apartment on some wild pretense, like the kitchen was on fire, or my neighbor was having a heart attack, but he'd certainly know what I was up to. Nothing for it—I had to man up and walk that tea out to the couch.

"Ah." He took a saucer from me and said nothing about the teabag or the lack of dairy products. He didn't drink it, though; he was Persephone and I was Hades, trying to trick him into staying in the Underworld after partaking of my pomegranate...or crappy cream-less tea bag tea, in this case. "Thanks."

I sat next to him. After the park, things seemed so tense, so differ-ent. It was as if we'd walked through some mirror into the world where what I wanted would never be. I wanted too much to shatter that stupid mirror and get back to where we were leaning against a tree and he was giving me a gift. But here we were, awkward.

"What did you want to tell me?" I sipped my tea.

He stared straight ahead, breathing hard. I could hear it...in, out, in, out. I had to fight the urge to put my head on his chest so I could be closer to it. Silly, silly, teenaged girl thoughts. Sipped again.

"Anna," he started, turning toward me. His eyes were full of pain. What if he were dying? "Oh, please, don't look at me that way."

"What way?"

"As if...as if I've run over your puppy."

"I don't have a puppy."

"I'm aware of that." He set his teacup on my side table, stood, and started to pace. *Come back! Sit down!* "Sorry. I...I have to tell you that—um—I've met someone."

How to respond? "I'm sure you meet people all the time. Why is that anything special?"

"Don't pretend you don't know what I mean." He licked his lips, shoved his hands into his pockets, and paced again. "I've met someone. A woman. I've met a woman, and—we've been dating. For nearly three months. And Anna, I know I've probably made you think that—" He stopped, blinked rapidly, and rubbed his hand over his eyes as if he didn't want to see what he was seeing. Which was, of course, me.

Waves of sound pounded my ears as if I were standing in the ocean. "You've met a woman?"

"Yes. I wanted to tell you several times, but honestly, it seemed too personal, and then you seemed to—well, in psychology, they call it transference. You've transferred all the feelings you've had about your life, your family, onto me."

"I see." I sipped my tea, placed the cup and saucer carefully on the table, folded my hands in my lap like a good girl. I waited.

He paced even more rapidly. "Yes, well. You *see*." He started several sentences, didn't finish any, and finally blurted out, "But do you understand?"

I knew that this was a moment in my life where a large portal had opened and I had to choose a path. It resonated with such importance, such unadulterated portent, that I had to catch my breath before I answered. I wanted to pull out the hair of my wig, although that wouldn't solve anything, and it would just make me seem even more unbalanced. I wanted to throw hot tea at his perfectly structured face, and I wanted to duct tape him to a kitchen chair, and I wanted to tell him to leave and never come back.

What I said was, "I understand."

I did. But understanding and accepting do not live in the same universe.

He sighed, relieved, and sat back down on the couch, slowly, as if he half expected me to claw his eyes out or tear off his shirt at the buttons, or cry hysterically. I did none of those things. I was numb, to be honest, but I knew that I needed to pretend to be a sane person if I didn't want him to bolt out the door, never to be seen again.

The silence. Awkward, pregnant, full of possibilities, a snow globe shaken and frozen, waiting to be thawed. I didn't want to break it, because once I did—once I thawed it—events would fall like dominos in the direction that they would, and whichever path I took, I knew I would regret it because it would mean ignoring the alternate path. I guess that's what normal people call "being stuck."

But as the minutes ticked by, I knew I couldn't wait there forever. He'd get uncomfortable, he'd leave, he wouldn't see me again. I had to say something. I prayed for the goddesses of wisdom and lust to have mercy and to give me the words I needed, the magic words that would take me where I wanted to go.

Instead, I said, "More tea?"

There are no goddesses.

. . .

I'm going to go. I glance out the window again—the sun has set, and for once, the darkness looks friendly instead of frightening. I shouldn't but...I open the window, just a crack.

In bed that night, I watch the moonlight make patterns on my ceiling. It is the first night I've left the window open since—well, I used to leave them open all the time, when I was in the old house.

Mmmm. For a fragment of a second, I smell lilacs. Those were in the yard, bursting in spring, a purple fountain of blooms, wild, almost swallowing the side of the house. I left the windows open then. Thin white cotton curtains used to dance in the night air, waving the dusky scent of the flowers into my bedroom—oh, and night blooming jasmine! That had been one of my favorites, a scent that promised mystery and excitement and things to come.

It's not the same now, of course. The smell coming through the window is not floral; it's a city smell, cooling asphalt, diesel exhaust, Chinese fried food—fried fair food. Those horrible things on sticks that they dip-dropped into spitting vats of rancid oil, Twinkies and cheesecake, and even pickles. Tom loved the fried pickles.

A glare of harsh light from some oversized semi washes through the room like a searchlight outside a prison searching for someone. Me? I've done nothing wrong. Everyone said so. Edward said so. Not my fault. The fault was in the stars, they say. Like Juliet, like Romeo, he had a Roman nose, they say, Tom did. It was one of the things I noticed first about him, and—

My face is wet. I close the blinds. I close the window.

I wake to the sound of a barking dog, so rhythmic it sounds like the scratching of a broken record. The sun is up and has been for at least an hour. Obviously, leaving the window open was unhealthy for me, and I got little sleep. My head itches horribly, as if an army of fleas has camped there overnight. I reach for a hairbrush and scratch my scalp, moaning at the pleasure of relieving the infernal skin affliction.

Despite my terrible night, I am determined to make progress on the trip. There are so many things I have to consider: How can I travel by car across this country without contracting several hideous diseases? Public bathrooms. I must purchase surgical masks and Purell in large quantities. Handwashing might be spotty at best. I've noticed that many modern restrooms refuse to stock soap or paper towels. This is all part of the 'green' movement, I suppose, but, ironically, it's simply promoting disease and poor hygiene. Most likely this will be the downfall of humanity.

I will be prepared, however.

I'll have to plan the route, of course. I'm not very good with maps, although if I plan carefully I should be able to construct a route that travels through fairly unpopulated, rural areas, which tend to be cleaner. I might need to stay in a motel to bathe, though, which will be difficult. My budget is very limited, and cost is usually inverse to cleanliness where accommodations are concerned.

I begin my legal pad list: *Go to bank. Get map. Cell phone. Supplies. Schedule.*

I'm going to need to plan my trip, day to day, and budget for it. *Need a calendar*, I add to the legal pad. I wonder if Petra has one. It probably features cute kittens in adorable poses.

Ugh. I'm going to have to go to the bank. In person. A stab of dread shoots through my stomach at the thought. Aside from public restrooms, banks are among the most germ-laden of institutions. Paper money, for example, changes hands so often that it should be burned—imagine if you could examine just one dollar bill with a high-powered microscope. Whole worlds of horrible germs exist on money. But I'm sure I'll need some cash. I could probably wash it. Plus, I need a credit card.

In the bathroom I adjust my wig, draw on my eyebrows (people *really* don't like it when those are missing), and lightly dust my face with blush to cover my indoors-only complexion. "You can do this," I tell my reflection. She doesn't look too confident. Annabella smiles at me from her perch on the wicker etagere. She believes in me. That's going to have to be enough.

The details of my preparations are cumbersome at best. I get to the bank, check my scanty account balance, and withdraw the money I need with minimal catastrophe (in my nervousness I tell the security guard that I absolutely do not have a gun, which of course makes him think I have a gun, and that sets off a whole search and seizure that frankly almost turns me away from the whole journey). I do insist that he wear protective gloves, at least, and that seems to make him even more suspicious.

They say no to the credit card. They suggest I buy a pre-paid Visa instead, and I can get those at any grocery store. I get more filthy dollar bills.

Cash in hand, I stop at the market next to get my supplies. I carefully count dollars out to the swarthy owner for a pre-paid Visa, although he has a hard time understanding why I want to pay him cash. I ask him how most people pay, and he tells me, seriously, "With a credit card." And why would a "One-Stop Shop" carry eggplants but not alcohol wipes? Humanity baffles me. I get what I can, and when I return to my apartment, I feel great satisfaction in crossing items off my list.

A knock at the door interrupts my preparation. "Anna?"

"Yes?" I call as I refold the items of clothing I plan to take (very few...I must travel light).

"It's Petra. Can I come in?"

Sigh. Of course. Now that she's given me the keys to my future, she feels she owns a piece of it. But I have to be pleasant. "Hi!" I go for perky, but probably sound like I'm on speed.

Petra smiles and barges into the apartment, closing the door behind her. An acrid odor follows her. "Just got my hair done," she says, doing a little ballerina turn to show it off.

"It's quite red."

"I asked her to make it vibrant. I wanted to really feel like I was showing the world who I am!" She glances at my suitcase. "You're getting ready to go on your trip?"

She knows I am. Why do people ask questions when they know the answers? But I paste a smile on my face and answer. "Yes. I've been getting everything in order. You'll keep an eye on my place while I'm gone, won't you?"

"Sure." She ambles to the table where my legal pad is open. "My, you do have a lot to do!" she glances back at me. "Will you really be able to leave on time?"

"I have to." Her comment reminds me of the deadline pressure. I don't really need the extra anxiety. Calm, calm, no panic allowed. "I think I'll be ready to leave on schedule. Sunday."

"Still seems rushed to me."

I continue folding. "There is a deadline. If I don't make it by the deadline, I might as well not go."

She sighs heavily and puts a hand on my shoulder. "Anna," she says quietly. "Really. Reconsider this. He's not going to change his mind."

Rage bubbles up from inside, acid rage, sudden and sickening. I swallow it. I say nothing. She stands there, immobile, as if waiting for me to be sensible and agree with her.

"Alright. If you're absolutely determined, then I wish you good luck. I do wish you'd take someone with you." She drums her fingers on the table. "Isn't there anyone?"

"No." And I realize: there isn't. *There isn't anyone.* This changes the acid rage into a wave of inconsolable sorrow, and I have to be alone. I turn to Petra. "Could you please leave?"

She looks shocked. "Well—I suppose. Sorry. I just thought—" She frowns, purses her orange-red lips and shakes her head. "I thought you might want some company before you leave, but I'll just go on and let you concentrate." The door slams as she leaves.

God, I hope I haven't blown it. I couldn't help it, though. Alone. *Alone.* I hate that word. It's a curse, a judgment, a deficiency, a yawning void.

And then, almost as if by magic, the box is in my hand. The box of Unwanteds.

I run my fingers over the smooth shoebox edges dotted with small nicks at the corner from being shoved here and there in moves and frenzies of discarding things from my previous life. Not now, though.

No time now. But what if I don't come back? I have to take it with me.

I try to touch it as little as possible as I ferry it to the bedroom, tuck it into a corner of my suitcase, and cover it with a dark blue towel.

5
PATH OF TRAVEL

It was my first appointment. Edward sat in his oversized brown leather chair, pencil in his mouth, reading my paperwork. I sat on a fabric-covered aqua couch with one coffee stain in the shape of the Virgin Mary riding a cheetah. I tried to ferret out some meaning in that stain, but nothing magically blossomed in my head.

"So, here where it asks about your family, you've left that blank," he said, a question lurking behind his velvety British baritone. I broke my concentration away from the stain and met his gaze, but immediately had to look away. "Anna, is there some reason you've omitted listing your family members here?"

"I have no family." I gripped the edge of the sofa cushion, and my knuckles went white. They were like small, blank faces pressing to escape from a thinly-stretched field of skin-colored canvas.

He made some noise, a guttural sound in his throat that communicated doubt. "If you're not honest with me, I can't be of much use."

"Are you calling me a liar?" Too confrontational. I willed myself to relax. "I mean, what makes you think I'm not telling the truth?"

I looked up and he was smiling, the edges of his eyes crinkled, his lips curled into a grin. "Are you? Are you telling the truth?"

I blinked. "No. Yes. Sort of."

Then he laughed. The rumble of it, the vibration, I felt in my chest. It chased just a fraction of the fear away, just the smallest crumb. But that was something.

"Let's just start slowly," he said, crossing his long legs. "Why don't you tell me why you're here."

Why was I there? I suddenly had no answer. "I don't know," I blurted out.

He paused, jotted something on his yellow legal pad. "You don't know why you've come to see me? Is it just a friendly visit to a fellow laundromat victim?"

And then I laughed. It was just a little chuckle at first, but it perked up from a deep cave in my heart and, like the tiny bubbles in champagne, floated to the top in a quest to seek air. It felt so foreign to me that I knew I had come to the right place. I needed this. "I think I need to talk to someone."

"Well, that's what I do." He closed the legal pad decisively. "I think we'll stop looking at your paperwork for today. "

"I'm going? Already?"

"No, no. But I think we have to go slowly. I think you'll tell me what you need to in time. But for now, let's just talk about something else. The weather." He looked out the window; the sky was gray, overstuffed with a patchwork of rainclouds. "Did you bring an umbrella?"

"No."

"Why not?"

"I don't walk in the rain."

"Why not?"

I shifted uncomfortably. "There are…things in the rain. Germs, you know. You just don't know where they're going to be. Water is the worst offender."

He frowned. "What about air, though? You walk outside, breathe the air, of course? Isn't that full of germs too?"

"Well, I can't very well stop breathing, can I?" Really. What stupid questions he was asking.

He stood, walked to the window, and gestured toward the ominous sky. "So, what do you do if it starts raining and you're out somewhere?"

"I wait."

He frowned at me. "You wait until it stops raining?"

I nodded. "It's usually not that long."

"What's the longest you've ever waited?"

I knew exactly. "Two days."

"Two days!"

. This was not going well. I didn't want him to think I was a crazy nut job, but even something as innocuous as the weather was turning into a revealing showcase for my neurotic eccentricities. "It wasn't like I sat in someone's doorstep for two days or anything. I was staying with a friend, and I just stayed a little longer."

"Doesn't that sort of thing get in the way of your plans?"

"I don't make too many plans. Plans are a waste of time. You know what they say about plans."

"No, what do they say?"

"Plans are what gets ruined when God fucks around with your life."

He seemed stunned, as if he'd never heard that old adage before. Perhaps because he was British. "Right." He checked his watch. He seemed to consider for some time, as if he were calculating a particularly important chess move. "We have another 20 minutes, but after that I actually have a gap of about two hours. Would you like me to give you a lift home? We could still talk. I could see where you live, and maybe being out of the office will allow you to speak more freely."

My heart fluttered, just a bit. Surely doctors didn't routinely offer their patients a ride home? "I don't want to impose."

"Not at all. I need to run some errands anyway." He scooped a dark gray raincoat from the rack, shrugged into it, and wrapped a houndstooth scarf around his neck. "Let's be off, shall we?"

I followed him out into the reception area, which was empty except for the uppity administrative assistant. Her neat auburn hair was tucked behind her ears, and she was slightly stocky with glasses; a bit pretty in a schoolteacher sort of way. I was sure after one look at her that nothing was going on between them; he would surely have chosen someone much better looking. "I'm going out for a bit," he said, waving to her.

She looked up and smiled. "Have fun." She looked at me. "Miss Beck, I have you down for next Thursday, same time. Is that alright?"

"Yes." I stared at her, mentally staking my claim to the doctor. Her bland face didn't register a thing.

"Great." She picked up the phone receiver and threw us one more smile as she pressed buttons to make a call. "Stay dry."

Happily, Edward's car was in a parking garage under the building, so there was no need to worry about looking silly in the downpour that had started. His slightly dented Range Rover surprised me; I had envisioned him driving a black BMW or something more doctor-ish. It was messy, too, which was challenging, but I knew that when you loved someone you put up with all kinds of things.

"Right." He turned the key and the Rover sputtered before starting. "Where are we going? Near that laundromat, I imagine, right?"

I gave him the address, and he knew right where it was. As he pulled out into traffic, fat drops hit the windshield. "Good timing," he muttered as the wiper blades swiped the water away.

I closed my eyes and breathed deeply. I wanted to memorize the scent of the car, his coat, the cold, the rain. As we drove on, he chatted about nothing, and I listened to everything.

. . .

It's near midnight Saturday night when I realize how tired I am. I've nearly filled two white legal pads with all the minutiae of my impending pilgrimage. That's how I think of it: a pilgrimage. A holy journey to a holy place.

I've visited the bank (tellers are judgmental), I've discussed arrangements for plant watering with Petra (Petra is judgmental), and I spent a good part of the day making sure the car was ready. This entailed wiping it down thoroughly with alcohol wipes, organizing the massive trunk into sections for my things, and laying in a large, rectangular cooler that is powered by the cigarette lighter (courtesy also of Petra's nephew, the one in jail.) I've hardly slept over the past two days.

So, tomorrow morning, Sunday, I will leave. As I stretch out on my bed for the last time (the very last time?) I allow myself the luxury of mentally touching everything in my apartment that I'm leaving behind. I realize there is not much to miss.

That shoebox in my suitcase. I'd like to leave it. I cannot. It's like a tumor twisted round my heart, and if I excise it, I'll die.

The dream:

Breathe in and out, a tide of life. In my breath I hear the waves washing to shore, shuttling a moonlit caress from the tropical breeze outside. French doors open onto a bamboo deck strung with tiny white lights. My hair, long, auburn, luxurious, cascades around my shoulders. It smells of cinnamon and lavender.

Something blocks the light coming in from the deck. I turn my head slightly, and I know who it is.

I know his form, his silhouette. Tall, almost taller than the doorframe, all angles and power, an athlete's body. He moves into the room, and I sense the hesitation, the fear of doing wrong.

"Come here," I whisper, sitting up slightly against the cool sheets. I'm naked, and the soft ends of my hair brush my shoulders slightly, sensually.

"I can't," he replies, but his body moves toward me as if pulled by gravity.

"Just sit. Talk to me." He eases himself onto the edge of the bed, taking up as little space as possible, as if that will make it permissible. He cradles his face in his hands, moonlight playing in his dark hair, touching it with silver. I do not touch him.

He turns his face toward me. Eyes anguished, hungry, he says, "We can't do this, Anna. It's wrong."

"I know." I lean forward, allowing my breasts to escape the modesty of the thin cotton quilt. His eyes find them, and his breathing becomes faster, more ragged.

"I shouldn't be here." He inches closer, slightly. "I— just came in to check on

you. Make sure you were alright."

"Why wouldn't I be?" I take a thin cigarette from the nightstand, gesture to him. He takes a lighter from his pocket, ignites it, flares the cigarette tip, and I inhale, exhale, like the sea, in and out.

"The wedding is tomorrow." He chokes slightly on the words. I inhale, exhale, in, out. He coughs slightly.

"And?" I am remarkably cool. I tamp ash into the ashtray, gesture with my cigarette. "Aren't you terribly excited? It should be a wondrous affair."

"Dammit." He knocks the cigarette out of my hand (and then picks it up and stubs it out in the tray. He is also safety conscious.) "Dammit, Anna, I love you. I don't love her."

He wraps the long, slender fingers of his left hand around my head, cupping it gently, and draws me to him. At first, he is tentative, brushes my lips with his as if seeking permission. I do not have the will to refuse.

The kiss becomes stronger, harder; his right hand finds its way around my waist, and he pulls me toward him. I do not fight. "Oh, Edward," I moan in his ear.

"Anna." He nuzzles my neck, his unshaven face blissfully rough against my soft skin. Sweat, citrus, some exotic flower—his scent makes me drunk.

He stops. He fixes me with jade eyes, intense and wild. "Do you want this as much as I do? I need to know. It's wrong, but I don't care. I can't live without having you."

"Edward," I breathe. "If loving you is wrong, I don't want to be right."

He pulls back and frowns. "What?"

"I mean—yes. Yes! I want it too."

"You just quoted a terrible pop song from the '70s at me. Didn't you? Is this a joke to you?"

"No, no of course not!" The spell is broken. He's pulling away.

"Cut!" the director yells from my spacious closet. "This isn't working. Come on." All the lights go on, and the room is suddenly an operating room, glaring, and Edward is wearing a surgical gown, and is surrounded by nurses who all look like April Fennimore-what's-her-name.

Edward snaps on latex gloves, leans over me, and says "We'll have to remove that, Anna. Can't have you running around with a broken heart." He pulls out a bone saw, revs it up, and the last thing I remember is a searing pain in my chest, a burning, torment, agony—

I gasp awake. Even my erotic dreams deny me happiness.

. . .

Early Sunday morning, when Petra sees me readying the car, she comes out of the shop to be sure I'm not damaging the vehicle.

"That's vintage," she says, shifting her weight from foot to foot, trying the patience of her small navy-blue pumps. "That car is a collector's item!"

"Is the dirt vintage also?"

She stops shifting and glares at me. That did cross a boundary, I realize, but I couldn't resist. "Just don't hurt anything."

I smile at her endearingly. "I will treat it as if it's my own child."

Anxiety slams me in the chest, breathing stops. Without thought, I clutch at my shirt and start to gasp. "Anna?" Petra trots over to the car. "Anna. Are you alright? What is it?"

I can't catch my breath enough to answer.

"Oh my god. Should I call 911?" I shake my head no. "Do you need mouth to mouth?" *Jesus*, no. "What can I do?" I shake my head, gesture for her to go inside.

I picture Edward, me, inside his office, lying on the dark green mat on the floor, him kneeling near my head. Steady breathing, steady breathing, in, out, like the waves of the ocean. I hear his voice: "Be still. Ride the wave. Be the tide." I feel his hand on my forehead. My heart slows. My breathing becomes less ragged. The pounding in my head becomes an echo.

"What in hell was that?" Petra has opened the passenger door and is kneeling next to me, dirtying up my alcohol scrub regimen.

"Something I ate."

"Something you ate? Are you insane?" I glare at her. "Oh. Sorry."

I take in two more deep breaths and try to explain. "I just thought of something that bothered me for a moment, but then I dealt with it. I dealt with it."

"What if you had been driving?" Petra touches the dashboard lovingly. "You could've crashed the car."

"That would never happen." I sit up, readjust my wig, and find a fresh alcohol wipe. "It was because we were talking. I won't be talking to anyone."

"We were talking?"

People are goldfish, glubbing away in their stupid glass bowls. I get so tired of explaining everything in excruciating detail. But I have to, at least this time. I put on the most patient face I can muster. "You were talking about me taking care of the car, it triggered a feeling, and then I dealt with it. But on my trip, I will be alone, and no one else will be able to intrude on my thoughts like you did there, so I will be perfectly safe. Does that make sense?"

Petra blinks, as if I've just recited *Bridget Jones' Diary* in Sanskrit, and exits the car. "I suppose," she says. "Just call me now and then. I'm going to worry the whole time."

"About me or the car?"

"Yes."

Being careful to snatch the keys, I brush past her and trot back upstairs to get ready for departure. My dining table is covered with a huge map of the United States. I have plotted the route meticulously and used Petra's laptop to note the most efficient locations for food and fuel (and printed copious pages since I will not have access to the laptop on the road.) I plan to sleep in the car since at the very least I can keep that environment clean. I know I will have to stop in motels along the way to shower, though, so I've also researched acceptable spots where I can hole up for the night without fear of bedbugs or stabbing. Nothing is a sure thing, though.

I take Annabella from the bathroom and place her next to my suitcase, which stands near the door as if it can't wait to get going. I put her in the box she came in (which I saved) so she'll be protected on the drive. I haul my things down the stairs, pack carefully, be sure the top on the car is secure (it's a convertible, I've discovered), make several trips to grab the map, the legal pad, my purse, food for the cooler and everything else I'll need.

One last look around the apartment, one last check in my purse to be sure I have the cash and the prepaid emergency Visa. I touch various things in the apartment, as if saying goodbye: the curtains, the little broken milkmaid sugar bowl, the quilt on my bed. A flutter of excitement, of danger, zings in my chest, just below my heart.

Petra stands silent in the door of the dog salon, like a disapproving mermaid on the prow of a sinking ship. "It's not too late to change your mind," she calls, cupping her hand over her mouth as if she's not loud enough.

"It *is* too late." I walk to the driver's side, open the door, sit in the over-large seat. I check in the rearview and see nothing behind me.

6
PARALLEL PARKING

I drive out of town, knuckles white on the steering wheel. I stop and get gas, uneventful except for the fact that I have to wrap my hand in paper napkins to keep from touching the pump. Thankfully, they have a box of latex gloves in the little mini store, next to the petrified donuts (why? Best not to ask.) I take them all. The gloves, not the donuts.

Before I take to the road again, I consult my legal pad, my constant companion. I have charted my course for the next five days and I know exactly where I am going. Day Six is Wedding Day. I have a running ledger in which to keep an accounting of the money I spend. Assuming all goes as planned, I should reach Colorado exactly one day before the wedding.

Being outside is, at first, a novelty. I've spent so much time indoors that I'd forgotten a lot. Billboards...I remember those whizzing by when I was a passenger, a long time ago, faces of smiling people and their smiling pets blurring as if the wind were erasing their features. Since I'm driving, it's a bit more difficult to see the details, but I remember. Traffic, too—that's something different. When I drove before, I don't think there were quite so many idiotic drivers on the road. Now, every second car seems to be piloted by a psychopath or a woman with dementia or an angry young man with an extremely thumpy stereo. Were there so many angry men back then? I certainly don't remember that.

I'd mapped my route to take highways that are less traveled, but I soon learn that in California, there is no such thing. Everywhere I try to drive, a hundred other people have had the same idea.

I'm mesmerized by license plates. Every one is different. Different state, different country. Guam, Mexico, Hawaii. I know Hawaii is a state, but still…that's a very long ways away. Bored. Bored. I believe this beast has a radio, but I can't stop to find it. The rumble of the car beneath me is comforting.

I wonder what he'll say when he sees me? Will he be happy? Surprised, certainly. I imagine him charging out of the church, arms open, and he picks me up, swings me around, and sets me gently on the ground. "How? How did you come?" he'll ask, tugging the restrictive tie from his neck and throwing it to the ground.

Doctor April will call from the entry to the church, and he'll turn, remembering where he is. And then he'll turn back to me, his face anguished. "I'm getting married," he'll say. I'll simply take him by the hand, lead him to the car, open the door, and, without words, show him his destiny. He'll pause, of course, long enough to shoot a deeply apologetic look toward April, and then he'll scramble into the car, slam the door, and we'll leave a trail of gravel and dust rising into the air, and a bride who had no right to claim him.

The traffic stops, and I nearly slam into a minivan with a sticker telling me that the person's family has eaten my stick family. I have no idea what this means. I know that I am not moving. A good opportunity to find some tunes.

The radio is old, the kind with a dial and no buttons. I punch it on, search past static and mariachi music for something, anything, in English. I finally hit on a talk radio station. Might be good to find out what's happening in the world.

"—expect significant delays throughout the day. In other news, police in Rafe's Mill, Oklahoma have uncovered a grisly scheme involving a local funeral home and a dog food manufacturer—" I twist the dial. I do not want to hear about that…news? Is that news? Maybe another channel.

"—so-called actresses who basically sex it up to get noticed. In the movie business today, you're either young and sexy or old and wise. There's no crossover, nothing in between. The message is that if you're over 25, don't bother trying to look good, because society has judged you unfit. You're washed up. You're through. The three-wrinkle rule, you know? If you have more than three wrinkles on your face, your photo has to be photo-shopped for any major magazine cover—" I twist the knob again, hoping for some classical music.

"—God's judgment falls upon all the wicked." A southern Baptist twang barks from the speaker, and my immediate reaction is to get it away from me, but something makes me stop. "If you have evil in your life, if terrible circumstances have befallen you, you cannot blame Jesus. You have to blame yourself. You brought it upon yourself, with sin. Sin is a magnet that draws calamity."

I shut it off. Fucking self-righteous religious dingbats give me migraines. Sin doesn't exist. I'm not even sure God exists, to be honest. God couldn't allow such awful things to happen here, unless he or she was some vindictive asshole with a huge cosmic magnifying glass frying us like insects crawling on this dirt ball.

What about the innocent? What about the people who do nothing wrong and are punished? Victims of war, victims of abuse, victims of random disease—

Must find music. My breathing is suddenly ragged. I know that I cannot drive a car without oxygen. I'd pull over, but there are solid lines of unmoving cars on either side of me, locking me into a lidless metal coffin. No one moves. I glance to my right—red pickup truck, windows rolled up, old man with grizzled beard smoking, staring straight ahead. To my left, a couple, arguing, window rolled up, dark-haired woman gesturing wildly to man waving cell phone. Behind me, in the rear-view, two burly Mexican men wearing dark sunglasses, staring straight into the back of my head. It feels like they could move my wig with a thought or two, violently. I grip it instinctively. Still there.

I have to have some classical music, some jazz. Since we're stopped, again, I cautiously turn on the radio, and vow not to stop if anyone is talking. After much careful tuning, I find a very faint, wibbly-wobbly frequency where tiny violins sing softly, as if they're afraid to draw attention to themselves.

Sunset marks the end of my driving time since my night vision is awful. Unfortunately, I am nowhere near my planned stop, so I am going to have to improvise. I see a sign for a rest stop that should be a mile away, so I'll pull off there and make camp for the night.

That, of course, takes me nearly an hour since we move like snails, so by the time I've steered the car into the rest stop it's pitch black except for one lone sickly light on a bent pole. I don't even know how to turn on the headlights of this beast. I steer into what I hope is a parking spot, turn the key, and relax into the relative silence. After poking around a bit, I find the button for the headlights, and they pop on, stabbing the darkness with two fingers of yellowish illumination.

I need to use the bathroom. This is huge. How did I not plan for this? I see the dark cement-block bathroom looming coldly outside the circle of the headlights. How can I get there? Terror rises up from my gut, nearly makes me vomit, but I tamp it down. What if someone's in there? What about the germs? The germs. The bacteria, the crabs, the warts, the leftover hitchhikers from all the dirty asses that have sat upon those unwashed seats. Maybe the bushes would be better…but there are no bushes. Just concrete and one lone tree standing near the exit.

My bladder insists that I solve this problem, and I am damn sure not going to pee in the car. So. Nothing for it. I need some form of protection, though. I grab a pair of the borrowed latex gloves—and delicately extricate Annabella from her backseat cradle. In a pinch, she could inflict some serious blunt-force trauma. I don't want to damage her, of course, but if my life is at stake…

I open the door. It creaks. There are exactly three other cars in this lot, all parked alongside each other in the shadowed section. Probably doing drug deals. All I have are my meds, and I don't think they're at all recreational. I pretend to be invisible, close the door as silently as possible, and tiptoe to the restroom. My bladder, knowing relief is at hand, suddenly wakes up and demands assistance.

I scuttle into the dark restroom that smells of disease-carrying bacteria. A small bit of moonlight throws silver slivers onto the oddly smeared walls (do not think about it). No one is in the room but me, so I hastily scuttle into a stall, shut the door and feel slightly sheltered. I cannot pull down my panties without setting Annabella on the filthy floor.

"Sorry, my dear," I whisper to her, setting her gingerly at my feet. After that, all bets are off, panties down, ass on the cold, cold seat, and I don't even care about the germs. I just want to pee. Ah, relief. It's almost orgasmic.

Nothing happens. No one bursts in with a machete. It's actually quiet. I finish, pick up Annabella, and exit the stall, bypassing the rusted faucets and sinks. Hand sanitizer beckons.

I realize I did not lock the car.

I realize I do not have the keys.

I realize that the whole trip may be lost before it's started. I peer out into the lot, expecting swarms of criminals to be jacking the tires off the Cadillac, but it's just as I left it, headlights still stabbing the gloom.

I run to the car, set Annabella down, get in, lock all the doors, breathe. Strip off the now-filthy gloves, roll the window down just far enough to toss them outside. I know it's littering. This is for a greater good. Hand sanny. Roll the window up again. Keys in ignition. Jesus, how stupid. I have to remember how real people live.

I feel safe inside. I consider re-parking, but I want to be near the bathroom in case my treacherous bladder decides to stage a middle-of-the-night assault.

For what must be half an hour, I stare ahead of me at the edge of the blocky bathroom building, past the pale watery light of the bent-pole fluorescent, into the gradations of gray and black that ink the world beyond. There may not be anything there at all. This rest stop might be all there is. How do I know? Our perception may be entirely false. What we think exists...does it exist if we don't see it? Does a one-pawed bear clap in the woods if no one hears him?

But the freeway behind me still undulates with sluggish life. I guess there must be something beyond the darkness.

"What now?" I ask Annabella. I turn her so it seems that her face is staring at me. Her luminous, peaceful visage and dark cherry lips pursed in amusement communicate volumes. "I am hungry, yes."

Time to raid the cooler. Twisting awkwardly, I open the lid, and things still seem relatively cool, but I don't think it's going to work for dairy or anything that will spoil quickly. I may be living on peanut butter. There are worse things.

Bread, peanut butter, a sterilized knife, a pint of white milk that I should drink before it expires. Not a bad little feast.

Darcy's favorite was peanut butter.

My throat closes. Air stops automatically pumping into my lungs, and the bite of bread threatens to kill me, stuck like a clog in a drain. Air, air...I can't...I kick against the car door, but it's locked and won't open. Finger fumble, unlock, open, head toward ground between knees, cough, get it out, spit it out, wheeze breathe in, in, exhale, cough. The offending piece of bread lies on the asphalt.

Why?

A scream tears out my throat, echoes off the cement bricks, envelops the bent-pole light, stabs the darkness beyond. No one seems to hear it.

I get control. I get back in the car. I close the door. Suddenly so, so tired. I find my pillow from the back, recline the seat as far as it will go, cover up with a fuzzy blanket, and drift off to sleep, the faint taste of peanut butter still on my tongue.

. . .

Bang. Bang bang bang bang bang. "Hey!"
I'm sleeping.
BANG! "Lady!"

One eye opens. A man, upside down, peers at me. He is floating in a clear blue sky. For a second I think I'm dreaming, but when I realize it's actually a real person, panic jolts me awake.

"You can't camp here." He shoves a star-shaped gold badge against the window, points to it, then as quickly pulls back. "Get up."

My back complains as I unfurl myself from the position I slept in. It appears I didn't move at all. I swallow, throat dry, and my wig has fallen off. I instinctively reach for the stubbled scalp, embarrassed. He'll think I'm a homeless nut. Homeless people don't have cars, do they? Certainly not Cadillacs. "What can I do for you, officer?" Isn't that what you're supposed to say?

Now that I can see him better, I see his name: Anderson, stitched above the right breast pocket. The gold star is on the left. I never realized they had actual stars, like a sheriff in an old-timey western movie. He also has huge reflective sunglasses even though it's barely morning. He motions for me to roll down the window.

I scramble to put my wig back on before I engage him. *Squeak, squeak, squeak* goes the window. I open it just enough for my words to escape. "Yes?"

"You do realize this is public property?"

I'm not sure how I'm supposed to answer this. "Yes?" I shield my eyes with one hand to block the sun that is rising behind him.

"Registration."

"Pardon?"

He is clearly annoyed with me. "I need to see your registration," he says slowly, as if I'm deaf, stupid, or foreign. It takes me a moment, but I remember that Petra said it was in the glove box. But it's not in my name. I don't know if Anderson will be able to understand the situation. Hmmm.

"I'm afraid that I can't show it to you at this time," I say through the small crack in the window. I have the keys in hand and I am ready to bolt.

"Why is that?" He shifts his weight to one polished black boot and crosses his arms.

"My glove box was melted shut." What? Really?

He stands there, stunned by my brilliance. "Your glove compartment was melted shut? Is that what you said?"

"Yes. That's what I said." Commit to it. Wishy-washy lies do not work. "Melted shut. Completely."

"You have your license in there too, I expect?" He grins as if he thinks he's brilliant.

"No." I tug at my wig just a bit and stare straight ahead. "My purse was stolen."

He shakes his head. "You've had a helluva trip, then, haven't you?" He backs up a step or two and gives the car the once over. "Sweet ride, though. How long have you had her?"

"Oh." I have no idea. "Many years. It was passed down to me. From my uncle. Uncle Edward." I slowly, slowly ease the key into the ignition. There is no front plate on this car. If I can back out suddenly, and then back down the exit, I can get away without him seeing the plate number, and then he won't be able to call it in—

The radio on his hip suddenly chirps and squeaks like a tortured monkey. He grabs it, listens, then responds. "Unit 42, on my way." He grins at me. "You got lucky. Someone got murdered."

He mounts his motorcycle, kicks it into life, and speeds off.

I doubt there are many places other than a California Highway rest stop where a murder would be good news.

There are several cars here now that weren't here last night. And if it's a public place, why can't I camp here? Doesn't public mean open for all? It belongs to the people. I'm a people.

I visit the bathroom once more (it's less horrible in the light of day, and also more horrible) and decide I need to eat a real, cooked breakfast despite the risks of foodborne illness. It is 7 a.m. and, after a dose of hand sanitizer and a quick brush over my wig, I am on the road.

It's congested again. I guess all the people in California had twenty children each while I was in my apartment. Within half an hour I see a gas/food/lodging sign, and gratefully follow it off the freeway and into a Perl's Family Restaurant. I wonder if Perl is a terrible speller or an excellent knitter.

The place is crammed full of unsavory people. There are little families generating clouds of noise, old trucker men with steel-wool beards, obese people who cannot be contained by the flimsy chairs. Their polyester-wrapped blubber gloops over the sides of the seats, inching toward the floor as if trying to escape.

"How many?" An iron-haired hostess named Dottie asks me.

"How many what?"

She huffs, exasperated. "How many in your party?"

Party? "I'm not having a party. It's just me."

"Great." Dottie already hates me. She grabs a grubby menu and walks away, so I follow her. Am I supposed to follow her? I think so. I clutch my purse to my side as if it might be snatched by the polyester gloop monsters.

She seats me near the window, in a tiny booth built for two. The orange vinyl seat is ripped, but I sit there anyway. "Your server will be right with you." She's gone.

I don't eat out. It terrifies me. The windowsill is littered with the bodies of dead flies, a dusty battleground. Fingerprints crawl up the window as if trying to find a way out. The place smells of rancid frying. Maybe eating is overrated.

Plunk. A scratched glass full of water appears. A man in an apron is already halfway down the length of the restaurant before I connect that he brought it. People come and go so quickly here.

I gently push the glass to the other side of the table. I cannot drink water from strange places. I should have brought my own in with me. Next time I will.

"Hi, welcome to Perl's. My name is Brinn and I'll be taking care of you." She's young, wrinkle-free, and her mouse-brown hair is tucked into an absurd pink paper hat. "What can I get for you?"

"I'd like something…well-cooked."

She blinks. That's not the usual answer, I take it. "We pretty much cook all of our food."

I haven't ordered food at a restaurant since—well, it's been awhile. I've forgotten the lingo. "What do you recommend, Brinn?"

She frowns and purses her lips. "I recommend you eat somewhere else."

"Really? Why?"

"I'm kidding." She pushes a stray hair behind her ear. "I can come back if you don't know what you want, but it might be awhile." She glances over at the iron-haired lady who is staring daggers at her. "I can't wait...they want us to turn over tables really fast here."

"Wouldn't that make a big mess?"

She blinks again, then laughs as if she doesn't want to. "Right. I'll come back."

She trots off toward another table, a huge circular thing ringed by a herd of children, two harried-looking adults, and a jaundiced prune of an ancient woman. They are going to take a while, I am sure.

I consider opening the menu, but it's so greasy-looking and dirty that I'm terrified to touch it, and I left the latex gloves in the car. What would I eat here? What would be relatively safe? I glance at the counter and see an empty stool. If I sit there, I can watch them prepare the food, and perhaps advise the cooks so they don't give me botulism. So, I migrate.

A burly man with one black eyebrow sweeps over to me immediately. "WhacanIgechu?"

I smile, and ask, "In English, please?"

He looks angry. "Funny. Youwannaeatorno?"

I will just answer anyway. "Coffee?" He nods curtly. "Bacon, well done, and when I say well done, I mean almost burnt. Toast, well done."

He stomps away, yells at the men in the kitchen, and glares at me as he plunks a white ceramic mug in front of me, pours a stream of steaming coffee, and moves away.

That chore accomplished, I glance at the people on either side of me. To the right, an attractive middle-aged man reading a newspaper and wearing a cheap brown suit. Mustache with egg in it. On the left is an old, old man who smells of cigarettes and unwashed clothing. One-eyebrow man slaps a chipped white plate in front of me. Two slices of nearly-black bacon lie prostrate on it, along with two anemic triangles of white toast with congealed butter seeping into the pores. I realize I'm starving.

I eat as quickly as I can, sip the hot coffee, wipe my fingers on a stiff white paper napkin after every bite. The crowd is getting to me. I start idly picking at the stubbly hairs on my forearm, although there's not much left to pick; it resembles a cornfield after a locust strike.

"Fuck you!" someone yells from the entryway. No one but me looks toward the commotion.

Iron-haired Dottie corrals a gaunt woman and a girl toward the door, and I overhear her. "I've told you not to come in here again. Do I have to call the police?" She turns toward the counter. "Fernando? Can you help me? *Ayuda me!*"

Eyebrow man wipes his hands on a grubby apron and shakes his head as he clomps over to the hostess stand. The woman being told to leave looks to be late 30s, bleached hair tied in a ponytail, skin tan and rough. The girl—I'd guess about 13—is slight, nose pierced, her hair bleached the same as the woman's, but cut short and sticking out at odd angles. She is hunched under the weight of an enormous blue backpack.

"You are not welcome here," Dottie says loudly.

"Fuck you," the woman with the ponytail croaks, then spits on the ground.

"Is that all you can say?" Dottie asks sarcastically. "Take your whore daughter and get out."

The "whore daughter" kicks Dottie in the shin. I'm secretly pleased.

Dottie howls as Fernando takes over and uses his bulk and massive eyebrow to herd them outside. He stands in the door, blocking them from entering again, as the woman screams and bangs on the glass. The girl stands back a few feet, staring at the ground. When Fernando sees that the pair is walking away, he comes back inside, whispers something to Dottie, and then comes back to the counter.

"What was that about?" I ask. He ignores me. "Excuse me, why did you kick those people out?" He moves away, starts wiping down the counter at the far end with a red striped rag.

"It's 'cause they come in here about once a week trying to get a free meal, like no one is going to remember that they were here before," says a cigarette-smelling man in a surprisingly smart-sounding voice. He rubs the gray stubble on his chin. "They dine and ditch on a regular basis."

"Dine and ditch?"

"They order, eat, and when no one is looking, they scoot out without paying. They wait till it's busy, so everybody's confused. It's not that hard to do. Nobody here pays much attention."

"Have you done it?"

He shakes his head and smiles with half his mouth. "Don't need to. I got money. No need to put myself through the stress. I got a bad heart."

I don't point out that eating at Perl's is probably not the best rehab strategy for a bad heart.

Outside, the woman leans against a light pole, sobbing. The girl orbits around her, helpless. Eventually they walk away, the girl still shouldering that enormous pack, following the mother a few paces behind. I watch them until they disappear around a curve in the road.

"Where do they go?" I ask the old man.

He shrugs. "They probably live under the freeway, or in the town, on a doorstep, in a dumpster. There's a lot of 'em. Blondie, though, she's pretty loud. Most people like that know that it's better to be invisible. You can get away with more. But she's not invisible. She wants people to see her."

I nod, and stare at my coffee.

. . .

"Why do you want to be invisible?" Edward asked me.

"I don't."

"You do. You hide from people. You hide under your wig, you hide in your apartment, you never go out. Why?" He crossed his long legs, leaned back in the oxblood leather chair, and tapped his pen on the legal pad where he kept notes of my madness.

He pursed his lips, steepled his fingers, and stared at me with those ridiculous blue-green eyes. I could not stare into them for too long; it would be like staring at the sun. I'd burn out. I'd burn out the part of me that kept me safe.

"Alright. You don't want to talk about that, clearly," Edward said. "Let's switch gears. Tell me about your childhood."

"Oh, that seems kind of trite." I glanced up at him to see if he was kidding, but he wasn't. "Really? My childhood?" He nodded, pen poised. "It was very normal."

"Oh, come on. Normal? That's boring. Give me something to work with, Anna."

Out the window, the autumn sun painted everything gold. "I was an only child, my parents were older when they had me, my father was a postman, my mother stayed home. It was the '80s. I guess it was a nice time to be a child."

"Why? Is it different from now?"

"Oh, of course." I realized he'd tricked me again. "I mean, I suppose it was. I can't really be a child now, so I don't know." I felt a well of unease bubbling up from my gut. I had a compulsion to scratch at my head, to pick at the hairs that were left (not many), but I was embarrassed to do that in front of him.

He watched me, a jaguar scouting its prey. "Tell me about your mother."

"So clichéd. Really?"

"It's clichéd for a reason." He crossed his legs in the other direction.

I picked at the embroidery on the couch pillow. "She was very nice. A perfect mother."

"Perfect?" He uncrossed his legs and leaned forward. "No one is perfect."

"Right. But she was a very good mother. She read to me, she

spanked me when I was out of order, she hugged me. She tucked me in at night." I got choked up thinking about her, of course. "She's been dead ten years now."

"Your father?"

"Dead."

He leaned further forward still. I thought he might fall out of the chair. "So, you're on your own."

"Everyone is on their own." I glanced up to see if he liked my comment. He grinned, and then relaxed back into the seat.

"This is true. You're quite bright." He tapped his pen on the pad of paper for a few taps, one, two, three, four. "Look. I have an idea. Let's go for a walk."

"A walk? Don't I have to lie on the couch or something?"

"I do somatic therapy. That means we use the body to help heal the mind. Walking isn't dangerous, I promise." He stood, extended his hand to me. I slipped my hand into his and felt an electric thrill race up my spine.

In the outer office, the receptionist smiled at us. "Going for a walk?"

Edward nodded toward her and gestured toward the door. I opened it and waited for him in the hallway as he spoke to the woman at the desk. "Let's take the stairs," he said, heading for a recessed door. I followed.

His deep voice echoed in the bright white stairwell. "No sisters or brothers?"

"No." My voice sounded scared, alone.

"Never married?"

I didn't answer.

He stopped on the landing and turned, blocking my way. "Married?"

I shook my head but couldn't look at him. I stared at the handrail and tried to discern the patterns of foreign countries in the peeling paint. Everything looked like Africa. "Africa has some of the worst problems with contaminated water," I said.

He didn't answer at once, but I looked into his eyes, and he was squinting, studying me as if I were a specimen on a slide. "I suppose that's true."

"It's definitely true. I've studied it." I brushed past him without looking at him and kept going down the cement steps.

"Say, do you drink coffee? Or tea?"

"Depends." Africa, Africa, Africa. I wondered if the painters did it on purpose.

"Depends on what? Hey, slow down. It's not a race." I'd made it to the bottom and was ready to bolt out into the fresh air. I waited. I desperately wanted to scratch under my wig, too, but I was determined not to do that in front of him. He opened the door for me, and we stepped out into a mild autumn full of golden leaves and long shadows.

"Here, let's go through the park. I took this office partly because of it." We crossed the parking lot and walked side by side along a winding stone path through two enormous hedges. Inside, the tiny park was truly beautiful. Liquid amber trees scattered California's equivalent of fall foliage onto green grass, and the hedges cut the noise of cars and people.

"I would never have guessed that there's a park here at all." I kicked at a small stone on the path.

"It's a secret garden." He chuckled at his literary joke. "It's a garden for secrets."

Was he trying to get me to tell him mine? I was determined not to let him see anything I didn't want him to see. "I don't really have any juicy secrets, I'm sorry to say. I'm just garden-variety crazy."

"So, you've had a diagnosis?"

"I don't really believe in those." A redwood-and-metal bench under a cast-iron streetlight sat at the curve in the path. I parked there and patted the seat next to me. He nodded and sat, stretching his legs in front of him.

"You don't believe in diagnoses? How can anyone get better if they don't know what's wrong?"

"Who says anything's wrong? Can't people just be the way they are?" I suddenly felt that any number of plague-carrying insects might be marching toward me.

He waited a moment before he answered. "I'm not saying there's anything 'wrong' with you. But you did come to see me, after all. There must be some reason."

"I suppose." My left leg started to shake nervously as if it had a mind of its own.

"So?"

My leg stopped because I willed it to stop. "So?"

"So, why did you come see me then?"

"That's a good question. I'm not sure I know the answer." I stood up. "Isn't it almost time for me to go?"

He shook his shirtsleeve to reveal an old-fashioned looking watch. "Not quite. We still have a bit of time. Tell me anything. Tell me whatever you want to tell me." He patted the seat this time.

I sat. Being close to him was intoxicating. I'd never really been drunk often, but what I remembered of it felt like this, the feeling when you've had just enough but before you've had too much. "So, just talk about something?"

"Yes." He patted my hand reassuringly, but it had the opposite effect. It caused my pulse to flutter and my heart to race. I'd say almost anything to get him to stay there like that, even though I knew it was a purely professional interest.

"Well," I began in that way that buys a person a bit of time when trying to discuss a difficult subject. "I live in an apartment. I'm modest in my habits and buy everything online because I cannot stand shopping. I listen to music, and I love the arts, but I don't go to live events very often because I generally dislike crowds."

"You dislike all crowds?"

"Yes. I don't really like people in general."

He chuckled at that, as if I'd said something very witty. "That must make it difficult to navigate through a job, or life, for that matter. There are people everywhere, aren't there?"

"That is sadly true. But I've found ways around it. You'd be surprised how easy it is when you're really motivated." He glanced up with his gorgeous eyes, which were studying me intently. "So?" I said, "Is that enough?"

He nodded, frowning thoughtfully. "Just one question, though. You said you have no family, but when I asked about your having been married, you didn't want to answer. Is that out of...some embarrassment? Or were you married, and it didn't end well?"

Sound roared around me as if the ocean had suddenly broached the shore miles away and sent a tsunami to sink the little park behind the hedge. What was it? I sat on the bench, covered my ears, and looked at the doctor, who was puzzled.

"Don't you hear that?" I yelled.

"What?"

"That sound. The loud sound, the roaring sound." It was getting louder, stronger, and I checked the sky to see if the giant wave was actually hovering, suspended, in the air. Nothing but clear blue sky dotted with cottony clouds.

"I think we should go back," he said loudly. He pulled my hand away from my ear and repeated himself. "I think we should go back now."

"Yes." The noise subsided...it flowed outward as if someone had drained a bathtub, away from us, away.

"What did you hear?" he asked as we walked the path back to the office.

"Just noise." I slipped ahead of him. "Just sound. I probably have a brain tumor or something."

"A brain tumor? I certainly hope not." He catches up to me, puts a hand on my shoulder. "You're running again. You don't have a brain tumor, but you are running from something. I hope you'll feel that you can tell me, in time."

I wave soundlessly at him, and, not looking back, make my way to the bus stop. Once aboard, I will have to crouch in the back, hoping to maintain a safe space between myself and the disease-ridden denizens of the MTS Local 244. A small price to pay to meet someone who understands. A small price to pay for someone who might make the ocean stop chasing me.

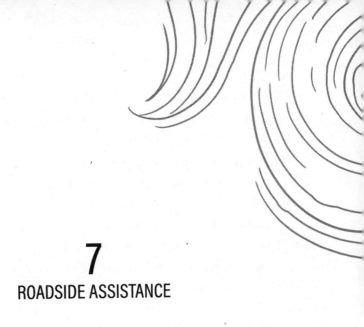

7
ROADSIDE ASSISTANCE

Although terrified to visit the restroom in Perl's, I risk it. I desperately need to wash my hands and face, and I would love to take the wig off for a moment. I suppose I could drive with it perched on Annabella... maybe a scarf. For now, though, I'm still not ready to let it go.

The woman looking back at me from the chipped mirror does not look great. Pale, purple-gray circles under the eyes, the beginnings of an eruptive zit at the edge of my nostril. If I squint, I think I can see bacteria forming tiny highways all across my skin. A shower is a necessity, and soon.

Someone flushes a toilet. A putty-colored door opens, and a tiny old woman with a hump on her back inches out of the stall. She leans on a cane, and her hand is impossibly gnarled like the root of a dying oak tree. Hobbling, she drags one orthopedic-shoed foot on the gummy tiled floor, and then leans against the edge of the porcelain sink.

Her breathing is ragged, and simply pumping a couple of shots of soap from the dispenser seems to be a chore. "Do you need help?"

She ignores me, continues her labored respiration, and uses one twisted hand to turn the handle of the faucet, but she can't make it budge.

"Here, let me help you." I reach over gently, turn the tap, check the water temperature.

She turns toward me as if just seeing me for the first time. Her watery, near-transparent eyes weep with old-person juice and are magnified by thick glasses. "I don't have any money," she squeaks.

I'm not sure what the appropriate response is. "Neither do I."

"You can't rob me, there's no point." She slips her hands, one at a time, under the water. "Too hot."

"Sorry." I adjust the temperature. Suddenly, I'm her handmaiden.

"You can't rob me," she repeats, as if her voice recorder is stuck.

"I wasn't planning to rob you." This is too much personal contact with someone I do not know. That's what I get for trying to help. "Have a nice day."

"Are you a man?"

"What? No." She dabbles her fingers under the water and makes that noise that old women make when they don't believe you. "I am not a man. Why would you even ask me that? We're in the women's restroom."

"You can't rape me," she says, as if she's commenting on the weather.

"Why would I do that? Are you crazy?" I turn to leave, and she says something unpleasant under her mealy breath. "What did you say?"

"She-male." Her dried-up lips prune in disgust. "Should be shot."

I exit the bathroom, and as I leave Perl's, I see Dottie leaning against the brick wall, puffing on a cigarette. Her lips are wrinkled in a perfect pattern around the tip, as if they've molded themselves there after years of repeating the same motion. A swarthy, teenaged busboy leans next to her, eyes closed, listening to headphones, also puffing a cigarette below the faint suggestion of facial hair. "I gotta retire," Dottie says to no one in particular. "Too many homeless comin' in here. Too many Mexicans." The busboy doesn't open his eyes but moves his head ever so slightly in time to the inaudible music.

I am beyond ecstatic to be back inside my safe haven, and I lock the doors for no particular reason. I take off the wig and toss it onto the passenger seat, gaze into the rearview. I do look like a man, especially without the hair. The old woman saw things clearly. How can I find him looking like this? I examine my face inch by inch, pore by pore. I haven't worn makeup since—but I might need to do that, I might need to. Of course, Doctor April will be painted like a San Francisco row house. I hadn't budgeted for such a trivial and ridiculous expense, but I am thinking I may need to stop off at a drugstore and find something that will lend me some color, some femininity. Damned old woman.

A vast expanse of gray highway stretches before me. I put the car in gear and roll slowly over the gravel in the parking lot, inching toward my destination. It seems like it will take an eternity for me to reach Edward. At this moment, it seems utterly impossible. Can I live on burnt bacon and toast, and be exposed to the madness of strangers for this long? I guess time will tell.

My attention drifts as it does when you're driving a monotonous piece of road. I just follow the cars in front of me, knowing that there are no turns, no decisions to make until I stop for the night.

I think about the girl with the bleached hair. She must be about thirteen, fourteen. The same age as—but I won't think about that right now. I refocus on the bumper in front of me, where a proud mini-van driver reminds me that his family could eat my family, for they are zombies. How wonderful. I'm not sure about this society's preoccupation with zombies; I once read that you can discern the direction politics will turn in the next election by examining whether vampires or zombies are more popular. Zombies mean Republicans (they eat brains and are slow and ponderous) and vampires mean Democrats (they suck the life blood out of you via taxes.) Which is most popular right now? I have no idea. I don't watch much television; I see some advertisements on it, but it's all a supernatural blur. I suppose that means it will be even, and nothing whatsoever will be accomplished.

The girl. Why did her mother make her carry that pack? It looked heavy. The girl was strong, obviously, but mothers should carry the burdens. Good mothers do that. Obviously, she wasn't a good mother. Good mothers don't use the word "fuck." I don't think I ever heard my mother say that, not once. Oh, maybe once. When she caught her finger in the car door and ripped off the index fingernail. Yes, I believe she did say that. But only that one time.

The sky is turning pink, so I suppose evening is approaching. Is it a motel night? I was going to wait until I'd been on the road a few days, but I feel like a colony of flesh-eating bacteria might be setting up shop in my armpits, and if I don't shower, I'm not sure how tomorrow is going to go. The wash up at Perl's just didn't satisfy.

I drive more miles, see more bumpers, more vanity license plates (MBTRAT puzzled me for many miles and kept my mind engaged. I'm a Bat Rat? Embitter A Tea? Embitiaraty? Is that a word? I don't know.) As darkness sinks over the concrete and car lights blink to life, I see a billboard advertising food, gas, and I guess a place to stay—the one icon is a person in a bed with a triangle over his head. Motel with roof (would a roofless room be cheaper)? Bed is greater than sky? Whatever. I'll turn off here.

The road turns sharply, and at first, there is nothing but dirt and a few suicidal bushes. The off ramp ends at a traffic light, which remains red despite no one coming from either direction. I wait, I count, I look for zombie hordes, I see none.

Finally, it changes, and I have to decide, right or left? No signs. Where is the man in the roof motel? I'll guess left. I hate Republicans. Vampires over zombies any day. At least they have a flair for fashion.

Scraggly palms suddenly sprout next to the road as if someone just left them there accidentally. They have that shaggy dead coat that makes them look like old dogs standing upright. I still see no lodging, nor food or gas for that matter. The road turns right sharply, and as I come around the corner a bit too fast, and, improbably, the woman and the girl from the diner are standing in the road.

"Shit!" I swerve to avoid hitting them and bump the Caddy into a stand of dried-out tumbleweed that is thankfully not hard enough to dent the car. Dust rises into the evening sky.

Is this an optical illusion? Didn't I just see this pair at Perl's, and didn't I drive away, alone? I look to Annabella for answers, but she remains inscrutable.

The mother stays put in the middle of the road, not registering that I nearly hit her and her daughter. I get out, and want to yell at her, but she looks numb and bewildered.

"Hello?" I call. No answer. The girl at least looks at me warily.

I remember that I'm bald and stubbly, so I grab my wig before proceeding. No need to scare everyone. I snug it onto my head as best I can, smooth my pants, and gingerly step toward the pair. "Hello?"

No answer. I lick my desert-dry lips. "I'm sorry, I didn't see you when I turned—"

"You're a shitty driver," the girl says, rolling her eyes, shaking her head.

"Weren't you and your mother just at that diner, Perl's? How did you end up here?"

She doesn't answer. "Do you have a cigarette?"

"No." I take a step closer. "You shouldn't smoke."

"I shouldn't stand in the road, but here I am. Probably won't be the dumbest thing we do today." She eyes me warily. "Were you stalking us, from the diner? Are you a creepy sex offender?"

I choke, offended by her implication. "No, of course not! You made quite a scene in the diner. That's why I noticed. And how *did* you get here?"

The girl waves a hand in front of her mother's face. "Hitched a ride with a toothless gypsy. He left us a mile back." I'm not sure if she's serious or not.

Now I'm within a foot of the pair. The mother still stares straight ahead. "Is she alright?"

"Does she look alright?" The girl walks around the mother as if she's viewing a statue in an art museum. "She's never been alright."

I don't get too close. I still have this nagging feeling that if I get within arm's length the woman will come to life and bite my hand. Human bites are much more toxic than animal bites. Plus, I doubt she has acceptable oral hygiene, which makes it even worse. Or she might be a zombie. Or a hallucination. "Is she on drugs or something?"

"Something." She shakes her head and walks toward the car. "Got anything to eat?" She opens the back door and dives in.

"Wait! Don't do that. Don't go in there! I didn't give you permission to get into my car!" I can't believe it. All that work making it as sanitary as possible, and there she is, polluting it with whatever she's picked up on her clothes and spiky hair. I don't want to come in contact with her, but I do, just to yank the back of her t-shirt to extricate her from the car.

"Hey! Don't touch me!" she squeals, jumping as if I've prodded her with a red-hot poker.

"Don't touch my things!" I slam the door shut. The girl frowns, her face a pierced storm cloud, cornflower blue eyes slitted with malice. She has a few freckles sprinkled across the bridge of her nose.

She stands there glaring at me when another car comes from around the curve, two tunnels of light piercing our little domestic scene. The driver goes slowly enough that he or she avoids us, but honks and salutes us with a middle finger hoisted like a flag toward the setting sun.

"Fucktard," the girl says, flipping the driver off with both hands, doing a sort of wiggly dance as she does so. "Eat me!"

"Let's get out of the road, shall we?" Someone has to have some sense. "You stay there, with your mother. I'm going to park."

The girl ignores me, goes to the passenger side, and climbs into the front seat. "Okay, go," she says.

"Get out."

"No."

I am utterly flabbergasted. I don't even know how to respond to this rudeness. "I said, get out of my car!"

She leans toward me, thin lips pursed, eyes squinting. "I said NO."

We stare at each other for a second, and when I hear another motor revving up the road behind me, I decide to move my car. I crank the ignition and pull off to the shoulder just as a motorcyclist takes the curve and nearly collides with the crazy blonde woman.

"Is there anything you can do about your mother?" I ask. She still stands, stock still, mid-road.

"We could probably pull her off to the side. She doesn't weigh much."

The girl picks absently at the nose piercing, which makes me shudder. I have to get her out of the car, at least. "Fine. Let's go move her."

We exit and approach zombie mom. "You take the left, I'll take the right," the girl says as if she's done this before. I copy what she does: she grabs the woman under the armpit (shudder) and we both tug her toward the car. The sour onion-skunk tang of body odor escapes as she moves willingly, trudging out of harm's way, but still doesn't speak. I lean her against the Caddy.

"Mom." The girl stands on tiptoe so her nose touches her mother's. "Mom!" She shoves the woman's shoulder, hard, into the car. Then she slaps her. Hard.

"I don't think you should—"

"Thanks, Mel." The woman blinks as if she'd just woken from a nap. Frowning, she examines the situation, and her eyes rest on me. "Who the fuck are you?"

I don't even know how to answer that. I just stand there, mouth agape.

"She almost hit you, moron," the girl says, digging in the mother's jacket pocket and producing a bent cigarette and a book of matches. She expertly lights the thing, sucks, exhales a cloud of smoke. A small circle of fire glows brightly in the darkening evening when she inhales.

Mom shakes her head, wipes her nose with the back of one denim sleeve, and then, with great concentration, focuses on me. Her eyes are the same cornflower blue as the girl's. "Sorry," she says, smiling crookedly. "Sometimes I lose track of where I am. I have these spells."

The girl snorts and walks a few paces away, blowing smoke at one of the shaggy palm trees.

"I'm sorry about that," I say. Isn't that what you're supposed to say when someone tells you that they have "spells"? I have no idea. "I need to move on, though. So, I'm glad you're alright. Please be careful."

I try to open my car door, but the woman blocks it. She's smiling now. "Fate probably brought us together," she says, smoothing her hands down the thighs of her worn jeans. "I believe in fate, don't you?"

"Fate is a bitch with a bad sense of humor." I try to elbow her away from the door, but she's stronger than she looks. "Please move."

"Yeah, yeah," she says, putting her arms in the air as if I'm robbing her. But she does take a few steps away from my door. "I understand. You have to look out for yourself. Single woman alone on the road. You don't know what kind of people we are. A mom and her kid. We could be notorious serial killers or something."

The girl snorts loudly and comes back to where we stand. "Mom, you are so full of shit." She turns to me. "Do not listen to anything she says, FYI. She can't help lying. It's her religion."

"She's a sassy bitch," her mom says, smiling. She ruffles the girl's bleached, spiked hair, and the girl dodges away. "Takes after me."

"I'm nothing like you, Rhiannon."

The mother's face clouds, turns vicious. "Don't call me that. I'm your mother."

"The only reason you're my mother is that you pushed me out of your vagina. Beyond that, you're just a crazy person who treats me like a personal valet."

It looks like the woman is going to hit the girl, and I can't tolerate that, even though the girl is incredibly rude. "Look," I say. "Let's all calm down. I'm sorry things are hard for you. If I had any spare money, I'd give you some, but I don't. I need to move on, though, because I need to be somewhere. I'm on a deadline. So, as much as I feel for you, I have to go."

The woman looks at me, and her face goes from vicious to meltingly sad. Tears roll down her sunburned cheeks, she closes her eyes, and she shakes her head. "I know," she says softly, walking in a circle with one hand to her forehead. "No, I hear you. I'm sorry. My daughter is right. I *am* crazy. Something is wrong with my brain. I don't deserve to be around decent people." She opens her eyes and takes a step toward me, and then lowers her voice to a whisper. "But...my girl. It's not too late for her. I need to find her somewhere safe. Kids should be safe."

Reason breaks inside me. Part of my brain is arguing with my good sense. I hear it clearly, like a conversation between two old maid school marms. *She needs help! Are you going to just leave her and her daughter here in the desert? To die?* to which the other brain responds, *Are you mental? She'll kill us in our sleep if we help them!* to which the other says, *Children must be protected. You know this above all else.*

"Are you talking to me?" the woman asks as she blinks, confused.

"No, not really."

"Oh." She turns to her daughter. "Mel, let's go. We need to find somewhere for the night."

Mel, the daughter, sighs heavily, then sinks to the ground, back against the tree. "I'll stay here."

"You can't stay here, honey." The mom now talks to her gently and kneels down next to her. "This place isn't safe."

The girl puffs the cigarette, then stubs it out in the sand. "No place is safe," she mutters. She looks up at her mother, her eyes teary. "Will you stay here with me?"

"This isn't a good place," the mother insists. "Too many cars. Somebody might see us and stop."

"Maybe they'll help us," The girl answers. I'm just a spectator in this drama, but I can't look away.

"No." the mother shakes her head. "People don't do that."

"Maybe some do," Mel says, but by the tone of her voice, I can tell she doesn't believe it.

"You can come with me," I say. What? What did I say? The words had popped out before I even knew I had formed them in my brain.

"We can?" The girl turns a hopeful, tear-stained face to me, her blond hair catching the last glimmers of sunset. "We can come with you?"

The mother oozes decency. "We've insulted you and put you out enough. Never mind. We'll be fine. Come on, Mel." She grabs the heavy backpack. I know she's playing on my sympathy, but I can't help myself. Why can't I help myself?

"No, you have to come with me." I take the pack from her, the cautious side of my brain throwing rocks at the compassionate side, trying to get it to shut up and sit down and be reasonable. *What are you doing?* The real me screams. *Danger! Danger!* Ignoring the internal alarms, I place the pack in the trunk of the car, trying to segregate it from my clean items. I ensconce it in a large plastic trash bag.

"Are you sure?" the mother says. She puts a hand on my shoulder and smiles disingenuously. "You don't have to do this."

"I do have to do this." I glance at the girl, who is now standing and staring hopefully at the car. "How long have you been hitching?"

"Three days," she says without hesitation. "Where are we going? What's your name?"

"I'm Anna." I gesture toward the road. "I am going to stay at a motel nearby. You can stay with me tonight. Get showered. Then I'll drop you somewhere tomorrow." *What? What?! Why? This is suicide, or at the very least, ill advised! Have you learned nothing from police procedurals?*

The mother extends her hand to me. "I'm Rhiannon. This is my daughter, Mellow." She licks her lips, and stares at the sand floor. "We forget how to act like nice people sometimes. I'm sorry." I'm not buying her contrite matron act, not for a minute.

"No drugs, though," I say. "You cannot have any drugs or smoke any cigarettes while you're with me. Agreed?"

Mellow asks, "Can I smoke if I go outside?"

I do not answer. Her mother slaps her shoulder gently. "We won't smoke," Rhiannon says. "Promise." To Mellow, she says harshly, "We can do without it for a night if it means sleeping inside, don't you think?"

The girl nods sheepishly.

. . .

"Nobody helped them." I was sitting, numb, on Edward's couch, recounting the details of a life that I'd distanced out of a sheer sense of survival. The fact was, I couldn't think of it without a black, bubbling cloud of suicidal pain enveloping my body, my mind, my soul. I didn't want him to see me that way.

"Why do you think that—"

"Do you have children?" I fixed him with a flat-eyed stare, unwavering. I imagined him pinned like a butterfly to a card, not dead, but unable to move until he answered my question.

"Sorry?" He frowned at me, shifted his long, long legs, leaned forward. I had intrigued him. "What?"

"I asked if you have any children." Iron gaze. No wavering.

He smiled slightly with one side of his mouth and then leaned back in his oxblood leather chair. Hands clasped, he covered his mouth, rubbed the right side of his cheek absently. He did this when he was thinking, I'd realized; my avoidance had offered him a delicious puzzle.

"No, I don't have any children." He ran a long hand through his dark, unruly hair, and said, "But we were talking about you."

"I want to talk about you, though." I blinked.

He smiled slightly and leaned further forward. "But Anna, if we don't talk about you, there's really no point in us meeting, is there?"

Touché. He knew exactly how to redirect me, which was impressive. In my experience, doctors could be sidetracked easily with a carefully placed question about themselves. I mean, doesn't everyone like to talk about their own lives? But this one…he seemed to know that trick, and he was trying to steer me back to the puzzle.

He opened a file sitting on his desk and thumbed through the papers. "This is the record of your hospitalization."

"What?" Goddammit.

"I have some friends," he said apologetically.

"You're not supposed to be able to see that unless I give you permission."

. "That is true."

"Who gave it to you?" My heart pounded, louder, louder, like drums, like blood, like waves against the shores of a killing lake.

"No need to worry," he said, closing the file.

"I am worried." My voice scratched and bled, sounded raw and savage. "You have no right to look into my personal life. You have no right unless I tell give permission. If I find out who—"

"Anna," he whispered. "I don't have your file." He rose and sat next to me on the sofa.

My eyes felt wild, my pulse pounded in my ears. I was an animal, trapped in a cage with no door.

He continued. "I'd never read your file unless you gave permission. You're right. I couldn't get it. But you just confirmed that you were, indeed, hospitalized." My jaw was clenched so hard that I felt I might crack the teeth out of my skull. I rubbed my hands absently over the velvet fabric of the couch, rub, rub, rub, to keep them from strangling this man. Betrayal. Manipulation. Like everyone else. He was no different.

"I know you feel like I played a trick on you." He held both my hands and I realized I was trembling violently. "I'm so, so sorry. I just needed to know where we were going. We've met five times and you've told me nothing, really."

And still I said nothing.

"I want to help you." He rubbed the top of my clenched fist, rub, rub, rub. I blinked, stared at the floor, felt hot tears threatening to drown me, drown me, drown me. "I can't help you if you don't tell me anything. Every time you almost give me some scrap of a detail about your past, you stop yourself. I know it's something painful, something you don't want to discuss. But Anna," he leaned forward even more, so our faces almost touched. "It's a wound. It's festering. It needs to be opened, cleaned, healed. I can help you do that."

I gazed into his other-worldly eyes. Like oracle pools, like the eyes of mystical dragons or magical necromancers or seers from the ancient world. I could be happy staring into them for the rest of my life. It would be enough. It would be enough. I could lose myself there. I could forget.

But only if I remembered first.

I breathed. I focused on those jewels of clarity. Breathe in, breathe out. Anchor to those eyes. I might be able to tell him…

"Nobody helped them."

8
HIGHWAY HYPNOSIS

"**W**hat the hell is this thing?" the girl asks from the back seat. In the rearview mirror, I see her holding Annabella.

"Please don't touch anything," I say. She grimaces in the half light and rolls her eyes.

"Mellow, you have to behave yourself," Rhiannon says, in her best preachy-mom voice. "Miss Anna won't let us stay with her if you're being disrespectful." She pulls a tissue from my anti-bacterial tissue box and blows her nose. It sounds like the walls of Jericho might come tumbling down. I have to focus on the road ahead (which is not well lit), but I am distracted by the inevitable snot storm that will be discarded onto the floor of my car.

"Please—please hang on to the tissue until we find a trash can," I say, an edge in my voice.

Rhiannon glances at me, glances at the tissue. "Okay, sure." She throws a glance at her daughter, who shrugs.

"I have to tell you something," I blurt out as I negotiate the curve of the road. "I am very, very clean. I need to be very, very clean. You have to respect that, or you can't stay with me."

"That's no problem," Rhiannon says, wiping her still-dripping nose on her jacket sleeve. "We're clean enough."

"No, you don't understand." I want desperately to stop breathing because now I'm suddenly worried that the small pocket of air inside the car is contaminated with whatever things Rhiannon has picked up from the road, from gas station bathrooms, from Perl's lunch counter—panic wells up in my chest and my heart starts beating too fast. I'm sweating and my hands slip from the steering wheel, but I grab it again.

"Jesus, are you okay?" Rhiannon leans toward me. *No!* Her lung air will be even closer! "You don't look so great." She reaches out to feel my face, and I jerk to the side, causing the car to swerve. "Shit, be careful!"

"Don't touch me." I say this as evenly as possible, but I suspect I sound slightly shrewish.

"No problem." Rhiannon moves back to her side of the car. Out of the corner of my eye, I can see her shaking her head. I've seen that before. People do that a lot. It means they think I'm crazy.

The motel looms in front of us, incandescent and welcoming, flanked by a gas station on one side and a seedy-looking bar on the other. I breathe a sigh of relief; at least there will be a shower. This particular place, the pretentiously named Princeton Motor Hotel, had many reviews mentioning its cleanliness and affordability. I am reasonably confident that I may be able to relax, at least slightly, and find a way to clean myself up while avoiding contact with these two undoubtedly germ-laden wayfarers. Why did I offer to take them with me? I shake my head. Sometimes I do things that are totally ridiculous and unreasonable. Edward would no doubt find it encouraging, but I did it in the heat of a moment, out of pity. Now it's too late to extricate myself from the situation. I have no way to ditch them. Do they plan to tag along with me for the entire trip? Oh, Jesus. I cannot let that happen.

As we exit the car, I turn to Rhiannon. "I'm very sorry for your situation, but you have to know something: this can only be one night. I have a mission, something very important that I have to do. I cannot be sidetracked. One night, and then you go. I'm leaving early in the morning."

Rhiannon leans against the car and smiles at me. "I get you. I understand. We understand, don't we Mel?"

The girl wrangles the pack onto her back and snorts in response.

Rhiannon, now all kindness and decorum, asks, "Can we help you carry anything in? Or would you rather we don't touch anything?"

"I'd rather you not touch anything. I can make multiple trips." I pick up Annabella from the backseat and make a mental note to sanitize her when we reach the room. "We'll get checked in, and then we'll discuss parameters."

"What are parameters?" Mel asks as she comes to stand next to her mother.

"Rules. Boundaries. While you're in the room, there will be a delineated area in which you can move. We will tape it off to be sure you don't cross into my area."

Rhiannon whistles. "Wow. You are…very kind. Really."

I don't answer.

"But God, I am grateful. Whatever you need, man. Whatever you need." She puts an arm around her daughter. "We are just so thankful that you have kindness in your heart. I have no idea why you do, or why you'd take a chance on us, but Jesus God, I'm glad you did. And one night? That's fine. That's more than pretty much anybody else has done. Unless they were getting something out of it." Her face clouds slightly and Mellow takes a small step away from Rhiannon. What did they have to do to find a place to sleep? I don't want to think about it.

"Of course," I say smoothly. "I'll check in. You stay here." I don't want the motel person thinking they're with me. I tuck Annabella under one arm, hitch my purse up onto my shoulder, and glide through the squeaky automatic doors as they open.

"Welcome to the Princeton Motor Hotel," a scrawny young man in an ill-fitting gray suit says enthusiastically. He's folding napkins behind the reception desk, and one dim bulb directly above him flickers. "Do you have a reservation?"

"No," I say, clutching Annabella even more tightly. "Room with two beds, please."

As the man (whose name, according to a red-plastic badge, is Rufus) taps a computer keyboard and frowns into an old, scarred monitor, I look around the lobby. It's not too bad for a cheap motel; it has a clean tile floor, a darkened dining area where the "continental" breakfast is no doubt served in the morning, and a hint of Pine-Sol clinging to the air.

"Here we go." Rufus hands me a plastic credit-card style key and a pink sheet of paper. "Your room is on the second floor. Take the elevator to your right, and it's right down the hall once you get off the elevator."

"Thank you." I am loath to touch the key, and I certainly cannot put Annabella on the counter, even if it does look deceptively clean. "Could you slip that into my pocket here?" I nod toward my shirt pocket. I can see this makes Rufus uncomfortable, but he leans over and swiftly pokes the card into the pocket with two fingers, then draws his hand away as if he fears being burned by my flaming breasts. "Breakfast is from six to eight." He wipes his hands surreptitiously on his pants leg. I like Rufus.

Outside, Mellow and Rhiannon are nowhere to be found. For one pulse-pounding second I fear that they've run off with the car, but it's still where I parked it. They are not inside. "Hello?" I call softly. No answer.

The car, which I left unlocked (stupid!) seems intact. I pop the trunk and grab the wig box, put Annabella into it, and tie it securely. I'll come back for the other things. This time I do lock the car, though. I have no idea what tricks they're playing.

When I reenter the lobby I nod to Rufus, who is reading a newspaper. We're old friends now. I walk down the hall toward the elevator, and at the end of the hallway, behind a smeared glass door, Mellow and Rhiannon crouch like wayward puppies. Rhiannon waves cheerily.

I push the bar on the door as quietly as I can. "What are you doing?" I whisper violently.

"We didn't want him to see us," she whispers in return, slipping past me into the hallway. Mellow follows her, both so silent it's slightly unnerving. The girl has pressed the elevator button, and stands absolutely soundless, waiting. Neither says a word. They could be statues, like those modern sculptures that guy does in New York, the one who creates what look like living people from the weird parts of society: maids, old people, tourists. I imagine the name of their piece: *Homeless Woman and Punk Daughter, Sneaking.*

Ding. The elevator door slides open, revealing an orange-carpeted box with faux blonde-wood paneling. We file silently into the box, I press the button for the second floor, and the metal door slides closed. Everybody exhales at once.

"I'm glad you saw us," Rhiannon says, laughing. "I thought we'd have to stay out there all night."

"What were you talking about with that desk clerk?" Mellow asks, grumpy. "Were you guys setting up a date or something?"

"I was just getting my key," I tell her. "I have to go back out and get my suitcases. I'll let you in, and you will just stay on the one bed, and then I'll get the tape from the car. But promise me you'll stay where I tell you."

"Yes, ma'am," Rhiannon says, saluting. "You are the captain." Mellow grunts and turns toward the wall. In small, rhythmic thumps, she taps her forehead against the fake wood paneling.

Inside room 225, there is an immediate problem. There is one bed.

Of course. Why would there be more than one? For all Rufus knows, I am one person. One person doesn't need more than one bed, unless they have illegal guests or unapproved orgies scheduled.

"So, you want us to sit on the bed?" Rhiannon moves toward it, and I yell "No!" so emphatically, I'm afraid Rufus might hear me. "Just… just stand there."

"Here? In the doorway?" Rhiannon pushes the door shut. "Is it okay if we use the bathroom?" Oh Jesus. The bathroom. I hadn't even thought—

"I do have to pee," Mellow says, casting sad puppy eyes at me.

"Fine. Please be as careful as possible."

The girl arches an eyebrow at me. "What, do you think I'm going to fling poo around the room or something?"

"Are you planning on defecating in there?" I'm starting to sweat.

"Uh…" Mellow looks at her mother. "I hadn't really made plans one way or the other. Mostly I have to pee." I nod. My stomach is in knots.

Rhiannon smiles and puts a hand on my shoulder. "Don't worry. I get it. You're a clean freak. I was in a clinic once with someone like you. I get it." She slides toward the wall and appears to make herself as small as possible. "We will take up as little space as possible. I will scrub down all the surfaces. I promise. Go get your bags."

I take a deep breath. Now that I'm here, in this situation, there is nothing to be done. I can't very well kick them out, can I? Nobody is helping them. "Yes. Thank you." I set Annabella's box in the center of the bed so it will be safe. "I will be back right away. Please don't—"

"I know," Rhiannon says, nodding. "Don't touch anything. I know." She puts her palms in the air to show me that she's not touching anything.

I pad out into the hallway, feeling faint. I could absolutely pass out. But passing out in a motel hallway is on a top-ten list of scenarios most likely to result in rape or death, so I know it's not an option. Where did I read that? I can't remember. Worse, lying facedown on that carpet—oh, no.

I do not want to wait for the elevator, so I look for the stairwell, but the door is jammed. Dammit! I press the elevator call button ten times in quick succession, hoping that the thing will arrive more quickly, but it doesn't. Press, press, press. Nothing. The floor indicator says it's stuck on four. Who's on floor four? Why are they taking so long? Press, press, press. Maddening.

I practice breathing, trying to calm my racing heart. I am battling a sense of urgency—I have to get to my car before someone breaks in, but I have to get back to the room before someone soils it. But I'm stuck here, between. Breathe, breathe. Press, press, press.

An eternity of breaths passes and finally the feeble *ding!* and the door opens slowly. Two enormous people of indeterminate gender take up the entire elevator.

"Are you getting on?" one of them asks.

Jesus. I never get a fucking break.

I step gingerly into the box, staying as close to the door as I can without getting my nose shut in it. I face the door, hoping not to engage the people in conversation. They smell. Jesus, please. If I believe in you, I would totally pray to you very hard for this elevator ride to end as soon as possible.

I notice a mirror mounted above the scratched metal button panel. The person on my right (I believe it is a woman, judging from the Hello Kitty necklace choking her neck) puts a thick finger to one nostril and inhales loudly. "Allergies," she says in a smoker's voice.

Now the inevitable cigarette smell hits my nose, and I cringe. Being trapped in a small, enclosed space with smokers is high on my list of hellish possibilities when going out into the world. I am apparently going to be checking off a lot of horrible things on my Bucket List of Hellish Things over the course of this trip.

The elevator is painfully slow. I can feel it descend, inch by inch, feel the air become damp and laced with germs and nicotine. I clench my fists, close my eyes, try to breathe. Edward was very big on breathing.

God, it's only one floor. How long can that take? Is it stuck? Have we stopped? But no. The holy *ding!* sounds again, the door opens onto the blessed freshness of the Pine-Sol lobby. I scurry away from the over-inflated people and scamper to my car.

The night air is a tonic. Clear, even here near Los Angeles. I take a moment to inhale the clean air, scrubbed by real pines and palms, and gaze at the silver pinpoints in the night blanket. I can imagine that Edward, too, is looking at these same stars from somewhere in Colorado.

I grab the suitcase from the trunk and lock the car (after wiping it down as thoroughly as possible under a candy-corn-colored sodium-vapor streetlight). Back through the empty lobby, back into the empty elevator where a faint whiff of smoke laced with pork-rind B.O. clings tenaciously.

When I get back to the room, Mellow sits on the floor, knees to chin, gazing out the wide-open window. "Where's your mother?"

"Bathroom." She continues to watch the sky. A quick check reveals that nothing has been touched, apparently. Annabella is squarely in the middle of the bed. My heartbeat slows, and I feel calmer.

"We need to discuss sleeping arrangements," I say. No answer.

I unzip my suitcase, find my blue painter's tape, and assess the room. There is a spot near the dresser large enough for a blanket and quilt, so I tape the floor between the bed and dresser. Conveniently, the window is on her side.

In the closet, I find extra blankets and pillows, so I pull them out and place them on the dresser. "I will have to cross into your area to access the bathroom," I tell the girl.

"Hmmm." She turns her face toward me. "Sure I can't have a cigarette?"

"Absolutely not." I shudder again at the elevator debacle. "Smoke clings to everything, and it ruins your lungs. Didn't you learn that in school?" I move my suitcase to a rack near the nightstand, prop open the top and remove my bag of cleaning products.

"I haven't done much school. Rhi doesn't believe in it." She stands up, stretches like a cat, and walks the blue tape line toe-to-toe as if she's a circus balancing act.

"Why is that?"

"Why is what?"

"Why doesn't your mother believe in school?"

Mellow snorts, and one toe skips onto my side of the tape. "Oops. *Mea culpa.*"

"How do you know what *mea culpa* means if you've never been to school?" I watch her turn, bow to an imaginary audience, and begin to walk the line again.

"I didn't say I'm stupid. I read a lot."

"You read Latin?"

"I read everything. Cereal boxes, pill bottles, wanted posters, stuff in churches—churches are excellent places to hide out, did you know that? They usually leave them unlocked at night. It's pretty easy to sneak in and just hide. Usually cold as fuck. Why do they make them all out of stone? Hardly ever have carpet. I guess God likes people to be uncomfortable. Except, oddly, Jews. Jewish places are usually pretty nice. But locked. I think they're more paranoid."

My box of Unwanteds is in the corner of the suitcase. Seeing it makes me feel nauseous. I knock on the bathroom door. "I need to use the bathroom, please."

No answer.

I knock again, more urgently. "Please. It's kind of an emergency."

I hear a faint "fuck" from the other side of the door, then hear the lock click, and it opens just a crack. "What?" Rhiannon's face is flushed.

"I really need to get in there. Could you let me in for just a moment?" Bile rises into my throat. "If you don't, I might vomit on the rug, and that stays with everybody all night long."

She rolls her eyes and puts a finger up (the wait-a-minute finger, not the flip-the-bird finger) and *she shuts the door again.* "Did you understand my veiled allusion to puking? Because that's what's going to happen." Clatter, clatter. Something glass hits the tile floor and shatters. Excellent.

"Oops." I hear more scuffling.

"I am going to kick this door in." I don't think I could, but she doesn't know that. Does she? Maybe so.

"Fine, fine. No need to get your panties in a bunch." She opens the door and the smell of patchouli incense wafts out, choking me. "Please, my queen. Take the throne." She makes a grand gesture to usher me into the crapper.

"Thank you." I shut the door behind me, lean against the cool (but likely contaminated) wood, eyes closed. Breathe, breathe, breathe.

When the nausea has abated, I open my eyes to a tidy little water closet. White towel on the floor for a makeshift rug, shower curtain smelling heavily of bleach, tiles scrubbed as white as they're going to get. The frosted-glass window is propped open with a block of wood. I'd love some water, but I'm not drinking out of the faucet.

The lid is down on the toilet. I sit, stare at my feet, still enveloped in my leather walking shoes.

A washcloth is stuffed under the plastic trashcan. I move it with my toe to reveal tiny shards of shattered glass. Drugs. I wonder what this woman is addicted to. I don't know much about drug culture. I do know I don't want to sleep with it in my room, though.

The good news: the nausea is totally gone, replaced by a blossoming panic attack. Silver linings.

Upon opening the bathroom door, I see Rhiannon sprawled out on *my* bed, legs working as if she's riding a bicycle. Mellow is back to staring out the window as if this is an everyday occurrence—which, sadly, it may be.

"She's on my bed!" I realize that sounds really callous, and try to breathe in calm before speaking again. "Is she alright?"

"You asked me that once already tonight, and I already answered you. She was not alright then, and she's still not alright. Isn't that pretty obvious?"

"Well, we need to get her off the bed. Help me."

I move Annabella's box away from Rhiannon's thrashing limbs and set it safely inside the closet. Mellow doesn't move.

"I said, help me move her."

"Let her sleep."

"Obviously, this was a bad idea. I'm not at all surprised. But here we are. And I need this bed. So, you have two choices. Help me move her, or I am calling the manager and I will report that you two snuck into my room uninvited."

Mellow finally looks at me, the orange light from the parking lot painting her face into a Picasso. "You wouldn't do that."

"I would." Would I? I don't know. But I need help moving this dead weight of a snoring woman.

The girl thinks about it for a second, then sighs heavily and stands up. First, she spreads a blanket on the floor (on their side of the tape, I notice), and places a pillow there as well. "Okay," Mellow says, "you take her feet. I'll take her arms. That's how we usually do it."

Since she's obviously an expert, I nod, and grab the woman's squirming legs. Although she's small, the girl is strong, and she fixes her arms under her mother's armpits like a seasoned firefighter.

We drag Rhiannon over to the blanket and try to place her gently on the floor. Mellow snatches the blue floral bedspread from the mattress and covers her mother with it. "She'll sleep it off."

"What is 'it', exactly?" I peer at the sleeping woman, who is now drooling, slack-jawed.

"Heroin, probably. Maybe PCP."

"What's that?"

The girl frowns at me disapprovingly. "How do you not know what PCP is? Don't you watch cop shows?"

"Not really."

We both stare silently at the sleeping woman. I'm sure PCP is not something that is good for anybody. I'm guessing it comes in a glass vial. It might explain her zombie impression in the middle of the road. All I can think about is the broken glass in the bathroom, and how badly I do not want to touch it.

"I need for you to get rid of that broken glass," I tell the girl.

She sighs and stares out the window again. "What broken glass?"

"There are small bits of glass in the bathroom, near the trash can. It must be cleaned up. One of us could step on it."

She nods wearily, and then goes to the bathroom, shoulders slumped. How many times has this girl had to clean up after her mother? An ache surges in my chest, almost like the beginning of crying, but not exactly.

I peek in the bathroom door. "How old are you?"

She doesn't look up but continues methodically removing the glass shards. "I'm fourteen. I look older."

I was thinking she looked much younger, too young to be tagging along from diner to freeway to wayward truck cab. Some people should not have children.

"Be sure you wipe down the floor with a wet cloth," I say. "It gets all the tiny pieces of glass. I don't want to step on it."

I watch her hunched form, blonde-spike hair bobbing up and down as she cleans. She starts to sing wordlessly, a tune I know but can't recall. What is it? Something Disney—something innocent and sweet. Wishing...something about wishing. "You have a pretty voice," I whisper, my throat constricting. She sweeps and scrubs, in rhythmic, circular motions, the Cinderella of the Princeton Motor Hotel.

. . .

There was the time I told him the truth.

An evening appointment. He didn't do those often, but I had stayed away, having gotten worse. I'd found I couldn't set foot outside, so he'd come to my apartment.

I watched from the window as the sun set in yellow-gray hard-boiled egg colors against the polluted sky. I imagined this foul air surrounding me, pressing me, coming closer every moment. If you watched it, it stopped approaching. As soon as you turned your eyes away, it moved again, a creeping shadow.

He exited a bright yellow cab in front of my apartment, and I had the pleasure of watching him without him knowing. He leaned in the passenger door, paid the driver, watched the cab drive away. He gave a second to the sky, straightened his dark coat, and turned toward the door. He hesitated before entering, and then, as if he could feel me watching, he looked up at my window. I moved away quickly. I didn't want him to think I was waiting for him.

I ran to the mirror. Wig straight. Annabella in her place of honor, right next to the tweezers. Very light tinge of copper blush on my cheeks (borrowed from Petra, sanitized and applied with sterile gauze) and a light coating of powder to cover the marks where I'd plucked hair from my brows and face.

I looked clownish. My heart sank. He would never be able to see me for who I really was.

A knock at the door, tentative but firm. My heart raced as I made myself walk slowly, slowly…I didn't want him to think I'd been perched on the other side of the door waiting (although I had been.)

I counted to five before opening it, five short seconds to compose myself, to put my best face forward. I pasted on a smile and turned the knob. "Hello," I said cheerily.

His thick, dark hair nearly touched the jamb. "Hello," he said nervously. Why nervous? Because it was evening? Because the night belongs to lovers? I felt myself blush. He asked, "May I come in?"

"Oh, sorry. Yes. Of course." I moved aside so he could negotiate the narrow door. He took off his long coat to reveal jeans and a t-shirt, definitely not regulation doctor wear. "I have to apologize for my attire," he said, gesturing vaguely at the clothing. "I had to do some errands between my last client and coming here, and I didn't have time to change into something more appropriate."

He was familiar; he laid his coat over the back of a dining chair and moved to the sofa. He knew my place. This gave me a little frisson of pleasure. "You never have to worry about appearances with me," I said. "Can I get you something?"

"Just some water would be lovely," he said. He turned to watch me in the small kitchen. "Are you feeling better than when we spoke?"

I had called him because I claimed to be having a panic attack. That was not far from the truth; the oppressive feeling of encroaching foul air had become increasingly bad, and I was having trouble figuring out how to get the necessities without leaving home. There were services, of course, but I could not afford them, and then I ran the risk of strangers bringing all odd assortments of new microbial tortures to my safe space.

I filled a clean glass with the last of my chilled bottled water and brought it to him. "Thank you," he said, smiling. I sat next to him. Did he move away slightly? Or was I imagining that?

He cleared his throat and absently rubbed his hands on the thighs of his jeans. He had long, slender fingers, graceful, musician's hands. I tried not to think of them caressing the bumps and scars of my belea-guered skin. "So, tell me about this panic. What's causing it? It sounded as if things had gotten worse after our last session. Do you know why?"

I turned sideways so I was facing him on the sofa, so I could gaze at him without seeming odd. "I just feel like things are pressing in on me."

"Hmm." His discomfort gave way to curiosity. I was a puzzle for him to solve. "Things…like what? Memories?"

"No. The air, time, the things in my apartment even." I looked around at the small space. "I know it's not real, but it feels as if the room keeps getting smaller, bit by bit, just a millimeter a day or so, but I can sense it. And outside, the air just seems dangerous. Yellow. Full of chemicals and toxins."

He shifted and crossed his legs, causing a phantom of scent to drift to me. Musk, silver-soap and fresh, moonlight on snow. I closed my eyes and breathed deeply, trying to memorize it for later.

"Are you having an episode right now?" he asked, squinting at me.

"No, no," I laughed. "I just wondered what scent you're wearing."

He moved uncomfortably, tensed. "Oh…does it bother you? I'm so sorry. I didn't even think—"

"No, no, it doesn't bother me at all. It's perfect."

"Oh." He seemed more disturbed by my last comment than my first. This was not going the way I planned. I certainly didn't want to tip him off, not yet…I loved him, but he couldn't know. It would scare him away, like an exotic animal in the wild. I needed to tread carefully so he didn't bolt.

"Sorry. I shouldn't have mentioned that. I didn't mean to make you uncomfortable." I folded my hands in my lap, a dutiful student. I desper-ately wanted to pick at the bloody skin around my thumbs, but I did not. I'd covered them with bandages, just to be sure I didn't. "I just can't go outside. I can't face the city, the air, anything. I need to know what to do."

"Ah." Given a professional task, he relaxed, as I knew he would. "You feel trapped."

"Yes. Exactly." Of course he would understand. "That's why I needed you to come here."

"Yes." He rubbed his hands on his thighs, which was his unconscious way of showing emotional discomfort. I had to make him feel comfortable again.

"But don't misunderstand." I stood, walked away from him. Perhaps that would help him relax. But how wonderful! My proximity agitated him! Wasn't that an excellent sign? I leaned against the mantle, hoping to look pale, wan, and distant. "I do know it's an imposition for you to come here."

"Not at all." His chin pushed his lower lip into an apologetic grin. "I'm sorry if I implied that it was an imposition. I'm here to help you."

"That's so good to hear." I turned toward him, gave him my most dazzling smile. "It's so wonderful to feel like I have an ally."

He smiled, nodded. I had to give him something here. He needed some bait, some tidbit of information to keep him interested. I stared down at my feet, as if I were carefully considering what I was going to say to him. Finally, softly, I said, "I don't think I can ever recover." I had practiced that line so many times, I'd spoken it to Annabella, to my mirror, in my bed, at my sink.

"Oh, don't say that." He jumped up abruptly. His impulse was to comfort, as I knew it would be, but he stopped himself from coming to me. I saw the struggle. His professional brain won, and he sat again. "Don't say that. Recovery is always possible."

"Is it?" I met his gaze. "What if the damage is so severe that death is the only answer?"

He paled. I'd gone too far.

Silence sat between us. He swallowed "You may need more help than I am able to provide," he said softly, pulling his phone from his pocket.

"No." I crossed to him swiftly, before he could think about it. I took the phone boldly from his hand and dropped it to the floor. I sat close enough to breathe in the moonlight silver scent. I whispered, "I need you."

With the comical awkwardness of a trapped suitor, he fumbled away from me, nearly falling over the end of the sofa, grabbed his phone from the floor, scooped up his coat, and ran for the door as if it was the safe zone in a game of tag. "Anna," he breathed. "I am so, so sorry. I have been so unprofessional. I've clearly misled— I am so sorry." His face was a violent shade of English rose. "Please call the office."

"But I love you," I said, too late. And with that, he was gone.

. . .

"Now, I am going to take a shower." I try to slow my breathing, try not to focus on the ragdoll heap of Rhiannon on the floor. "If you can bring your mother to consciousness, that would be excellent."

"I can't do anything when it comes to her," Mel says, flopping down on the bed as she reaches for the television remote. "We sort of orbit different planets." She switches on the box and starts to flip, channel to channel, without really watching anything.

"As I said, I need a shower. Please don't touch any of my things," I say lamely as I pick up the box containing Annabella. Of course, they've both been on my bed, and now I don't know if I can even sleep on it. Is this how they mark their territory?

The bathroom is clean, as promised. I nearly get my nose to the floor inspecting for drug-laced glass shards, but I see nothing. The girl did a good job cleaning up. Probably not the first time she's had to do that. I'm not looking my best; a quick glance in the mirror reveals dark circles under my eyes, and an uneven wearing of the face powder that gives me the look of a human patchwork quilt. I place my wig on Annabella carefully, as far from the shower as possible.

The water is blessedly hot; I carefully unpack all my instruments of hygiene, place a stiff, white towel within arm's reach, and duck into the waterfall. As the warm water cascades over my head and face and back, I feel the stress draining away. Water is such an amazing element. Is it because we are made of it? Is that why it soothes? But we're equal parts fire and earth and wind—the heat of the blood, the clay of skin and bone, the respiration of sighs and crying.

I imagine Edward here. I imagine him embracing me in this blissful waterfall of warmth, the world shut out by a cheap vinyl curtain the color of vanilla ice cream. Our bodies fit together, skin on skin, pulsing in waves of wetness and pleasure and—

Bang, bang, bang. "Hey! Hey, get out here!" Mellow screams on the other side of the bathroom door.

"What?" I frantically turn the creaky faucet and shut off the water. "What is it?"

"She's having a seizure or something!" I hear the fear in her voice.

I wrap the towel around me, fling open the door. "What happened?"

Mellow's frightened little-girl face breaks into a huge grin and she laughs, twirls, points at me. "I got you!"

I just stand there, dripping. "So, she's not having a seizure?"

"Not right now." The girl does an impromptu dance, fist pumping in the air. "I got you, I got you," she sings.

"Why did you do that?" I try to be as even as possible. I am at a distinct disadvantage, being naked and wet.

Mellow takes a step into the bathroom and gazes studiously at my head. "Jesus, you're totally bald."

"Really? Thanks for telling me. I wasn't aware." I reflexively put a hand to my scalp, as if to shield it from criticism. "You've had your laugh. Now can you get out so I can finish my shower?"

"So, do you, like have cancer or something?"

"Something."

She flips the toilet lid down with a loud plastic clunk and sits, pulls her knees up to her chin. "You've been in here for, like, twenty minutes. I'm starving."

I don't even know what to say to this hubris. "Get out," I manage to squeak.

She frowns. "Geez, you don't need to be a bitch about it." She grumbles and saunters sullenly out of the bathroom, leaving the door wide open. I slam it shut behind her.

Obviously, this was a brilliant idea.

I finish my shower, but the lovely erotic illusion is shattered. I just wash quickly, get out, towel off, shuck into clean clothes, and fix my wig onto my freshly-scrubbed scalp. The mirror is blessedly steamed, so I see a hazy outline of my face rather than the harsh lines and pits.

Steam follows me into the short hallway. I see Mellow's calves and feet tapping to some inaudible music as she sits on the floor against the wall. She has a tattoo on her leg—I hadn't noticed that before. I don't recognize it, whatever it is. A bird? A plane? The eye of Sauron?

Her mother is still twitching under the floral bedspread, likely drooling on the sheet. Mellow does, in fact, have white earbuds jammed into her ears, and she's pummeling the air with invisible drumsticks. "Where did you get the iPod?" I ask. Her eyes are closed, and since I can hear the raw metal sound coming from the headphones, I guess she can't hear me. I nudge her foot with my toe.

Her eyes pop open and she sticks her tongue out, gives me a devilish rock-chick squint and sings something unintelligible. I extricate some clothes from my suitcase, and head back to the bathroom for a tiny bit of privacy.

The mirror is less fogged now and frames my beleaguered face in a wreath of steam as if I'm an old-time photograph faded with age. I do feel that way, sometimes. Like my life has faded and eventually will simply be the absence of all color. Then it's just...invisible. Maybe that wouldn't be so bad.

The clean clothes refresh me. I adjust my wig and feel almost human. I walk out of the bathroom and call "Mellow?" Oh, she can't hear me. It's almost like having a teenaged daughter.

Suddenly, a pain skewers my eye as if someone hammered my head with a piece of granite. The pain travels the length of my spine like a lightning bolt, and then I'm looking up at the ceiling. The paint is flaking.

"Shit, are you okay?" Mellow stands above me, upside down, an angry totem. "What are you doing?" She grabs my arm and pulls me upright.

"I don't know," I mutter, pushing my wig into place. "I just had a horrible pain in my head."

She squats, her face nearly nose-to-nose with mine, and peers into my eyes. "Your pupils aren't dilated," she says matter-of-factly. She sticks her black-polish index finger in front of my eye, moves it back and forth slowly. "You're tracking, so I don't think you have a concussion or anything. Are you a mystic?"

"What?" I grab the doorjamb and hoist myself up, lean against the wall.

"A mystic. A shaman. A witch. You know, hocus pocus. Visionaries often travel to other realms and abandon their bodies." She nods as if this is common knowledge, like the recipe for the best chocolate chip cookies.

"I usually take my body with me when I travel." Not nauseous, not feeling sick—did I hit my head on something? I examine the frame of the door...nothing.

"I'm starving." Mellow prances from one foot to the other. "And I have to pee again. Move, please." She shoulders her way to the bathroom, slams the door, and I'm plunged into semi-darkness. I feel my way along the wall. Why did she turn out the light near the bed?

I wait a minute, so my eyes can adjust. I don't want to stumble over Rhiannon and wake her. When I can see, I move toward the bed, which now sits invitingly in the moonlight...and I'm suddenly exhausted.

But something is wrong. My suitcase, which I know I closed, is open. Mellow has looked into it, and carefully tried to put things back where they were, but I know how things should be folded. Why would she go through my suitcase? Looking for money? A shiver runs down my spine.

The bathroom door creaks open, spilling fluorescent light onto the dingy carpet. "Why were you in my suitcase?" I ask.

"Oh." She freezes. "I—I just wanted to find out something about you." She creeps forward, carefully, as if I might hurt her.

"What did you find out?" I stand with arms folded over my chest.

She comes no closer. "Nothing. You're neat, I mean, you keep all your stuff very tidy." Rhiannon suddenly snores like an apneic lion. "Sorry. Really. I know I shouldn't go through your stuff. I was just curious." She folds her arms over her chest, as if she's waiting for me to shoot her in the heart. Then she sighs heavily.

I push back the urge to panic about someone's fingers touching all my things. She's a kid. "It's fine. I mean, it's not fine, but I understand." I arrange my things and close the suitcase. "You said you were hungry."

She says nothing.

"Let's go find some food." I glance at the snoring lump on the floor. "Should we try and wake her up?"

Mellow nudges her mother's blanketed body with one foot. "She won't know we're gone. Hope she doesn't choke on her own vomit or something. Of course, she wouldn't know it, so I guess that would be an okay way to go."

"You're a very morbid young lady." I grab my purse and try to extinguish the vision of a vomiting drug addict from my mind's eye.

"I am." She slouches past me, opens the door, and then turns to me. "Do you have your key?"

9
FOOD, LODGING

The night smells industrial, a mix of diesel and dirt, exhaust and exhaustion. "Where should we go?" Mellow asks excitedly, as if we're going on a big adventure.

"I'd rather not drive at night. So," I glance around at our choices, "gas station or bar."

No hesitation. "Bar." She starts marching toward the pink neon OPEN sign. The letter O flickers off and on, so it goes from being OPEN to PEN. I follow her across the gravel parking lot.

"Wait for me," I call.

There is no evidence of care or pride of ownership in the tavern named The Monkey Bar. It is dark and reeks of old beer and fetid carpeting. I'm not sure I can even go inside, but the girl dashes in and I have no choice but go in after her. Shit. I take a deep breath and plunge through the door.

The place is blessedly underpopulated, which should minimize the biohazard. Two scruffy men, one skinny, one fat, play pool under a dismal fluorescent light in the back. A scarecrow woman sprouts from a stool at the long black counter, and Mellow is standing, hand on hip, in front of an old-fashioned juke box near a sign that says TOILETS hung on the head of a moldy, unlucky deer above a doorway.

"Do you have some quarters?" she calls over her shoulder.

The bartender, a woman whose face resembles a topographic map of Death Valley, sucks on a cigarette and blows a cloud of bluish smoke. "It don't usually work," she says, gesturing with dinosaur hands. "Tell your kid to save her quarters."

"She's not my—do you have food here?" I try not to touch anything. The woman behind the bar grabs a menu from under the counter and slides it to me. I'm afraid to pick it up. "Do you have a clean napkin?"

She frowns at me, then rips a paper towel from a roll next to a neat row of alcohol bottles. "Here you go."

I feel her watching me, so I wait, hoping something else will draw her attention. She just puffs away.

Mellow trots up and leans her elbows on the bar. "I thought you couldn't smoke in public places anymore," she says sweetly. "Can I have one?"

"No." The woman frowns at her, becomes a Shar-Pei dog squinting under a straw-dry thatch of blond hair.

The girl wriggles up onto a barstool next to me and grins as if she's the happiest person on earth. "Can I have a beer?" she chirps. Shar-Pei squints and walks away, waving her cigarette, mumbling about kids these days or something. Then she leans over my shoulder and peers at the menu. "Anything good?"

"Good? No." It's tough to read beyond the greasy fingerprints and unidentifiable stains. "What would you like?"

She grabs it from me, touching it, making me shudder. "Cheeseburger, I guess. Nobody can mess up a cheeseburger, right?"

"No meat." I feel bile rising in my throat. "Do you know how sick you can get from a tainted piece of meat?"

"I like that. 'Tainted piece of meat.' Maybe I'll make that my band name." She stabs at the menu. "Salad?"

"Here? Do you know how long the lettuce has probably been rotting

in that biohazardous kitchen? No. I think the only thing that's safe is…"
I scan the plastic-coated paper. "Baked potatoes. Possibly pancakes, no
eggs, if they'll make them this late. Or anything prepackaged."

Mellow curls her lip at me as if I'm a freak. "Seriously, do you ever
eat out? You cannot be that picky."

The bartender has meandered back to us since the skinny barfly
has apparently fallen asleep nestling her cocktail. "Want something?"

"Yes, we do." I smile, hoping that I look normal and engaging. I
doubt it. "Can you still make pancakes?"

"Only 'til 10. In the a.m." She stands, waiting.

"Baked potatoes?"

She shakes her head in disbelief, as if I've asked for blowfish sushi.

"Grilled cheese," Mellow pipes up. "Two grilled cheese sandwich-
es, please. With pickles."

As if they speak the same language, the squinty woman nods, pulls
an old-fashioned paper waitress pad from her hip pocket, and scribbles
something on it. She walks it over to a clip near the kitchen window and
rings a bell, three times. Everybody in the place wakes up, stares at the
bar, and appears to wonder if it's a fire drill or a vice bust.

"Sit," Mellow says, patting the stool next to her. I wait until the
other bar people have gone back to their desperate musings, and then
I quietly slip onto the stool.

"Grilled cheese?"

"Pre-packaged cheese slices, bread, butter, heat. Not too much to
mess up, unless the cheese has gone bad, and that stuff never goes bad."

"Smart."

"Clarice!" A booming voice from the depths of the kitchen calls out.

The bartender flinches a bit, then hustles to the kitchen window.
"What?"

"What kinda bread for the grilled cheese?" A dark face peers out,
sees us, and laughs. "White bread. Never mind."

"Well," Mellow says, huffing. "That was racist."

"We can change it. What kind did you want?"

She pauses for a moment. "White." She puts her fingers to her lips and lets loose a wolf whistle worthy of a truck driver. "Bartender! Two Cokes here, please. In the can. Wipe them off first."

The woman brings us the cans of soda, two paper-wrapped straws, and two glasses of ice that look relatively clean. Mellow makes a ritual of opening each one, pouring it a bit, waiting, pouring, waiting, until the caramel-colored foam reaches the rim. She hands me a straw.

. . .

"Just water please. From a bottle." I looked up at the seasoned waiter, who sniffed at my request. He'd expected I'd order wine, or something more expensive.

"Tea, please." Edward smiled at the tuxedoed gentleman—oh, what I'd give for that smile to be directed at me!—and handed him the menus. "That's all. Thank you."

The waiter stood, blinked unbelievingly. "Will you be ordering anything else, sir?"

"No." Edward grinned cheerfully at him.

The man's stodgy face was a raincloud. He blinked rapidly, then scuttled away. "I hope he doesn't spit in your tea," I whispered, nearly giggling.

"I suppose we should have ordered a biscuit or something, but I didn't like his attitude." Edward bobbled his head comically. Looking down at his hands on the table, he grew serious. "So. I'm really glad you were able to come outside. This is progress."

"I'm still not comfortable."

"Of course. I know. But here you are." He smiled at me across the table, and my heart fluttered. "I've asked you to tea today because I have a proposal."

I nearly fainted. Obviously, it wasn't *that* kind of proposal. But for a nanosecond, my foolish, romantic heart believed it, so I blushed red as a sunset.

"Oh." He looked worried. He had seen my reaction. "Uh...sorry. No, I meant...a proposal for treatment. Bollocks." He shook his head and sighed heavily. "Sorry. I'm...I'm not always good with the words I choose. I know I should be, I'm a doctor after all, but even we make mistakes. I meant that I wanted to discuss a treatment plan for you. I thought it would be nice to do it here rather than at the office."

"I've been seeing you for nearly a year. Don't we have a treatment plan?"

The waiter returned with a bottle of Pellegrino, a crystal glass, and a tea service. "Could I have a straw?" I asked. The man cringed (really) and stalked away to fulfill my request.

Edward grinned at me. "You're such a contradiction, Anna. You're terrified to be outside, but then when you're here, you seem fearless. We have to try and get that fearless person to make more decisions."

"I'm fearless because you're here too." A harried young woman pops by the table, drops a straw on my bread plate, and runs away as if she's being chased. "I guess our waiter felt it was beneath him to deliver a drinking straw. Thank God for underlings."

I unwrapped it, poured the water into the glass, and took a sip.

"And you're so funny. You have a dry, cutting wit." He tapped his teaspoon on the edge of the table absently. "You just...you need to be out in the world. The world needs people like you. To counteract the people like them." He nodded toward the waiter, who hovered near the kitchen door, glaring, no doubt willing my Pellegrino to boil and scald my face.

"I know this sounds strange, but the world doesn't deserve me."

He arched an eyebrow, poured tea into the delicate china cup.

"What I mean is that the world has made too many mistakes," I fumbled, suddenly unsure. "I...can't trust it to do the right thing. It's abusive. It's cruel. If it were a person, you'd tell me to avoid it at all costs, wouldn't you?"

Edward set the teapot down gently, and just stared at me. He looked toward the ceiling, as if some answer would be written there. He cleared his throat. He sipped his tea. "Your logic is quite sound."

"You're supposed to tell me why I'm wrong."

"I can't." He stirred a bit of raw brown sugar into the tea and poured the cream. "The world is harsh. It's abusive. I can't argue with that."

I was flustered. Of course, I knew that I was right about that, but he was supposed to pull me out of the swamp of despair I'd fallen into since making that realization. "But…if all that's true, then why try at all? Why pretend that there's hope, or that things can change?"

"You're entirely too smart for me." He sipped his tea and smiled wanly at me.

Rather than feeling like I'd won, I felt panicked, as if I were drowning and the only rope I could grab was being slowly, inevitably pulled up from the water. "No, no, I'm not too smart." I leaned forward and grabbed his hand. "You have to help me. I don't want to be like that. I don't want to think like that. I want to have hope."

He almost covered my scarred hand with his much larger, softer hand, but drew it back as if I were a hot stove. He leaned toward me. "Do you, really? Do you want to have hope? Hope comes with responsibility."

"What?"

His green eyes were so close to me, mesmerizing. "Hope is the admission that things might get better. It's a risk, though, because there is no guarantee. Despair is absolute. Giving up requires no risk. Brave people hope. Cowards despair."

A loop of energy flowed between us, and I could not take my eyes away. I was held, an insect in amber, exposed and examined.

"So, tell me, Anna. I know you're brave. Where is your hope?"

"It died." I broke his gaze, stood up too quickly and knocked the Pellegrino bottle over so the contents flowed over the side of the table, a sparkling waterfall. "Excuse me."

I blindly ran toward the door, knocking into the tables and chairs, snagging tablecloths, the world a kaleidoscope blur. *In my mind's eye, I see a lake, a sunny day, a girl in a daisy-patterned bathing suit, hear bird song woven into breezes—this blurs and transforms into sterile white hospital walls. Bird song becomes the monotonous rhythm of uncaring machines.* I grabbed onto a wooden bench outside, gripped it as if a great flood was coming and it was my anchor. My face was wet.

I heard his footsteps before I saw him. His hand on my shoulder. Traffic noises. Footsteps of people walking by, no doubt wondering why the strange woman on the bench was sobbing uncontrollably.

"May I sit?"

I nodded. I felt his body next to me, the warmth of his hip, his hand on my shoulder leaving a scarlet imprint of sacred touch. "What happened?"

"I'm a coward," I said, turning toward him with weeping eyes. I mashed my face into the lapel of his jacket, breathed in the things buried there in tweed fibers, and he reluctantly put his arms around me, and patted me like an inconsolable child.

. . .

"Hey. You there. Did you take some of my mom's drugs?" Mellow snaps her fingers in front of my face. They smell of burnt butter and gooey faux cheese. "You were, like, in the twilight zone or something."

A sandwich sits on a paper plate in front of me. It doesn't look bad; she's right about the relative safety of grilled cheese. Suddenly, I'm ravenous.

"Easy there. If you eat too fast, you'll get stomach cramps or something." Mellow savors a small nibble of her own sandwich. She's already taken tiny bites around the edges. "I make it last. I memorize every bite."

"That seems like a lot of love for white bread and Kraft singles." However, I do slow down, and try to really taste the crispy edge of the bread, the melted golden cheese product.

Mellow brushes crumbs from her face and wipes them on her pants. "So, okay. What's your plan?"

"My plan?"

She slurps soda loudly enough that the squinty bartender glances over, puzzled at the noise. "Yeah. Where are you going? Why? What's your final destination?"

"I'm headed to Colorado." I nibble. I don't particularly want to share my personal details with her. Sharing connects people, and I cannot afford to make random connections, especially not now.

"Colorado." She nods, drums her fingers on the sticky brown bar top. "We can go that way."

"I can't take you with me."

"Why not? Is it because of Rhiannon?" She snorts derisively. "She fucks everything up."

"You shouldn't talk about your mother that way. It's disrespectful."

"She hasn't earned my respect." She rolls her eyes at me, then rips the remaining crust from her sandwich and lowers it into her mouth as if she's being fed. "Best part."

What am I going to do with this girl? With her mother? Stupid, stupid, stupid. My plan has derailed before I've even started. I realize that in order for me to get to Colorado in time, I have to do this alone. I cannot start wandering or caring about other people on this journey. We've already had too many conversations. We've eaten together. All bad.

"We should get back," I say firmly, putting a twenty-dollar bill on the counter.

Mellow frowns, slowly sipping from her glass. "I'm not done."

"Well, be done. We need to get back."

"What's the rush, Roadrunner?"

"Hmm?"

"You're the Roadrunner. Like the cartoon."

I tap my foot impatiently. I think that's what people do. "I don't watch cartoons."

She tears a tiny corner from the remainder of her sandwich and dangles it in front of her mouth. "Wile E. Coyote? Roadrunner? Did you even have a childhood?" She snaps at the food like a hungry fish. "Roadrunner is super clean, always preening, always running from nowhere to nothing. Always in a hurry. Running away from Wile E."

"I'm not running away. I'm running toward something." I grab her arm and force her off the stool.

"Is there a difference?" She giggles, finger waves to the bartender, and lets me hustle her out of the bar.

We walk back to the room in silence. It's a clear night, and our shoes crunching on the gravel sounds like a monster chewing rocks.

"I'm not even sure she *is* my mother, you know," Mellow says as she dances across the parking lot, making patterns in the stones with her foot. "I think I'm a princess and someone dumped me on her doorstep. Look at me." She stops, stands, hands on hips, chin to the stars. "I'm elegant. I'm smart. I'm unusual. She is none of those things."

"Oh, I'd say she's pretty unusual." I walk by her but can't help grinning, just a bit. She *is* entertaining.

"Not really. There are more crack whores out there than you think." She catches up to me and matches my walk, step for step. "Why don't you have any kids?"

I do not answer.

"You do, huh? Or you did. That was the picture in the shoebox, right?"

A rock has lodged in my throat. I find, suddenly, that I cannot breathe, and my heartbeat gallops in my ears. I am willing my legs to keep walking, but they've stopped, and I'm paralyzed in the motel parking lot.

Mellow knows she's overstepped. She goes quiet. She stops prancing. I sense her, just over my left shoulder, but my eyes are closed. I concentrate on the *blink, blink, blink* of the neon, the constant pulse, the hum of traffic.

She says nothing. Silence—I could stand here, eyes closed, until sunrise, feel the light change on my eyelids, feel the temperature rise with the sun, and I could stay here for days, and I could just stand still for the rest of my life. Would I become a tourist attraction? *See the paralyzed woman! The living statue!* And would my blood and bone eventually petrify, grow brittle, crumble to sand, leaving only a pair of shoes and a few wisps of cloth?

Breathe. A puff of air. Another, on my face, deliberate. It smells of…cheese. And burnt butter. "Sorry," she says as I open my eyes. She is inches from me, enormous, blotting out the moon. "Come on."

She loops her arm in mine and is towing me, like a shipwrecked trawler, toward the motel building, through the thickness of night air and memory.

She fishes the plastic key card from my purse, swipes it, and we are assaulted by frigid air, the smell of pine cleaner, and blinding light. Wordlessly, she guides me toward the elevator, pushes the button, and we ascend.

Somehow, I end up on the bed, shoes off, with a thin sheet covering my shivering body. The girl sits in a chair, facing me, and I see the glowing red eye of a lit cigarette that I'm too tired to object to. "I'll make sure everything is okay until morning," she says. "Go to sleep."

I don't know why this means anything, but I close my eyes and beg for darkness to fill my mind. I beg for sleep. I beg for an absence of everything. And I hear a voice humming, *"Hush little baby, don't say a word / Mama's gonna buy you a mockingbird,"* and then an exhalation and the chalk-gray smell of smoke.

10
ILLEGAL DRUGS

"Hey," a voice yelps in my ear. I am asleep, and for a moment I don't know where I am. The bleach smell of the sheets reminds me: motel. "Wake up."

I open one eye. Mellow looms above me. "Yes?"

"She's gone." Thinly disguised panic tinges her voice.

"Who?"

"Rhiannon. My mother." Mellow gestures toward the haphazard pile of bedclothes in a pile on the floor. "She's not here."

Sit up, scratch my head. The wig is still on, which is really, really not acceptable. "Did I fall asleep without washing?"

She doesn't even hear me. She's rifling through the pile of sheets as if the woman might be hiding under them. "She's not here," she says again, anxious.

"She probably went out for—I don't know. Why would she go out?" Scratch my wig, take it off, and blessedly massage my itchy scalp. I feel like a bowling alley shoe that has been worn and not cleaned. A vague memory of something unpleasant nags at my mind, but I push it away. Mellow skitters to the window, where pink-orange crème light is just peeking over the sill: dawn. Rhiannon got up before dawn? That seems impossible. "Are you sure she isn't in the bathroom?"

"Don't you think that's the first place I checked?" Mellow's voice squeaks as she angrily yanks the curtains shut. "I'm going to go look for her."

That doesn't seem to need a comment from me, so I watch her hastily pull on shoes and bolt for the door. She slams it, and the sound echoes off the blank walls. Of course, now that I'm awake, I won't be able to go back to sleep. Once I get a few hours of shut eye, my brain wakes up and decides it's ready for the day even if I am not.

Why did I ever, *ever* pick these people up? I just hope Rhiannon isn't lying in her own vomit at the bottom of the stairs, or floating face down in the pool. I don't know how I'd handle a grieving teenager—would she grieve? Or would she feel relieved?

I pull the cheap sheets up and try to make the bed, but it's futile; the bottom sheet doesn't fit exactly—its elastic tired and flabby—and the top sheet is almost transparent from so many washings. At least they're clean.

I pull on my slippers and pad to the bathroom, turn on the hideous light, and see in my face that I haven't slept enough. When I was younger, I could get by on a few hours of sleep and look bright and chipper—well, maybe not bright and chipper, but functional. Today, I see the face of a worn, tired woman with days on the road ahead of her. I am certainly not starting out well. A missing person, a wild child, and me.

I hear Mellow charging back up the stairs. She yanks at the door but it has locked, so she pounds *boom, boom, boom*, a SWAT team knock. "Let me in!" she screams.

"Jesus." I open the door to a tear-stained face veined with mascara rivulets. "People might be sleeping, you know."

She brushes past me, wiping her eyes on the sleeve of her jacket. "I can't find her."

A short, sharp pang of worry begins to sprout in my belly. "I'm sure she'll turn up."

"She doesn't get up early." Mellow paces, eases a cigarette from the crumpled pack she carries, and flicks a lighter to life. She sucks the Virginia Slim like a deep-sea diver on an oxygen line. "Do you think she was kidnapped?"

That's so laughable, I snort. "Why would anyone come in here and kidnap *her*? And don't you think we would have heard something?"

A fluttering panic starts to flood my brain, and I suddenly feel the need to organize, wash, control. I ignore the recalcitrant sheets and haul my suitcase onto the bed, unzip it, and find a clean pale green shirt and beige pants, simple linen, plus a brand-new pair of French-cut briefs, cotton. The thought of carting around dirty underwear from state to state is too hideous, so I've purchased enough underwear that I can discard every pair I wear.

"Could you please stop unpacking or whatever?" She flops into the chair, puffing away, blowing smoke wantonly into the room.

"This is a non-smoking room, you know."

"You didn't say anything about it being non-smoking last night." *Puff, puff, blow*—a huge cloud emerges from her cupid-bow lips petulantly.

Tom hated cigarettes. When we went to hear music, if people were smoking, he would swoosh his arms in an exaggerated way—"Last night—" I remember. Like a hammer hitting a bell, the memory rings, and I remember. I push it away. I put it back. I lock it down.

. . .

One day, Edward and I took a walk and happened past an Italian restaurant near his office. It was late in the day, and everything was cast in a golden glow. It almost felt normal. This was toward the end of our time together, although I didn't know it then.

"Let's sit for a moment." He gestured toward a wrought-iron bench. I sat, gladly. My stamina for walking had diminished a lot since I never left the apartment.

We sat silently for a while, watching couples arm in arm coming in and out of the restaurant. "If you would just talk about it—"

"I can't." He had been pushing every session. My resistance was wearing down. Now, watching these happy people, I felt my loneliness acutely. I had no one to talk to, except this man, whom I paid. Wasn't that worse than prostitution, really? Paying for sex seemed trivial compared to paying for intimacy.

"Tell me. Please."

One little family—a sweet-faced woman, pudgy man, and a little girl—exited, laughing about some joke that only they understood. It was enough to break the dam inside me, and I started to shake with sobs that I could no longer contain.

On a bench outside a restaurant, while he reluctantly held me, sobbing, I realized that if I told him, if I really told him everything, this would end. *We* would end. My secret was what kept him coming back. Once it was exposed, he would have solved the puzzle, and he would disappear.

I hiccupped, but was still clinging to him like a lifeboat in an ocean storm. I didn't trust myself to speak. I wanted to share my secret so badly, *so badly*, but I couldn't do it. So, I stayed silent, clinging, tamping down the tears as best I could.

"You can tell me anything," he whispered in my ear. A frisson of pleasure swept through my body at the sensation of his breath. He pulled away then—had he sensed how much I longed to stay there? I was caught, a schoolgirl in trouble with the headmaster. Would he scold me? Would he leave me here on this bench with strangers carrying little white boxes of fettuccine Alfredo to their cars?

The brief magic popped like a bubble, leaving us exactly as who we really were: two people on a bench, bound by nothing more than a secret and client-doctor confidentiality. He pulled back slightly so our bodies were not touching. "This was a terrible idea," he muttered dejectedly.

"No, not at all." I wiped my eyes on the edge of my blouse, leaving a dark rose stain on the light pink fabric.

"Here." He pulled a white linen handkerchief from a pocket and gave it to me. Always the gentleman. I dabbed at my eyes, leaving tiny black particles of mascara on the snowy fabric.

"Oh, sorry," I said, noticing the dirt. "I'll take it home and wash it."

"No need." He gave me a pale, weak smile.

Head down, he was studying the pavement, tapping one brown oxford shoe, scratching an itch on the back of his hand. A prism of understanding suddenly clicked into place for me: contrary to what I believed, I wasn't just a *client*. I was someone with whom he clicked, and it was *wrong*. Why else would he be so uncomfortable?

I felt color rise into my cheeks and I tried not to look too happy. This miniature breakdown had given him a chance to comfort me, to show me that he really cared. It was a gift.

"Alright now?" he asked, concern in his eyes.

I nodded, adjusting my wig discreetly. "I appreciate that you care enough to talk to me here, away from the office."

"It's important that you begin to come back to the world," he said. "You need to become part of it again."

I was staring at him, gazing at him as if he were a star on the horizon and I were an astronomer calculating the great distance between us. "I don't want to be part of this world."

"I know." He grinned ruefully, and turned toward me, as if to share some privileged information. "But, here's the thing, Anna, if I—"

The heart does not think. I knew this from before, and I had vowed never to let it run my life again, but in that moment, with the sunset painting the sidewalk in a wash of gold, I swallowed hard, took a breath, and kissed him. I kissed him with all the pent-up passion and longing I had locked away for the years since the accident, and I poured it all into the tender place where our lips met.

He was startled, frozen in place by my rash action. The kiss felt as if it lasted for an eternity, as if I could feel every nerve electrified, and the current ran down my body, a river of sensation. Music—something classical, violin, scent of lilac, rough touch of a linen shirt, and then his hands, grabbing my wrists and pushing me away.

My eyes were closed. I didn't want to see this moment, I wanted to live in it forever in my mind, be preserved in it as if I were an insect in amber. This would be enough. No going back, no moving forward, just this perfect, perfect moment.

When I opened my eyes, he was gone.

. . .

In my mind, I am in a tranquil desert, in a silk tent waiting on a British archaeologist who will bring chilled champagne and expensive cheese on a silver plate. I feel his breath on my face— but it smells of cigarettes and is followed with a chaser of body odor, which make me bolt straight out of my reveries. Mellow's bright blue eyes are even with mine.

"What do you want?" I ask.

"I want to know where you went there. You were having, like, an episode or something. Are you schizo? Do you have multiple personality disorder? Are you going to strap me down and give me a Coca-Cola enema?"

"Why would I do *that?*" My muscles are ridiculously sore, and I can't remember why.

"That's what freaks do. I watch movies." Mellow tamps another cigarette from her dwindling stock, taps it on the dark-wood dresser, and lights it.

"I don't watch the same movies you do, I don't think." I shook my head, trying to clear it a bit. Something…something bad had happened. What was it? Oh. Oh, *yes.* "Did you find your mother?"

"No, I did not find my mother!" she screams. "And then you just checked out, mentally going to planet Pluto or something."

"Pluto's not technically a planet anymore."

"I don't give a shit!" she yells. "I learned it as a planet, and it is still a fucking planet!"

"Fine." I breathe, and realize I desperately need a shower. "I'm going to get cleaned up. Then we'll call the police."

"We can't call the fucking police!" she screeches, pounding her feet back and forth, an angry cartoon character. "They'll arrest you or me, or both of us, and we still won't know where she is."

"Why would they arrest me?"

"You're traveling with a minor who's not your kid," she says snottily. "You don't think they'd frown on that?"

"Could you just stop shouting?" I will get out of this. I will get to Colorado. I will leave after I've cleaned up, and I will not look back. "I will be out momentarily."

I walk wordlessly to the bathroom, and as I shut the door, I see Mellow's angry, mascara-streaked face framed by the window behind her, a pale balloon unmoored. Despite all the bravado she puts on, I know in this moment that she's a scared little girl. I close the door gently. "I won't be too long," I say in a tone of voice usually reserved for talking your way out of a grizzly bear attack.

The closed door is a relief, a barrier to the crazy that I've welcomed into my life. The lock is loose, but I turn the little button on the knob, hoping it holds. The tap runs, filling the room with steam that softens the edges of everything. I imagine the shower washing away the past day, letting it circle down the rust-tinged drain to a river of past mistakes. I step into the hot stream, and I zone out, and I take it in.

The calm is broken when Mellow bursts into the bathroom in a cloud of profanity and smoke. "How long are you going to be in here?" she shouts.

"I locked that door!" I clutch the thin plastic shower curtain. My heart beats so fast I worry that I might need a jump start.

"Sorry," she says, as if she's not at all sorry. "How long are you going to be in here?"

"As long as it takes," I reply through gritted teeth as water trails down my back.

"What am I supposed to do?"

"Leave and shut the door. I'll talk to you when I'm finished." I continue scrubbing my stubbly scalp with the shampoo provided, something called Day Lily Explosion. Mellow stomps off in a huff, slamming the old door practically off its hinges.

"So, this is what it would be like to have a teenager," I mutter to the running water. I do hurry up a bit, despite the fact that I feel I shouldn't have to. I use the bleach-scented rough towel to dry off and get dressed before taking my wig from Annabella and placing it gently on my head. It's a bit curly from the steam, as if the hairs all decided to go their separate ways.

Mellow sits by the window, longingly staring at the parking lot. I go to her and put a hand on her shoulder. "We'll leave our things here, check in at the desk. Maybe they've seen her." This seems to offer some comfort; Mellow nods, blinks rapidly, and we head for the door.

In the lobby, a different clerk is at the desk, a young woman with a spotted complexion and alarmingly red hair. "Excuse me. Have you seen a woman, about how old?" I ask Mellow.

"About 30, but she looks 50," she replies, hiding a cigarette behind her back.

"About 30, sallow, tired, somewhat...used up?" Mellow nods. She approves of the description.

The redhead, whose name is Sheila, looks up at the ceiling as if she's searching there for Mellow's mother. "Um...I don't know. I don't remember seeing anyone go out this morning. I've been here since 5 a.m."

"Are you absolutely sure?" Mellow leans over the counter, eyes fixed on the girl. "It's a matter of life and death."

"Oh." The clerk blinks rapidly as if just coming out of a trance. "Well...uh...I don't think I saw anyone. Really. I'm sorry." She licks her chapped lips. "Do you need me to call the police?"

"No." I smile as reassuringly as I can. "I'm sure she just went out for some food or something."

Then the stunning truth hits me like a brick: Rhiannon has no money. I move aside, thanking the girl half-heartedly, and begin rummaging through my purse. "Oh, no. No."

"What?" Mellow peers over my shoulder. "What happened?"

"She took my cash. She took what was in my wallet." I quickly checked the zippered compartment in my suitcase where I had stashed the prepaid Visa card and another 200 dollars. Not *all* gone, at least. How could this be happening? This is certainly not how things were supposed to go. I glare at Mellow.

"Why are you looking at me? It's not like I told her to do it." Tears trickle down her cheeks, and her voice becomes a strained whisper. "I'm not surprised, though. That's just like her. She's ditched me before."

"I thought you said she'd never leave without you?"

She swipes at her traitorous tears. "I lied. She's done it before."

"That would have been good to mention."

The clerk notices our exchange. "Is everything okay?" she asks in a high, strangled voice.

"Not really," I mutter. I need time to think. I need to sit. The breakfast area is open, so I walk numbly to a small table by the window that is pre-set with cutlery, plates, and red napkins. The chair scrapes when I pull it out.

Mellow hastily sits opposite me. "What are we going to do?"

"What are *we* going to do? She's not *my* mother."

Her face goes ashen and she leans back as if I've slapped her. After a couple of seconds, she shakes her head, wipes her nose on the red napkin in front of her, and nods. "No, you're right," she says quietly. "She's not your problem. Neither am I."

She gets up and walks out to the parking lot.

Good, I think. *Let her go. There's that problem, solved.*

But as I sit fiddling with packets of sugar, rearranging the salt and pepper shakers and lining up and sorting the jam packets, a feeling nags at me. As every second ticks by, I feel more and more panicked. I have to go get her. I can't leave her abandoned out there, alone in this world. She's just a girl, and somebody has to be responsible.

But this is perfect. She'll just go, and it will be as if she were never here. I can go on with my journey, I can move at my own pace, I will make up for lost time.

She's been abandoned. Again. By you.

I scrape the chair, knock over the pepper shaker, scatter the jam packets in my haste to bolt out the door—the automatic doors are too slow, so I push them open. The parking lot is empty except for my Cadillac and a couple of other dusty cars.

I run to the car, fumbling in the purse for keys, and finally find them. The engine complains but finally turns over, and I pull out of the lot, trying to figure out which way an abandoned girl would go. I see no sign of her. Right, left?

I go the way she hasn't been, because if I were abandoned, that's what I would do. The past is known, and a failure. The future might be brighter. The eternal optimism of youth. Left turn.

The road is all ruts and patches. After driving for a few minutes, I see her. She's sitting under a sprawling oak tree, smoking. I ease the Cadillac off the pavement. "What are you doing?" I yell out the window.

She does not reply.

I get out of the car and walk slowly to her as if she's a wild animal. She shows no sign of movement; I'm not even sure she sees me at all. "Mellow?" No answer.

Drought-dry leaves crunching underfoot, I make my way to the tree and crouch down next to her.

"I'm sorry about your mother." Is that the right thing to say? I have no idea. A voice in my head is screaming at me, asking why I'm seeking this girl out when I could have let her go. I have no answer. "Come back."

"It's pretty clear you don't want to be stuck with a fucking kid," she says viciously.

I know my answer will determine the course of this, whatever this is, so I have to choose my words carefully. Her mother may or may not come back, but I can't wait. I have to decide, now, in this moment, the course of the rest of this trip, the course of my life as it is now.

"I would welcome your company," I say. I'm not sure if that's a lie or not.

She turns to me, the hard façade dropped in surprise. "What?"

"I'd welcome your company."

"But you just said—you said it's not your problem." The hurt crosses her face again, visible as a bruise. "Not your responsibility. She's not *your* mother." Bitter. I think she's had lots of practice with bitter, even at her age. "I'll be fine," she insists, but she looks less than fine. Her small, dirty fingers shake as she motions with the cigarette. "You don't have to worry about me. I've been on my own before."

"I'm sure you would be fine. But maybe I need someone to travel with." It's as if my mouth and my brain have become disconnected, and some altruistic pixie is speaking for me.

"Really?" A tiny, tiny spark of hope shines in her voice.

That hope hooks me in. I am a sucker for hope, apparently. "Yes. Really." I motion to the car.

I ease myself up by pushing against the sturdy tree, but she's still sitting on the ground looking up at me suspiciously. "What do you want?" she asks.

"Hmm?"

"What do you get out of this? Nobody does anything to be nice."

This breaks my heart because it is so true. I realize, I'm not doing it to be nice. I'm doing it because…because… "I just don't want to abandon you."

"Ah. Pity. Sure." She hops up, sunny, as if no crisis had occurred. "That works for me. Let's go."

As we drive back to the motel, she hangs her head out the window like a happy dog from Petra's shop, makes her hand ride the air currents heating up in the California summer. Watching her sun-lit face, a sudden stab of unexpected joy jabs my heart, a foreign sensation that feels somewhat familiar, like something from a half-forgotten dream.

11
UNCONTROLLED INTERSECTION

There is no sign of Rhiannon when we return to the room. "I can't wait long for her," I start to say.

"Are you kidding?" Mellow asks. "You left money out where she could get it and fell asleep. She couldn't pass that up."

"Has she done this a lot?" I am folding clothes and putting them neatly back into my suitcase, sorted by color.

"A couple of times," she says, her pack thrown over her shoulder. I'm guessing it's more than a couple of times.

"But will she come back?" I can't leave this girl alone, abandoned and homeless. But I also can't wait for her flaky mother to grace us with a visitation.

Mellow looks out the window, contemplating the odds of return. "I don't think she'll come back. Because she thinks you'll take care of me."

"That's a pretty bold assumption." Am I that transparent? I guess so.

"She only cares about me enough to be sure I'm not dead. Past that, I'm kind of inconvenient." She says this bloodlessly, as if she's reading a grocery list or reciting the pledge of allegiance. I choose to ignore the comment.

"I have to tell you some things about myself if we're going to travel together." I close the suitcase and zip it so that the two zippers meet exactly in the middle. It's much easier to open that way. "I have some… challenges."

"Right." She flops into the armchair. "So, it takes you a long time to pack, I'm guessing, since you sort all your clothes and stuff."

"I have a touch of obsessive-compulsive disorder. I'm not sure if you know what that is—"

"Of course I do. I read. I watch TV. I watch that show, *Girls*, on HBO whenever we find a place that has it. That main girl has to count stuff and put things in a certain order, and she twitches like an electro-cuted cat. Like that, right?"

"Something like that." Clothes are packed, I move on to the bath-room. "Are you going to shower before we leave?"

"I did last night." She clears her throat as if preparing to ask me something difficult. "Uh…so, what's with the hair?"

Holding Annabella, I come out from the bathroom. "You mean why am I bald? Why is my skin scarred?"

"I guess." She doesn't look at me.

"It's the illness." I cart Annabella to the bed and gently place her on the pillow, and then go back to the bathroom for toiletries.

She follows me. "Like cancer? Do you have cancer?"

"No." I brush past her, carrying my newly dried shampoo bottle and brush. "I pick at my hair. I pull it out."

"Oh." She's like my shadow. A teenaged, rude shadow. "Why would you do that?"

"It's not like I want to," I begin, but realize there is no easy way to talk about this without going into details I don't want to think about. "It's just something I do. Like you smoke. Which you can't do in the car, by the way."

She sits on the edge of the bed and watches me pack. I don't think anyone has ever done that before, mostly because I rarely pack. It makes me uncomfortable. "So, tell me about this freak ceramic thing," she says, tapping Annabella lightly.

"Please don't touch her," I say defensively as I move the head out of her reach. "She was a gift."

"A gift? From who?"

I don't answer. I continue folding, sorting, tucking, packing.

"Oh. It's a big secret, huh?" She swings her legs, thumping them against the edge of the mattress. "Your boyfriend? Or are you gay?"

"I'm not gay."

"This looks like a pretty gay gift." She motions toward my wig head again. "Very fem-Deco Erte sculpture Gertrude Stein."

"I don't even know what to say to that."

I feel her watching me. The panic that seemed so intense has vanished, and is now a high cloud in a rainless sky. She hums and drums her fingers on the side table as I square away my belongings. I cover the box of Unwanteds with clothes and bury it deeper inside the suitcase. I need to find a better place to hide it, clearly.

"Alright." I snap the locks decisively on the case. "Ready to go. Are you sure you want to do this?"

"Are you sure *you* want to do this?"

"I don't think I have a choice." I lift the case off the bed, and she grabs it from me. "You don't have to do that. You're not my maid."

"I know." She grins and tilts her head to the right, a movement I'm starting to recognize as her attempt to be endearing. "But I want to help. I can't pay my way, but I can help you out with carrying stuff, and pumping gas, maybe even cooking a little. "

"Cooking."

"Yeah. I'm actually really good with a microwave. You can make a lot of stuff in them." She ambles to the door, yanks it open, and glances over her shoulder. "Let's go...uh...what should I call you?"

"Anna, I guess."

. . .

"I'd really rather call you Edward," I said at our third meeting. "Dr. Denture sounds so old fashioned."

"I'm a rather old-fashioned type of person," he responded, grinning. "But Edward is fine, if that makes your more comfortable, of course."

The weather, gloomy and gray, stood in stark contrast to his dark wood and brass office. He even had a fire glowing merrily on the hearth. I yearned for a cup of tea and a Jane Austen novel, although in general, I despise romantic literature.

He sat in an oxblood leather armchair, stork legs crossed, a large manila folder spread on his lap. "Last time, we talked about your issues with germs. I'd like to talk more about that."

"I don't want to talk about that." I picked at the stubbly hairs on my left forearm. Whenever one started to grow, I felt the need to root it out and pluck it, but when they're relatively short, it is so difficult to get a good grip on them. Usually I need tweezers. Of course, I wasn't about to pull the tweezers out of my purse right there in front of Edward. I didn't want him to think I was crazy.

"Talking about things you don't want to talk about is kind of the point of therapy." He tapped a pen, muted gold and expensive-looking, on the paper.

I said nothing, just stared at the unwanted hairs on my forearm.

He leaned forward, hands on knees. "I know that you are very intelligent. And you suffered a trauma several years ago that has impacted your life. I want you to tell me about it."

"You want me to tell you." I crossed my feet at the ankles, stared at my sensible canvas shoes. "There's nothing to tell. It's in the past, that's where I leave it."

"But have you?" He stood, walked to the rain-spotted window. His reflection in the glass seemed to be watching me. "Have you really left it in the past?"

I couldn't answer. That act of thinking about what happened made it real again, and I had used all of my energy to keep it from being real.

He turned toward me and shot me a generous, compassionate smile so full of radiance that I felt as if I would melt if I were too close to it. Those blue-green eyes crinkled at the corners, amused at my self-deception, I suppose. He turned to a neat collection of audio components and CD cases, chose a disc, and fed it into the music player.

A lovely, sad, piece of piano music cascaded from the wall speakers. "Oh," I whispered. "What is that?"

He said nothing, letting the notes fall like fat raindrops trickling from the leaves of trees. I closed my eyes imagining the beauty in the rain, and when I opened them, he was sitting next to me on the tapestried sofa, uncomfortably close. My heart beat uncomfortably, and the firefly voice deep inside sounded a warning, but I silenced it.

"This," he whispered, gesturing to the air, "is the music of Eric Satie, a French composer. The album is *After the Rain*, and I always play it when the day is gloomy like this."

"It's sad. But beautiful." I wanted so badly to grasp his hand, to bring it to my face and guide it across the contours of my cheeks, my lips, across the geography of my eyes and throat.

"Lie back," he commanded, and my heart skipped. My rational mind knew that he was asking me to relax, but my little vixen of a subconscious wanted darker motives to be present in that statement. I demurely reclined.

"Close your eyes."

"I don't like to do that."

"I know." He stood at the foot of the couch. "But it will be fine. You trust me, don't you?"

"Completely," I sighed as my lids shut out the watery light.

The piano music seemed more present with my eyes closed. I could hear it winging around the room, a ghost frequency touching all the surfaces. I imagined a small orange bird flitting and landing in time to the staccato slow rhythms of the piano notes. I felt my breath.

"Good," he said from behind my head. "Now, imagine the music is a silver curtain of rain. It does not dampen your clothes, but as it falls on you, from your feet to your head, gradually, it brings peace and relaxation to your muscles, to your heartbeat, to your breath."

"I feel it," I breathed, and wasn't sure if I spoke aloud or not.

"Good." His voice, velvet, wrapped me in warmth like a dusky liquor. "Now, rest for a moment, be in this peaceful state. Feel your breath in, out, like the tides of the seas, like the waves on an ocean."

Tide. Waves. Water. Suddenly, I was drowning. I gasped for air, my lungs filled with something, what? Not water, surely, because I was here in this office—but something. My heart thundered too fast, and the music disappeared as the sound of rushing water roared over me.

"Anna," someone called, far away on the shore. "Anna." The wind took the voice and scattered it like sand grains. "Come back. Wake up."

A high-pitched whistle sucked all the sound from the room, and as if a vacuum seal had been activated, everything instantly became still as death. I opened my eyes. My palms were slick with sweat, with blood where I'd dug my short fingernails into them. Edward stood a foot away from the sofa, horrified, face beet red.

"What was that?" Edward asked, his expression at odds with his calm, doctorly voice.

"Hmm?" I sat up. He took a step away from me, as if I were suddenly contagious. "What happened?"

Edward sat in his armchair again, steepled his tapered fingers in front of his lips. He stared, unblinking, at me, as if he were studying a puzzle. "You are full of surprises," he said finally, closing the manila folder he'd placed on a side table, tapping it with one finger. "Definitely intriguing."

"Was I hypnotized?" I moved my legs off of the couch so I could feel the firm, hardwood floor. "All I remember is the music."

He looked down and nodded slowly. "I believe you were in some altered state—I think you were reliving a repressed memory, perhaps. Do you know why water has such a resonance with you?"

I said nothing.

"Do you have a memory of water? Something painful or traumatic?" He continued to gaze at me, and I at him, unbending. We sat like that for what seemed like hours but was not. "Anna, I can't help you unless you give me some information."

"I have no memory of water," I said, rising and grabbing my purse. "And I am late for something, so I'll see you again another time."

He blocked my exit, which both thrilled and annoyed me. I took the opportunity to push closer to him, close enough to feel the heat from his shirtfront, to catch the scent of his cologne, something musky and wild that didn't seem to match the button-down office.

"Anna," he whispered near my ear, "we will find it. Together. You don't have to do it alone."

Breathe. Breathe. I tried to memorize the moment to examine later, the closeness of his chest, the gravitational pull of our bodies. But he stepped aside, opened the door, and in a much louder and more professional voice, said "Miss Leonard, could you please schedule Miss Beck for next week, same time?"

I walked away and did not look back at him, although that's all I wanted to do.

. . .

Three hours pass, and it's as if we're both alone. Mellow says nothing, which surprises me. Instead she stares at the blurred landscape outside the window, a landscape of concrete barriers, green road signs, and speeding cars. Occasionally she sighs.

"Are we going to stop?" Her voice shocks me after so much quiet. I could almost forget she's there.

"Do you need to?"

"Yeah."

I glance at the horizon for a sign of a clean bathroom. I cannot do gas station bathrooms. It has to be a restaurant. Those aren't always much better, but at least they have occasional inspections. I'm not sure anyone with the health department ever sets foot in a gas station restroom. I'd rather pee on a tree. "Watch for a sign. A restaurant, preferably not a fast food place."

"Do you consider Denny's fast food?"

I glance at her. She's smirking at me. "I'm on the fence about Denny's. It's probably alright. It depends on how badly you have to go."

"Denny's then." She rolls down the window, letting an exhaust-infused gush of hot air into the car. "Why do you think we have bodies?"

"What?" The dry gusts, the noise, the dust—they all annoy me, perhaps as much as her question. "What are you saying? And roll up the window. I can't breathe with all the dirt and noise."

I see her grimace at me before grudgingly rolling up the window. The poor air conditioner seems to choke with relief. "Why do you think we have bodies?" she asks again.

"I thought that's what you said." The Denny's sign hovers above the horizon, a duck-yellow promise of cheap food and a place to rest. "Why would you even ask a question like that?"

I glance in the mirror and merge to the right so we can exit. I'm too slow, and other cars honk at me angrily. How can horns sound angry? It seems impossible, but they do. People who have no control over their lives get so angry when they drive. It's odd when you really think about it. But understandable. No one really has control over anything.

"Did you even hear me?" Mellow leans toward me, waving a hand in front of my eyes.

"Jesus! Don't do that! I could wreck the car!" I swat at her.

"You weren't even listening."

"That isn't as important as not dying." My heart pounds, so I breathe to slow my pulse. The exit appears; I ease our behemoth to the ramp and slow down. "Why are you even asking me something like that?"

I can sense that I've wounded her somehow. She huddles against the door, silent. She stays that way until I ease the car into the gravel lot next to the restaurant, pull into the furthest spot, and turn off the engine. "Wait," I say as she opens the creaky door.

Her eyes blaze with fury. "Why?"

"I'm sorry if I hurt you. I just needed to concentrate on driving. I...I haven't done it for a while, and I haven't driven with a passenger since—"

She sees something in my face that I'm not even aware of. The anger vanishes, replaced by a wide-eyed wonder. "Why?"

"Why what?" I get out of the car and lock it. It's too damned hot to sit inside. My skin suddenly goes clammy. I feel sweat trickling down the small of my back, a ringing in my ears, and I'm cold and hot all at once.

Gravel crunches under my shoe. I imagine my foot parting the gray sea as I step, creating dents in a field of stones. Would the dents be there tomorrow? Would they change when someone else steps near them, rearranging the pebbles? Are the pebbles different once someone steps on them, at some cellular level? I imagine myself tiny, invisible, a single-celled entity gazing up at the craggy rock face of one of the gravel pebbles, worshipping it—then a massive, unexpected force from heaven crashes down, and in an instant, the rock under whose shadow I had lived moves, changes, is crushed, and my world changes forever.

Mellow plants herself in front of me and I nearly run into her. "What are you doing?" I sound annoyed.

"You just sort of go in and out of consciousness or something." She leans in so her eyes are inches from mine. "Who else is in there with you?"

"Let's go." I dodge her, trudging through the gravel toward the sticky-finger-printed glass door of the restaurant. She scrambles, catches up, and grabs the door handle, ushering me in with a formal wave of the hand.

The place is fairly empty. Still, it takes several minutes for anyone to notice that we're waiting, which give Mellow ample time to natter at me. "So?"

"So what?"

"Are you multiple personality disorder?"

"No one *is* multiple personality disorder. You *have* it." I wave to a flat-haired mouse of a waitress who ignores me. "Could you please find someone to seat us?" I say to Mellow. Maybe giving her an errand will give me a few moments of peace.

"Sure!" She seems excited to have a job and prances off like a puppy into the dining room. Oh, what was I thinking? This has got to be the worst idea in the history of bad ideas. I don't travel well to begin with, but why did I ever think taking an adolescent nomad with me would be a workable idea? You really can't help anyone. It all just prolongs the inevitable and taking Mellow with me will probably only make her lonelier when we part. It was probably quite cruel that I allowed her to come with me. What if her mother comes back to look for her? But of course, wouldn't that have been even more cruel, leaving her to the incompetent mothering of Rhiannon and her drug addiction? She probably didn't come back anyway.

Mellow bounces back, trailed by the mousy waitress. A gray net the exact color of her hair has flattened her tresses. Her face is sickly too, and her mouth puckers all around as if it's a string bag someone's pulled too tight. Patterned with dandruff and smudges of grease, dirty glasses perch on the end of her nose. According to her tag, her name is, dissonantly, *Pretty*.

"Two?" she mumbles. She has few teeth, which accounts for the puckering. I nod, and she grabs two plastic-covered menus and walks wordlessly into the dining room. We follow, Mellow jumping about as if it's Christmas. Despite everything, I smile at her enthusiasm.

"Drinks?" Pretty may only speak in single syllables. I guess that makes sense if speaking is painful and embarrassing.

"Hot tea, no lemon," I say, plucking open the menu from the one clean corner.

"Dr. Pepper." Mellow is a blur of motion, restlessly bouncing in her seat.

"I don't think Dr. Pepper is a great choice," I say, but the waitress has already walked away.

"Why?" *Bounce, bounce, bounce.*

"Because you're already hyper. Plus, it will make you have to go to the bathroom."

"It's good to go to the bathroom. It keeps your kidneys fresh." Bounce, bounce, bounce. "Can I have a quarter for the claw machine?"

"What?" I try reading the menu, but the bouncing is distracting.

"The claw machine. Can I have a quarter?"

I focus on her and feel a headache beginning to excavate my skull cavity. "What is a claw machine?"

"Geez. I guess you never had kids, huh? The claw machine is that." She points to the foyer where a large plexiglass box stands stuffed with cheap Chinese plush toys. "You put in your money, and then get a chance to make the claw grab a toy."

"And it never gives you a toy, am I right?"

She shrugs. The waitress Pretty has come back with our drinks. Lipton tea, of course, and hot water in a cheap chrome-plated pot. Mellow attacks the bubbly brown beverage and drinks half in one gulp. Pretty asks, "Are you ready to order?"

Nothing looks appealing, honestly. I imagine that everything will give me heartburn or diarrhea or both. But Mellow is raring to go. "I want Moons Over My Hammy," she says, giggling. "I just love to say that. Extra hash browns. Extra toasted on the sandwich."

"I'll just have the tea." I realize now that feeding a teenager is going to put a dent in my carefully planned budget, and without cash, it's going to be even harder. A trip to a grocery store will be in order very soon. We absolutely cannot eat at restaurants every day, and she obviously needs to eat more than I do.

Pretty scratches the side of her hair net with her pencil. "You want a biscuit or anything, hon?" she asks me. Her watery brown eyes loom large behind thick glasses.

"No, I'm fine."

"You really should eat," Mellow says. "Could you bring her a Moons Over My Hammy too?"

"No, I won't eat that." I smile at Pretty patiently. "She likes to take charge."

"Give it to her," Mellow commands.

"No," I say through gritted teeth.

The poor waitress is outmatched. Her head swivels from me to Mellow, back and forth. "So, one or two Moons?"

I say one and Mellow says two.

"That is quite enough," I hiss at her. "I'll just leave you here if you're going to act like that."

Pretty gasps. "Now, it's not my place, but a mother should never talk like that to a daughter," she says.

"She's not my daughter."

Mellow shakes her head sadly. "No, I'm not. She kidnapped me."

I clank my spoon on the table. "That's it." I stand up, place my napkin on the table, and grab my purse. "I am going to the restroom. We want one, and only one, order of that disgusting thing. And when I come back, we are going to forget this conversation ever took place."

I shove out of the booth, barely touching Pretty (who feels as if she's made of twigs and twine, not flesh).

This was a huge, huge mistake.

In the horribly yellow bathroom, I can see the stress on my face. Even though my wig is sitting where it should, it looks as if it doesn't belong there. Bruise-colored circles have bloomed under my eyes, which are tinged red at the corners. The tiny cracks around my dry lips look like moon canals, and my face sports patches of flaky, red skin next to grayish-white spots. I look a mess. I absolutely would not want Edward to see me like this. If I keep traveling with Mellow, it will just get worse, won't it?

"Jesus," I murmur at my reflection. "Maybe you should just go home."

The restroom door swings open, bringing with it the unmistakable smell of burnt bacon. Mellow's face pops up in the mirror next to me. She looks pretty good. But then again, she's young.

"I'm sorry," she mouths silently at our reflection.

"For what?" I ask aloud. She just stares at us, her lips pursed, eyes blinking rapidly. I turn to look her in the eyes. "Why are you sorry?"

We're close enough that I feel the warmth coming from her body. She looks up at me, her eyes filled with sadness. "I'm sorry you got dumped with me. It's not fair. I'll leave. I know I'm making whatever it is you're doing harder." Then she hugs me.

I haven't been hugged for a long time, I realize, and my body goes rigid with shock. But she doesn't let go, and I recover in enough time to put my arms around her and hug her back. Leaning into her hair, the scene of jasmine and young sweat reminds me of bathtubs full of toys, mountains of suds, hunting for dolphins with a red plastic boat piloted by a tiny man with a plastic yellow head…

Darcy's bath time.

Feel like retching, cold to the bone, I hate this cold light and the yellow tile and the cracked porcelain sink. I push the girl aside and run back into the dining room, hoping to forget, but I only feel lightheaded, so I grab for a chair near the door.

"Jesus, are you okay?" Mellow squats on the floor next to me, trying to look up into my face, which I've covered with trembling hands.

"Not really."

I cannot look at her. Her cold hands pry mine from my face, and she offers me a wadded-up tissue and a worried smile. "I'm sorry."

"For what?" I wipe at the tear tracks on my cheek.

"For whatever happened."

Whatever happened. As if it were the same as catching a train, or buying fruit, or going swimming in a lake that seemed safe enough. These are all just things that happen, one as important or trivial as the next. If I keep them all in order, contained, they cannot force me into feeling anything. Not anything. Nothing.

But here I am, at a rural Denny's restaurant, with a grimy-faced transient girl, and my mind is breaking into tiny puzzle pieces, and I'm running from a porcelain sink.

12
ESCAPE ROUTE

"**S**o, what was that, back at the Denny's?" We're back on the road after a two-hour eating spree that put a sizeable dent in my food budget. The road is long and almost deserted, some backcountry side road that I mistakenly found when looking for a freeway onramp. This old car has no GPS.

"I'd rather talk about how we're going to get back onto the freeway." A gas station, improbably, looms over a rise in the road. "Finally. Maybe somebody there can help us."

"But you're still not answering my question," she says in a sing-song voice.

"I'm not going to answer your question."

I ease the behemoth onto the chipped asphalt lot. "Did you ever think that broken pavement looks like the bottom of a cheesecake with Oreo crust?"

"Why are you obsessed with food?"

She pouts. "I was just pointing out an interesting fact. I'll just shut up."

Oh, how I wish that were possible. She's done nothing but yammer since we left the restaurant. I exit the car, close the door, and stretch before checking my watch—we've been driving for nearly two hours.

Two hours of yammering. Two hours of mental avoidance. Two hours of wishing I had left her in a hotel room.

The bearded clerk inside the Gas 'N' Go stares at a small television screen, hardly blinking. I don't think he sees me. "Excuse me." He doesn't blink. I wonder if he's dead. "Hello?"

His hand moves, motioning for me to be quiet. His eyes still glued to the screen he leans forward a bit, as if something is happening on the soundless monitor. Is he watching a game? The news? An ad for some medicine that will change his life and brings with it the risk of never waiting on another customer? I don't even want to touch the counter, which is covered in peeling plastic and indeterminate stains.

"I need to fill up my car," I say slowly. Still no response.

Something small and fiery pops in my belly. I can't say exactly what it is, but it bubbles up like magma from the core of the earth and I feel it travel the veins and arteries until it reaches my mouth. "Goddammit, motherfucker, I want some gas!" Did I just say that?

It does snap him out of his stupor. His brown eyes, punctuated with hairy caterpillar eyebrows, open wide, as does his mouth full of crazy white teeth. "No need to scream, ma'am." He moves cautiously, as if I'm a predator poised to pounce. Now he doesn't take his eyes off me. "How much?" he asks warily, as if this will trigger another profane bout of verbal diarrhea.

I wad up the twenty-dollar bill I have in my hand and throw it maliciously at his head. He dodges as if I've thrown a hand grenade. "And I want these." I pile five packs of Oreos onto the counter.

He nods slowly, his eyes never leaving my face. "How much gas?"

"Twenty. Didn't I just give you a twenty?" My voice does not sound like my voice.

He nods enthusiastically.

"Give me a bag for the cookies." Am I now robbing this gas station of Oreos? I think this is possible. He hastily sweeps the cookies into a plastic bag and hands it to me at arm's length, as if he's afraid to catch the crazy. "Thank you." I grab it and feel somehow exhilarated with my newly minted crime life. Free cookies, just for the asking. As I exit, I turn to him and call over my shoulder, "Have a nice day."

. . .

"I think you have a great reserve of untapped anger," Edward said at our next session.

"I don't think so. I'm not an angry person." I couldn't stop picking at the nonexistent hairs on my forearms. Now there were scabs and I'd started picking those, too. I had to keep emergency tissues and bandages with me wherever I went, in case I went too deep and started to bleed.

He made a noncommittal sound from his leather chair. He sat there now instead of near me. His desk was between us. I guess I frightened him. That's certainly not what I wanted. *Pick, pick, pick.*

He cleared his throat. "Let's talk about something different today." He waited for me to reply, but I didn't. "I'd like to talk about when you were a child."

"That was nothing special." Damn. I'd picked a scab and now I had to triage it. I dug in my purse for a bandage and a Kleenex.

"Do you want some antibacterial ointment for that?"

"No." I cover it up with the snow-white tissue, and a blossom of red appears. "It's fine. It's nothing. I just scratched a scab. I'm sure your office is very clean. I have some in my purse, in any case." I did carry it with me, because you never know when you'll pick a scab and start to bleed, and if it had been in a public place without proper sanitation, I absolutely would have slathered it on.

He was frowning when I looked at him, as if he were puzzled. "Well, what would you like to talk about?"

I couldn't tell him what I wanted to talk about; it would have been obscene. Ever since the last session, I'd been having nothing but erotic dreams about Dr. Denture. Whenever I closed my eyes, he appeared in various states of undress, in various locales, always rescuing me from some dangerous dream demon. "Fine. My childhood, then. It's extremely boring, though."

He relaxed a bit. "That's alright. Better to have a boring childhood than one full of trauma. So, tell me about your parents."

It almost pained me to meet his gaze; I felt that he could see into my soul, and that he would strip me bare of all my pretenses. But then, what a pleasure to feel his attention on me! "My parents. Both dead."

"I'm sorry," he murmured.

"That's what everyone says, but I'm not that sorry, actually. They weren't bad or anything, just a bit rigid."

"How so?" He steepled his fingers again in that classic black-and-white movie doctor pose. Hmm. What if we had been in one of those classic movies? I could be Rita Hayworth and he could be...not Cary Grant. Too comedic. Cheekbones. Someone British, with cheekbones. Basil Rathbone. Yes!

"Sorry, what?"

"I asked you, in what way were they rigid?"

"My parents?" He nodded, smiling so that his eyes crinkled. "Oh... you know. Just, very rule-oriented."

"You were an only child?"

"Yes. How did you know?"

He shook his head. "Just a guess. So, did you fight against these rules? Were there any in particular that you really hated?"

I cast my memory back to when I was younger, but the memories, as always, were a bit hazy. Truth was, I hadn't had a fantastic childhood, but I didn't want to tell him that. I hate when psychiatrists pin everything on how badly you were potty trained, or how cruelly your father treated you, or how cold your mother was. In the end, we're all responsible for our own actions if we're adults. Children can't help it, but adults can. Adults can be responsible, and really, there is no excuse when they aren't there to help—

"Anna?" He was suddenly sitting on the edge of the sofa, next to me, as if he'd teleported over there. "Sorry to startle you. What were you thinking about?"

"My parents." This was a lie. I moved slightly away.

"What I asked you—did it trigger some memory?"

"Not really. I mean, a little, but no. My parents were just normal parents. They loved me, I suppose. I don't remember that much about them."

"When did they die?"

The word "die" always got my attention. It just seemed too plain, too curt, for what happened when life ended. "It was—I think I was 12."

"You think you were 12? You don't remember?" He tilted his head slightly. "That's a pretty significant event. I would think you'd remember."

I sighed. "I haven't thought about it for a long time. I guess it was pretty traumatic."

"You guess?"

"Are you going to parrot back every word I say?" Anger started to bubble up. I certainly didn't want to blow up at him, but...if he kept pushing, I might. I just might.

He put his hands up as if to surrender. "Fine. I'm not going to push. It just seems significant. But if you don't want to talk about it, that's okay." He glanced at the wall. "It's almost time, anyway. I feel like we're making progress." He stood, went back behind his desk, thumbed through his appointment book. "I won't be here next week, though, so I'm hoping we can pick this up again."

"Where will you be?"

He seems surprised that I asked. "Uh...I'll be traveling. Just for a week."

"Where are you going?"

He turned scarlet. It was adorable. "I...uh...I'm going to...the Midwest. For a conference." I knew he wasn't telling the truth. Why would he lie to me, though? Would it be...because he was doing something he didn't want me to know about? What would that be?

Delight rushed through me, a shot of adrenaline. If he wanted to hide something personal from me, then he must care for me beyond just the limits of the patient-doctor relationship. But this was wonderful! It was confirmation of what I suspected all along. He was in love with me.

"That made you unpredictably happy," he said, a puzzled look on his face.

"Your conference?" I smiled dazzlingly. "I'm happy that you're doing something to further your career. You're so talented."

He gulped, clearly uncomfortable. I felt so powerful. This moment of power erased all the anger and painful things that had nearly bubbled to the surface during the session. All forgotten now. All replaced with that firm suspicion that he held me closer to his heart than he even knew, perhaps.

"Anna," he said, taking a step toward me. He looked as if he wanted to say more, but was afraid. Something held him back.

"Yes?" I imagined my eyes bright with promise, eager to receive all the subliminal messages he couldn't help but send me.

This seemed to draw him closer. He took another step toward me. "We need to be careful. You need to be careful."

I smiled, nodding. "Of course. I will be. I promise. No accidents."

He looked confused. "No, I don't mean that—" He seemed to catch himself as I walked away. "I'll see you in two weeks," he called after me. His voice shook, didn't it?

"Have a nice 'conference,'" I said, not looking back.

. . .

I throw the plastic bag of Oreos at Mellow through her open window. She squeals with delight when she sees what's inside. "Do you know how to pump gas?" I ask her.

"Sure." She's already crammed two cookies in her mouth and black crumbles trail from her lips like ants at a picnic. She hops out and expertly wrangles the hose and spout, shoves it into the place for gas, which is near the rear license plate.

"How did you know where to put the gas?"

She chews, motions for me to wait. "I need some milk to go with this."

"Well, I stole the cookies, so you have to steal the milk."

"For reals?" She's stuffed the remaining packs into her bra. They stick out like thick blue antennae.

"I guess. If you want milk." I glance at the gas station store to see if the eyebrow man is on the phone to the police to report the cookie heist. He's back to watching the screen. From outside, I can see that he's watching some kind of sport, but it's grainy and I have no idea what sports really look like anyway.

Mellow chomps and waits as the gasoline flows into the reservoir of the Eldorado. I'm truthfully glad to have someone to pump the gas; I am always afraid that I'll get it on my hands and onto my food, and I am fairly certain that ingesting gasoline, even in small quantities, might cause brain damage. I'm not so worried about her; I think the damage has been done.

"Okay. Done." She squints at the pump. "Jesus, this thing takes a lot of gas! Did you already pay for it?"

"Yes. I gave the man twenty."

"Oh." She smushes her lips sideways as if she's thinking. "Sweet." She replaces the pump gingerly, as if it might explode, and then ambles into the store, short patchwork shorts riding up her legs. I would never let a daughter of mine walk around in those shorts. I should tell her.

I consider using the restroom, but it's certainly filthy, so I decide to wait. No sounds but the rustle of tree limbs, and the distant hum of the sports on the television. The sky is so blue; it's open in a way that I never see in the city, as if there are more possibilities here.

Mellow scuttles out of the store toting a plastic jug of milk. "Hurry," she hisses.

"Did you actually steal that?"

"You told me to!" She pouts indignantly.

"This is the first time you've done what I told you to do," I mutter, jerking open the car door. It weighs a ton, and when you slam it, it sounds like the door to a women's prison.

"Let's go, let's go," she says, her right leg vibrating nervously. She rips the orange cap off the milk and slugs it as if she's taking a tug off a whiskey bottle. "Come on!"

The engine complains but turns over, happy for its petroleum breakfast. As I check my mirrors, Mellow does some gymnast move, swings her legs over the center console, and jams her foot into the gas pedal, making the car lurch forward.

"What are you doing?" I screech, wrenching the wheel.

"We gotta move!" She contracts back into her own seat as I push the pedal.

"What is the hurry?"

"We stole a bunch of stuff!" she yells back, craning her neck to look out the back window. "That dude might come after us with a fireman axe!"

In the rearview mirror, eyebrow man is, indeed, chasing us down the road, waving. I gun the engine and try to focus on the road. "What in hell did you do?"

"I didn't do anything!" she screeches. "You just ripped that dude off for, like eighty bucks or something!"

"What?" I glance at her, then at the rearview (in which the man is blessedly smaller), and back to the road. "What do you mean?"

"You gave him twenty bucks, but I put, like, eighty in the tank. I filled it up."

"You what?"

"You didn't tell me not to." She grabs for the cookie bag and I swat it out of her hand. "Hey!"

"You made me a criminal!" My hands are shaking, and my breath is shallow. "I knew this would happen. You are just no good. It's not a surprise."

She is stone silent.

I drive on, my breathing still ragged. She stares straight ahead, her jaw set tight. We go on like that for about 20 minutes before I pull the car over to the shoulder. I turn off the engine but keep my hands on the wheel. I study my fingernails, bitten, short, warped from years of saliva and stress.

She says nothing, just opens the door and smoothly slides out, slamming it behind her. She starts walking.

This is my chance. I can get rid of her. I can let her go. It would absolutely make this trip easier, and if I get stopped because of the theft, I can pin it on her, conveniently, since she won't be with me.

But I don't do that. Instead, I turn the key, slip the car into drive, and follow ten feet behind her, gravel crunching under wheels. Her body is rigid, her footsteps angry, arms crossed across her chest as if she were a petulant toddler. My heart breaks a little.

I speed up, pass her, and park the car so she has to go around it. "Stop," I call from the open window. She does. She's breathing hard, her chest heaving more with emotion than with exertion. Mascara has left tiny black rivulets down her face. I get out of the car and walk to her.

I touch her arm. "I'm sorry," I whisper. She blinks rapidly, wipes her face with a dirty sleeve.

"Why?" she croaks.

"Why?"

"Why are you sorry?" Puffy, red eyes stare at me, irises brilliant blue.

I don't know the answer. There is an unraveling inside me, some spool of spider silk that's been tucked behind an attic door for many years, and I feel it wending its way into this reality. "I have a hard time caring about other people."

Her interest is piqued. "You do? I don't think that's true."

"No, it is." I cross my arms across my chest. "I live alone. I do everything alone. Caring for other people is careless, and useless, and in the end, it all comes out the same. And I'm sorry for that."

"You can't be sorry for how the world works." Her tears have dried. "And I think you do care about people. That's why you say you don't."

That's as much as I can do for the moment. "Come with me," I say gently. "I—I want you to."

The blinking slows. Her shoulders relax. "You don't have to take me with you."

"I know I don't. I want to."

She nods, as if she already knew that. She walks silently to the car, opens the creaking passenger door, and slides back in as if she's been meant to sit there.

So, the decision has been made. I'm still not sure why, but I know it's the right thing to do. And although I hate to admit it, I think I would miss her, just a little.

13
EVASIVE ACTION

Mellow slumps with feet up on the dashboard as we continue to drive through endless, flat, sand-colored fields of nothing. She asks, "Why do you do that? Why do you bite your fingers?"

"Please get your feet off the dash."

She grunts and drops her feet, straightens up against the high leather back of the car seat. "So?"

"So what?" It's been two hours since we left the showdown in the road, and I'm just slightly regretting that I didn't leave her there to face the wrath of the gas attendant.

"Why do you bite your fingers?"

"Everyone does that." I fix my gaze on the road ahead, although there is absolutely nothing to see. "Can you look at the map again?"

"I just looked at it, like, ten minutes ago." Still, she unfolds it and sets it on her lap, then pulls it up to within an inch of her face. "What's the nearest cross street?"

"There are no cross streets. We're on a highway. We left Barstow, or near there, and now we're going east. Finally."

She disappears behind the map. "Mmm. Mojave National Preserve is this big green part with nothing in it. Maybe we could go there."

"There's nothing in it."

"There has to be something in it. There's a road that goes in there. It's got the coolest name. It's Z-z-y-z-x Road. How do you say that?"

"What is it? Spell it again."

"Z-z-y-z-x. Zi-zix? Somebody must've been on crack when they named that road." She laughs at her own joke, but I don't. "So, why do you bite your fingers?"

"Everyone does that," I tell her again, with an edge to my voice. "Why this obsession with my fingers?"

"I'm just watching you while you drive. I can't read because I get motion sick when I read in the car. See? You're doing it again."

And, in fact, I am. I unconsciously bite at the loose ends of skin around my thumbs and fingers, because I cannot stand the feel of them being ragged. I have a need to smooth them out. But you can never really smooth them out, because once you bite off a piece to smooth it, you create another jagged edge.

"You bleed sometimes too. Doesn't that hurt?"

I don't answer.

"You do know that you do it, right? I mean, you're not just eating your own fingers and not knowing it?"

"I don't eat my own fingers." A claustrophobic feeling, a tightness, rises up from my gut into my chest, and I start to feel as if I can't breathe, like my head is being held under water. "We need to stop for a bit." I scan the horizon for a turn out, or an exit. Of course. There it is: Zzyzx Road.

Mellow lets out a delighted squeal as I steer the car off the exit into unknown territory. It certainly doesn't look like anything exists on Zzyzx Road; it's long and empty, a stretch leading to a serial killer's barn or a miles-deep sinkhole. "I wonder what's at the end of this road?" she asks in a hushed whisper. I slow the car, drive with one hand, nibbling the skin of the index finger of the other as I steer.

"I don't think we should follow it to the end." I pull to the side and put the car in park. "I don't think there's anything here at all. Just dirt."

She yanks open the door and jumps out of the car, takes off running full speed toward a slight rise twenty feet away. "What are you doing?" I call lamely. Dammit. Now I'll have to follow her, I suppose.

It feels good to stretch, but I'm still not excited about taking a stroll on serial killer land. Or maybe it's a military installation where they practice using land mines. Wouldn't they have to put a sign up if that's what they did here? But it *is* the military. Maybe they figure that if you're spying on them, you deserve to have your bloodied fingers blown off. I saw a film once, an old 1950s civil defense newsreel, showing a town full of mannequins and houses being blasted by a test bomb. This place felt like it could have been ground zero, minus the mannequins.

At the top of the rise, Mellow jumps and waves both hands in the air like an inflated balloon person at a cheap car lot. "You gotta see this!" Her words carry through the dry air and sound as if she's right next to me.

Trudge, trudge. It feels good to put my feet in dirt, actually. Too much concrete in this life. Not enough natural surfaces. I concentrate on my feet, the patterns they make in the moon surface of this desert area. Even though it looks like dead earth, there are tiny white flowers poking timidly through the surface.

I get to the top of the rise and realize how dreadfully out of shape I am. "Look!" Mellow shields her eyes from the sun and points to a green-brown lake lined with desiccated palm trees. In the middle of this stain of a lake is a little island. On this little island perches a building made of rocks, with one snaggle-tooth of a window, black as a crow.

"Hmm."

"Is that all you can say? Look at this place. It must be, like, a Harry Potter portal, or a spy hideout."

"Really? Those are the two options? Hogwarts or CIA?" She's so excited. I forget what it's like, to be excited about things, to suspect that magic might be all around and to look for it.

"Let's go see!" She skitters down the dirt hill toward the lake, and when I realize what she's intending to do, I run so fast I nearly trip and fall.

"No." I stand in front of her, my hands firmly on her shoulders to stop her forward momentum. "No, you cannot go into that water."

"Why?" She strains against my hands, but not too much. Just enough to show me that she doesn't think I'm her boss, but she'll still do what I say. For the moment.

"Look at it. It's filthy. Do you know how many microbial agents are hiding in that water?"

"Ooooh. Microbial agents. That sounds very James Bond." She relaxes against my hands and laughs. "Seriously? You're afraid of a little dirty water?"

Afraid of a little dirty water.

. . .

He'd found out about the water. I was never sure how it happened. He brought it up on that day he returned, and it changed everything.

He was gone for two weeks, as promised, and at my next appointment I was determined to find out why. That was how far gone I was. I didn't even realize that even as I was solving the puzzle of our relationship, he was solving the puzzle of my dysfunction.

"How was your week?" he asked casually as he pulled files from his briefcase. I had worn something thin and sheer for this meeting. It was hot outside, so it was excusable, but I also realized that he had probably gone off somewhere to meet a lover or someone he didn't want to tell me about, which meant I needed to accelerate my seduction.

He wore a charcoal-gray suit despite the heat. I watched his back as he moved about, shuffling papers, moving files. Was he trying not to face me?

"I'm ready to talk," I said. This got his attention.

He turned to me, blinked rapidly, and forgot his paperwork. "You're ready to talk."

I nodded. He grabbed a steno pad and pen, shrugged out of his jacket, loosened a blue-green tie, and dutifully rushed to his chair so we could begin. He crossed his long legs, set the pad on his knee, and leaned toward me expectantly.

He said softly, "Whenever you're ready."

I sighed, stretched my arms to heaven. I visualized the edges of my sheer blue shirt stretching and gapping to show just a peek at my breasts. I had left my bra at home. He looked at the floor and blushed slightly, so I knew he had seen this.

"Ask me something." I felt as if I were the doctor. I felt in control.

He stared, unsure of what to do now that I was steering things. "Uh...tell me about your parents. You said last time that they'd died, and that—"

"My parents dying wasn't important at all." I reclined on the leather sofa, hoping my silhouette looked as good as I thought it did. "I told you that because it was what you wanted to hear."

He cleared his throat. "You...lied? About your parents? Are they really dead or not?"

"Oh, yes. They are really, really dead. But it was just normal stuff. Heart failure, smoking. A few years ago. It hurt, yes, but that's not what's going on here."

"No?" he asked.

"No. But before I tell you, I need for you to tell me something. I need to trust you."

He frowned, uncomfortable with this. I knew he didn't want to tell me about his mysterious meeting, but that was going to be my price. I had only one truly valuable piece of information to trade, and I wasn't going to give it up unless I got something in return.

He closed the notebook and set it on his desk. He steepled his long fingers as he did whenever he had a puzzle to solve. He leaned toward me. "Alright. What do you want to know?"

I sat up again, leaned toward him. "Who did you go to meet?"

"When?"

"At your conference. The one you just returned from."

He frowned, uncomprehending. "I didn't go to meet anyone. I was at a conference. I mean, I met people, but…are you asking something else?"

It was not going as planned. I had imagined the scenario, and it included a tearful confession, and passionate, apologetic sex on this leather couch. It had not included confusion.

He coughed slightly and sat back in his chair. "Look, I think we need to address something rather important, Anna." He cleared his throat again and ran his hand through his thick, lovely hair. "I really didn't want to talk about this, but I don't see a choice. Do you know what I'm referring to?"

"Yes, I think so." He was inviting me to move. Of course, he could not look eager, or attempt to push the situation forward. It would be unethical. But I, on the other hand, could do it. I could move it forward. I rose and slowly crossed the few feet between us until I was standing directly in front of him, his eyes level with my breasts.

"Please go and sit down," he said weakly. He looked toward the door.

"You don't really want me to." I took a step closer. "I know what you want."

"Anna." He jumped up, shoving me aside, and bolted to the window. "I really do think you've misread something. I'm so, so sorry. I…this is so awkward."

"It doesn't have to be awkward." I moved toward him, but he put his hand up as if to stop me. He turned so the golden light from the window framed his angled face.

"Anna. You understand that I'm your doctor, yes? That I am unable and, indeed, prohibited by law from having any kind of relationship with you other than that of a client and physician?"

"Laws are for people who don't live with their hearts." I heard myself say it and something jarred in my head, tipped and swayed, like a cardboard construct of a building that looked real but was truly hollow inside, simply giving the illusion of reality. My confidence waned. The lovely scenario, like an old bit of celluloid, started to dissolve and fly apart as if heated by a too-hot bulb.

He stared down at his notes for the longest time. I wanted to jump up, embrace him, forget all the things I knew were right, and those that were wrong. Instead, he looked at me, pained, and said, "This is really about the water."

The room reduced to a small, black, closed-in tunnel straight to him. I was plunging down a dark, dank hole toward an unknowable end, and I had no reason to think anything would save me. A high-pitched whine like an electronic field of static or a far-away siren enveloped the room, closed in toward me as if to seal me in a mesh bag of sound.

A man's face floated to my consciousness as if it were surfacing from the bottom of a deep, murky lake. Different from the doctor, so different—an earthy man, sandy hair, he had smelled like vanilla and fresh grass. Brown eyes, always crinkled in laughter—everything was funny to him. The world was comical. Until it wasn't. He was so much mine, and so much hers, and we were a family, but more—we were a united front against the cruelty of the world. But the world made sure to show us that we were wrong.

I choked, blindly finding the couch so I could curl up in a ball. "Water will kill you," I whispered.

"Alright." He was next to me, his hand on mine. "Alright. Now we can talk. Now I can help you."

. . .

"If you go in there, I will drive away and leave you," I say, my voice shaking. Mellow stops abruptly, and the teasing smile melts from her lips. She says nothing. She just walks forward.

"Wait!" I scream so loudly a flock of black birds rises from behind a chaparral hillock into the dusty silence. It's enough to stop her. She stands frozen where her footsteps stopped, rigid, as if my words have suspended her.

Breathe. I'd like to fall asleep here, right now, bake in this desert oven into a hard-clay figurine of a woman. "Please," I say more gently.

"Please come back."

She turns her head slightly toward me but does not look at me. "Why should I?"

I take three tentative steps forward. "I need you to come back."

This must be the right answer, because she does an about-face and stands, arms folded across her chest, staring at me across the heat haze. "You need me to come back? I thought I was just a pain in your ass." The hard, well-practiced mask she wears crumbles just a bit, and her rigid, protective mouth quivers. "I thought you were going to leave me."

Then I'm hugging her, trying to draw her inward like a deep breath, trying to make a cage of my arms that will never be, have never been, long enough to protect anything. Unwashed hair, the scent of the young and careless, still-malleable bones beneath my fingers, I sense she is a clay figurine in her own right, but she can still be transmuted into something else, not baked hard and left to crack.

I close my eyes, and an image clicks into place as if it's in an old View-Master, technicolor and golden like the pictures from the past always are. The image is of a flat green lake, still as glass. It looks beautiful and welcoming, but I know what's in there. I know what it will do, and the knowledge bubbles up from inside me like a well of ichor or tar, black and sticky and laced with the dinosaur bones of a million guilty, sleepless nights.

I open my eyes abruptly to stop it. I am here, in this hot, dry desert, with this petulant, scared little girl. And we are running. "Let's get in the car," I rasp through cracked lips. She nods, and neither of us speaks again until we are outside Las Vegas.

"Wow." Mellow chomps on the last surviving cookies in a pack of Double Stuf Oreos. "Las Vegas is really lit up."

"That's sort of the point." I've never been to this place, and I never really wanted to go, but I've lost quite a bit of time, and according to the maps, it's the most direct route. My skin crawls just thinking about the all the disgusting bodily fluids secreted on a daily basis, not to mention the amount of alcohol-sweat this desert Sodom milks out of its customers. "Please be sure you clean up any crumbs. I don't want the car to turn into a garbage can."

I can feel her roll her eyes without even looking at her.

"Are we going to stop at a casino?" Her voice is hushed and excited. "I've always wanted to gamble."

"You're not old enough anyway." Is this true? I have no idea. Las Vegas (or my image of it) seems like the kind of place where they would encourage children to throw away their allowance whenever possible.

"My mom was from Nevada," she offers up off-handedly. I don't ask a follow-up question. I'm afraid of what else I'll learn. "I have to pee."

"I'm sure there's nowhere to park," I tell her as we follow a line of cars onto the main drag.

"Ooh!" She squeals. "Look at the pyramid! I want to go to the pyramid!" There is indeed a huge, black glassy pyramid right off the road. I guess that fits with the desert theme. "I think it has parking." She turns puppy dog eyes on me. "I really need to pee. It'll only take a minute. I promise."

I follow a sign and find myself driving down a palm-ensconced drive toward the looming structure. "Free valet parking!" Mellow screams, jumping up and down in her seat. It's as if she's discovered the Hope Diamond hanging from the rearview mirror.

Anxiety rises in my chest proportionate to every inch we come closer to this cesspool of faux-Egyptian excess. I hear my own breathing become shallow, as if I'm being held under the Nile without a hollowed-out reed. Mellow, blissfully unaware of my cresting tide of panic, bounces in her seat, eyes round and expectant.

"We need to be quick," I mumble. I am loath to hand the keys over to someone else. I am sure that all of these valets smoke, and I'm sure their nicotine-stained fingers will no doubt contaminate my things. The thought of one of them in my car—it's too much. I come to a slow, slow stop and Mellow jumps out of the car, leaving the passenger door hanging wide open.

"Wait," I command. She stops, amazingly. "You wait for me. I'm not letting you go in there by yourself."

"But I really have to go!"

I just put a finger in the air, and she nods. "Stay there and shut the door." She does.

A young man with sandy blond hair and a cut above his lip—knife fight, perhaps?—leans into my window. "Afternoon." He opens the door as if I am a starlet or a person of some importance. I grab my purse, clutch it to my chest, and come close enough to sniff his shirt-front. No smoke.

"Whoa," he says, backing up slightly. "What's up, McGruff? Sniffing for crime?" Another kid, skinny, Mexican, slugs water from a crushed plastic bottle and laughs at David's joke (his nametag says David. I'll bet his name is something much more urban, like Kid or Rocko or Razor.) "Keys, ma'am?"

"Keys?" I breathe in response. Mellow is waving both arms, dwarfed by the great glass pyramid. The sun here is brutal, a bare bulb in an interrogation room.

"Are you going to give me your keys so I can park your car?" He speaks slowly as if I am deaf or infirm.

"No." I face front, trying to ignore him, but he's straightened up his torso so it is exactly centered in my peripheral vision. He takes a step back from my window.

He motions to someone else, and within a second, another torso is hovering near my window. David-Rocko is waving other cars around me as if I'm a road hazard. Another head is in my window.

"Good afternoon, ma'am." The older, deeper voice is smooth, soothing. The crazy-person wrangler. "I'm afraid this line is for valet parking only. You'll either have to move and take your chances in the far parking lot," he gestures toward a point on the far horizon, "or let us park your car for you, free of charge. You don't want to walk in this heat, do you? I promise, we'll take good care of your vehicle. No worries."

People are driving by me now, their faces scrunched in distaste, their middle fingers held high in salute to my slowing their roll toward destitution. Smooth-voice crazy-wrangler crosses his arms. "Ma'am? I need for you to decide, please. You're holding up traffic."

Oh! The new original sin: holding up traffic. God forbid anybody should stop for five minutes to think about what they're doing! "Fine," I mumble, grabbing my purse, adjusting my wig, and shoving the door open. It bangs into the wrangler's knees.

He's taller than I am, so I have to stand on tip-toe to see him eye-to-eye. "Do not eat, smoke, spit, or ejaculate in my car." I hand him the key reluctantly.

He frowns at me and tosses the key to some pimple-faced moron holding a 7-Eleven cup that is bigger than his head. "No!" I scream, scrambling to get the key back from the pimple pilot. "No. You personally park my car." I press the key into Wrangler's palm and stare at him pointedly. "YOU park my car. I'll know if anyone else touches it. Believe me, I will know."

"Yeah, I believe you," he says, shaking his head in disbelief. He slides into the leather seat, key in hand, and cocks his head in my direction.

"Fine. Now drive away. I'll wait."

"Hurry!" Mellow whines.

The other valet boys are snickering. They all think I'm an eccentric crackpot, but I might be a really rich eccentric crackpot, so they don't want to piss me off too much. I might not tip. Which I will not.

14
DRIVING DISTRACTIONS

L as Vegas encompasses every horrible thing about America. I feel
like bubble wrapping myself and hiding away forever inside a sterile
cocoon.

It's a sensory overload of epic proportions, first of all. The smells
of tanning oil mingle with cigarette smoke, fried food, body odor, Chinese herbs, and a distinctive processed, forced cool-air scent that is
only found in desperate places like hospitals and casinos. Sounds: bells,
whistles, screams, shrieks, moans, drunk tirades, babies crying (why
babies crying? Jesus, people.) A constant aural wallpaper of unappeal-
ing sounds designed to keep you moving forward, subconsciously forc-
ing you to put money into the greedy mouths of behemoth machines.

I tuck my chin down, eyes forward, visualizing a clear path toward
wherever I am headed, Mellow trying hard to keep up. The Luxor pyramid is designed like a huge rat maze so you can never truly know where
you are, and you get lost, and finally sit down, disgusted, at some movie
tie-in slot machine just to simply *stop moving.* After 15 minutes of passing the
same cocktail waitress (or do they clone them?) we find a bathroom.

"I'll be fast," Mellow promises.

I park at the Golden Girls slot machine, which is the closest seat to the bathroom. A large white plastic cup filled with dime wrappers (the shed skin of some legal tender caterpillars) has been abandoned.

Sitting, I can breathe a little bit better. Things swirl around me, but I'm not in the middle of it. The smiling faces of Blanche, Sophia, Dorothy, and Rose beam at me, happy to welcome me to their oasis. "Shut up, ma!" the machine blares at me.

"Hey." I turn. It's her. Tapping my shoulder. "Told you I was quick. Are you going to gamble?"

"I don't gamble." The crowd starts to make me feel lightheaded, and I realize I have a limited amount of time in here before I curl up in a ball in a broom closet.

"Do you need to pee? The bathroom is really nice. Lots of marble and recessed lighting, real classy stuff. Avoid stall four, though, because somebody dumped out a whole buffet and didn't flush." She plops down on a stool next to me and spins slowly. "So? Hurry up. We don't want to stay here all day, do we?"

"Right." The bathroom still looks very far away, and I guess Mellow senses my reluctance.

"I can go with you," she offers. I nod and we both go in.

She hums a tune as I sit in the marble-encased stall. A golden Egyptian goddess-head purse hook glares at me from the door.

When I open the door, Mellow is standing under the hot air dryer, pits to the airstream. "I washed in the sink and now I'm drying," she explains. "I saw it in an old movie I watched with my mom. Madonna was in it."

"*Desperately Seeking Susan.*" I scrub my hands with soap that smells of lavender and greed.

"Yeah, that's it!" She dances like an '80s virgin, hearing the tune in her head.

When we exit the relative peace of the restroom, the sheer mass of humanity smacks me in the face. I can see no path through the undulating crowd, and my breathing becomes ragged. I am frozen.

"What's up?" she asks, still flapping her arms to dry her pits.

"I don't know if I can get through this crowd."

"We got through it to get to the bathroom," she points out logically.

"We had a reason...I guess I didn't notice as much. Now it seems—I just don't think I can get out of here. Not with all these people in the way."

Mellow frowns, looks around, and has an 'a-ha' look on her face that scares me. "Be right back," she says. "Don't move. Ha."

She scampers off, leaving me clutching at a fake golden pillar for support, eye-to-eye with a flat hieroglyphic face of, presumably, an ancient Egyptian high roller.

Within a minute or so, intensely loud sirens wail throughout the casino. A calm, recorded voice announces "Please exit the casino at this time. An emergency situation has arisen. Please exit the casino at this time."

The sea of humanity, with great cries of disappointment and some bad language, drifts toward the exits. Security personnel swarm the floor, looking for something on fire. Mellow reappears, smug, and gestures toward the exiting crowd. "Now you can walk to the exit with no obstacles."

"You did that?" I whisper, alarmed.

She nods happily. "Wasn't that hard. Alarms are just there, you know. You just have to push the handle and scoot."

Now I'm worried that she might be arrested. Is it a crime to throw a fire alarm in a casino simply so a crazy lady can walk to her car? Probably. But my anxiety does lessen significantly as the crowd of grumbling losers thins. Mellow links arms with me and we walk, in an orderly fashion, to our car.

The hot oven slap of Las Vegas greets us as we exit into the parking lot, which is now a flat field full of cranky, sweaty, indignant people who had to leave what was surely the next big-money spin in Wheel of Fortune. The flat mass of humanity reminds me of the Burning of Atlanta in *Gone with the Wind*, except almost everyone still has all their limbs.

The valets are standing around looking like a herd of maroon-vested deer, but I find the guy who was supposed to have personally parked my car. "We need to leave," I tell him. He stares blankly past me at the hotel. "Hello?"

"Hmm?" He focuses on me. "Oh. Nobody can leave right now. They have to figure out this fire alarm thing."

Mellow eyes the pavement sheepishly.

"Fine. We can walk, then." I grab her arm and haul her toward the long, long exit from the parking lot.

"I'm not walking in this heat!" She yanks her arm away.

"You *will* walk in this heat," I tell her, "because this is all your fault and I am not sitting out here waiting for my wig to catch fire."

"It's all her fault?" the valet asks, eyeing the girl incredulously.

"No, no. I mean it's her fault we're in this horrible city in the first place." I try to put on a calm, adult smile. "I just need to get something out of the car, so can I have my keys please?"

"No can do," the valet answers.

"Can you at least tell me where my car might be? Generally speaking?"

He points to a far lot shimmering on the horizon. "Someplace over there. The overflow."

Mellow slips away while I argue with the heat-addled attendant. She slips back a moment later and grabs my arm, smiling at the young man. "Sorry we bothered you. We'll just go find a shady patch and wait 'til this emergency is over." She tows me away and calls over her shoulder, "I certainly hope they catch whoever is responsible."

When we're out of earshot, I turn on her. "What in hell are you doing? We need to leave. I don't have time to—"

She waves my keys in front of my face and grins.

I'm furious, but I have to hand it to her—in the world of small-time hustles, she definitely outranks me. "Let's go find the car," I sigh.

. . .

Two hours later, we pass a sign that tells us we are in Utah, although we briefly flirted with a neglected corner of Arizona. Nothing looks much different; it's all dry and rough and the air seems made of sand. Mellow has said nothing the entire drive from the city. She's curled in a tight ball, knees to chest, hair in her eyes, earbuds jammed into her ears so she can shut me out along with everything else.

I pull over again to look at the map and to see where the next motel stop is. After Las Vegas—I feel as if somehow oily fingerprints migrated to my body even though I was very careful not to touch anything—I definitely need a shower, and Mellow's unwashed pits need a rinse, judging from the scent wafting across the driver's seat. Looks like another hour of driving before we reach the designated motel. I wordlessly spark the protesting engine and pull back onto the empty road.

The wig is so hot here, itchy, and I wonder if I can just take it off and let my scalp breathe a little. When I reach under the front, I'm astonished to feel small, bristly hairs sprouting on my head. When did this happen? I contort so I can reach the back seat and find Annabella, carefully transfer the wig to her and safely ensconce both in the box and yank the rearview mirror down so I can get a better look.

My eyes, ringed by dark circles, stare back at me, and above them, the thinnest caterpillar tracks of eyebrows are beginning to form. And above them, a fine shadow of coarse stubble spreads in an even shape around my forehead, as if someone planted a garden on my scalp in the middle of the night and magical stalks are suddenly sprouting.

"Leaving Las Vegas," Mellow croons, as she leans out where the car's window would be. She's rolled it down despite my protests. "Leaving Las Vega-a-a-as—"

"Could you please roll it up now?"

She shoots me a pouty eye roll. "You hate nature."

"I hate sand in my eyes."

She begrudgingly cranks the squeaky handle, sealing the hot air outside. "Will you turn on the AC, then?"

"It might overheat the car. Do you want to get stuck in the middle of this horrendous sandbox?"

"Jesus. Then we have to roll the windows down!" She cranks the handle again, opening the pane halfway. This has been our routine for the last half hour.

This trip is making a believer of me. I believe that God has decided to curse me, and that he, she, or it has laid out a plan of infinite torture to test me. I'd like to think that this means I am like Job, the favorite of God, the one who perseveres through all the slings and arrows (and I do realize that I'm mixing literary metaphors, but my brain has melted in the Nevada hellhole). Perhaps this means my reward will be all the more rich for the obstacles I've endured. Or perhaps God has a wicked sense of humor and likes to see people fail. Perhaps God looks at humanity like one huge reality show, and the degradation and suffering just boost ratings.

Mellow has put in her earbuds, and the mosquito hum of her head-banger music sizzles in the dry air. At least she's not talking. The dash-board clock says it's 5:15, and assuming that the earth's rotation hasn't been altered by the intense heat, we should be reaching our overnight destination within the hour.

I wonder if Las Vegans (Las Vegasites? Las Vaginas?) have many words for sand just as Eskimos have many words for snow. Gritty sand would be rockdust; soft, white sand would be roughmilk; course, dark sand would be tarcutter.

The buzz of Mellow's music abruptly cuts out. "What the fuck?" she shouts as she yanks the earbuds out of her ears. One thin, white wire snags on an earring and she howls in pain. "Fucking batteries."

"You should probably try to cut down on how many times you say the word fuck," I suggest, keeping my eyes on the rockdust, roughmilk, tarcutter horizon.

"You should probably try to cut down on how big of a douche you are," she mutters as she slides the back off the iPod. "Do you have any batteries?"

"Douche?" I ask, glancing at her for a reaction.

"What? Are you asking me if I want to douche, or if I have a douche, or what it means, or what? You need to work on your communication skills." In my peripheral vision I see her mocking sneer.

"I was asking why you'd use a word like that. What is it supposed to mean? You're not giving me any context."

I feel the waves of contempt rolling off her teenaged body. Sarcasm is apparently fine for her but frowned upon when returned. "Only real douches don't know when they are being douches."

"Douche is French. Did you know that?"

The ball of contempt threatens to explode. I know that I am pushing her, and for the moment, I don't seem to care. It's as if my uglier self is just flinging verbal weaponry with no regard to the result.

Then she smacks me hard, on the arm.

I don't say anything. I just calmly pull the car over to the side of the road, ditching the driver side into a slide of dirt and sand. I turn off the engine and sit, gripping the steering wheel so hard my knuckles are white.

She says nothing. We sit, staring at the horizon.

. . .

"Staring at the wall is not going to help you get better." Edward crossed his stork legs. He wore grey flannel trousers, and bright blue socks with his black loafers.

"It's very peaceful, just staring straight ahead."

He shifted again, uncomfortable with the silence. Therapists loved talking, that much I knew.

The spot on the wall where I focused was familiar. It was a small dent in the oxblood paint, perhaps left by an old photograph or a pissed-off patient with a tiny fist.

"Right." He steepled his fingers in front of his mouth again and studied me. To have him focus on me like that, it was almost worth the cost of being there. "Let's try something else."

He stood, straightened his trousers a bit (did he have an erection? I so hoped that was true.) Then he sat down on the couch, right next to me. My kneejerk response was to move over—I cursed myself for it, but instincts do what they do.

"Why did you move away?" Did I imagine the tenderness in his voice?

"I don't like to be so close to people."

"Why?"

"You know why."

He slides an inch closer. "I want you to say it. Out loud."

"I can't." Simple. Direct. True.

"How can I help you so you can?"

Mmm. I closed my eyes so I could more easily absorb the sensory experience of Edward. The woodsmoke, cold-weather smell of his jacket, some odd tinge of bergamot. Reminded me of tea, of course. So English.

I put my hand on his leg, just above the knee, and studied it. He flinched, I could feel it. I was crossing a boundary. My hand, scarred, picked, punished. Two blue river veins running from the fingers into the wrist, where small cuts showed, angry red. He did not remove my hand. I took this as a good sign.

"What do you see?" he whispered. I could live in the space between the breath he took and the words he uttered.

"It's a mess. It's all ugly and scarred."

"That's not what I see." This made me turn and meet his gaze. His eyes were full of pity, I guessed, not desire, not love. Pity.

I pulled my hand back, hid it in my lap with the other, equally scarred hand. "I don't care what you see."

"I think you do." He reached over, gently took the hand I had hidden, and turned it, palm up. "These hands still have a lot to do, Anna. You can't hide from everything. You're much too intelligent, you have too much to offer the world."

I kissed his hand. Swift, light, the briefest brush of skin on skin.

Delicious, an electric current through my lips straight to my core.

I dared to open my eyes, to see his reaction. He was shocked, stunned really, and so still, I wondered if time had stopped. I ran from the room, leaving the door ajar, ran into the office, ran into the hallway, out to the street, blindly.

. . .

"Staring out at the desert is not going to fix anything," Mellow says as she chugs the last of the water. The car is stuck in the sand, unwilling or unable to move forward, just like I am. "If you are trying to punish me, it's not working, because I don't care if you kill me. I can die here and no one will care."

"Why would I want to kill you?" My bristly head itches like crazy. Scabs, left unpicked while we were in the casino, are now blooming ripe, red blood like a field of poppies on my arm.

"Because you are clearly psycho." She pitches the empty plastic bottle out the window.

"You shouldn't litter."

"Maybe the vultures can use it. It *is* recyclable, and they are the ultimate recycling machines." She doesn't get a response from me. "Look, seriously, are you going to drive this heap somewhere or is your plan that we both just dry up and blow away?"

I have no plan. I just got stuck here, stuck in a memory of a kiss, and I can't move forward. It's an elegant solution, dying in the desert, since water essentially took my first life, my real life, the life I thought I was destined to live. Poetic, really. Tragic.

Quiet snuffling sounds come from the passenger seat. Mellow, her knees to her chin, arms over her head, shakes quietly with strangled sobs. "Why are you crying?" I ask her.

With a trembling voice, she says, "I don't want to die."

I lick dry, cracked lips. "Of course, you don't want to die. No one wants to die, do they?" *Not true*, my inner self, my old self, screams. *I want to. I wanted to. I still want to. Past, present, future.*

"Do you? Do you have a death wish?" She furiously wipes at the tear tracks on her face. "Seems like it. My mother does too. Seems like everybody has one these days. It's the new mid-life crisis."

"That's very witty." Still staring. Counting grains of sand and wondering: How much sand would it take to absorb all the fetid water in every contaminated puddle in North America?

"Could we please get going?" Her yelling has turned soft, desperate. "Let me see the map."

"No."

"Let me see the map!"

I slap her, hard, across the face. My hand stings, and a bright, red handprint develops on her cheek like an emerging Polaroid.

"I'm sorry," I mumble, although I know it's too late.

She yanks the door open, stumbles out of the car, and starts running through sand, looking like a drunk trying to find the next bar. I can't leave her here.

"Wait! Mellow, wait!" I, too, wade through the thick dunes which seem to pull at my feet, willing me to stay. "God dammit! Slow down! I'm too old to run through a desert!"

"Fuck you!" She disappears over the top of a scrubby hillock.

I'm breathing so hard my chest threatens to collapse, but I make it over the little rise. She's fallen next to a stubby cactus, and she's holding her bare foot.

"This whole empty litterbox and you manage to step on a cactus?" I wheeze. She clutches the foot and rocks back and forth, biting her lower lip.

"Fuckfuckfuckfuckfuckityfuck." She glares at me. "This is your fault. I'm probably going to lose my foot."

"Did you read about that in *Ripley's Believe it or Not?*" I squat down next to her, shield my eyes from the glare. "Cactus-induced limb loss?"

"It's not funny. Everybody knows cacti are laced with deadly strains of bacteria."

"I don't think any self-respecting bacteria would live in this climate. They need water. Come on." I offer her my hand and she shakes her head. I say, "Don't be stubborn. You can't walk on that."

"I can. I have great inner strength." She tilts her chin toward me defiantly. "Just leave me here."

"Oh, like I'm going to just *leave you here*." I plop down next to her, displacing a dusty cloud of sand. "I can wait."

"Leave. I don't want your help."

"It doesn't matter. You need my help."

"I doubt you can help anybody, Anna. You can't even help yourself." I can see by her expression that my face betrays me. "Uh...I mean...I didn't mean that."

"No, you're right." The scabs on my left arm make a pattern. It's like a constellation. It's Aquarius, I think. *Pick. Pick. Pick.* If my arm were a map, the red streams running would join somewhere near the elbow, then flow on to the delta, the palm of my hand. This must be how God feels, watching from far above, seeing the course of rivers and lives flow in inevitable currents toward certain destinations.

"Please, Anna," the girl whispers. "Stop doing that." *Pick, pick, pick. Pluck, pluck, pluck.* Stubble hairs harvested too soon, a dead crop. "Why are you doing that? You're scaring me."

"I can't help anyone." I hear my own monotone voice.

"Yes, you can. I was just being a bitch when I said that. Don't listen to me. I'm just—I had a shitty childhood."

"You had a childhood, though." I rub the blood into a smeary daub, painting my arm, the Sistine Chapel. God's finger points toward me, accusing.

"What the fuck happened to you?"

The emptiness echoes around me. Sound of splashes, laughter, silence, and then, I'm here again. "Something I can't talk about. That's what happened."

"Maybe you'd feel better if you talked about it." Her face softens a bit. "I'm a good listener, when I want to be."

"Let's get you out of here. We need to get to the motel, clean that wound, rest. You need water, and so do I. Water. It always comes back to that, doesn't it?"

Puzzled, she takes my hand, climbs up my arm and grabs my waist, and we wade through the sand toward the car.

15
UNCONTROLLED INTERSECTION

I relent and run the air conditioning on the way to our destination, the Nighty-Night Inn near Richfield. The parking lot is bordered by dead and dying wisps of yellowed trees, and the asphalt is full of cracks, over-baked by punishing sun.

I get the key from a wilting desk clerk and return to the car. "We're on the first floor," I say, and Mellow nods.

At room 111, we drag what we need into a small, neat room. We do not open the curtains. It feels like a blessing to be in a dark place.

"We're sleeping here, right?" Mellow asks from a prone position on the jaunty goldenrod-harvest orange bedspread.

"I hope so." I place my suitcase on the flimsy rack, put Annabella on the desk/dresser combo, and adjust my wig (which looks like a dead animal).

"What time is it?" Mellow's eyes are covered by her bracelet wrist.

"5:45."

"Are we driving any more tonight?" She sounds somewhat afraid of the answer.

"No, of course not. We've driven enough today. I'm going to check the map and see how we need to adjust the rest of the trip. We're behind, of course."

"Because of me."

"Well, yes. Because of you."

She hops off the bed and hovers near my shoulder, a punk angel. "So, where are we going again?"

"You need a shower. Why don't you do that while I do this and then we'll eat."

She hunches down so her face is parallel to mine. "Hey."

"Hmm?" The ripe, teenaged-girl smell reminds me of a wild animal. "You really do need to shower."

She unexpectedly pecks my cheek before skipping off to the bathroom. The door slams and I hear her humming. Where she kissed my cheek, it hums with a different frequency, alien and transformed.

. . .

"I can't meet you outside of the office," he said over the phone.

"Why not?"

"You know why not." I heard the muffled voice of Ms. Leonard, his receptionist. By the way it sounded, I could tell he was covering the receiver with his hand so I couldn't hear what she was saying.

"Doctor. Doctor!"

"Please, Anna." He sounded desperate. I had suspected that the receptionist might be trying to steal him away, and this confirmed it. "We—you—I don't want to mislead you into thinking that this is anything other than a professional relationship. I think you misunderstood my…intentions. And I'm so, so sorry for that. I really do want you to come back to the office so we can talk about it."

Why did it all have to be so difficult? I loved him, he loved me. I knew what society said about therapists and clients, but the heart wants what it wants. I would tell him that when I saw him. "Fine. I'll come to the office. Can I come on a Saturday, though? I'd really like to have uninterrupted time with you."

I hesitated. "Yes, I think that would be best," he agreed.

So, two days later, I found myself outside his office door. The building felt ghostly, deserted, which suited me. I knocked softly. "Come in," he said with his rich British baritone.

I opened the door, and he was sitting at his desk, wearing a cobalt-blue t-shirt. His hair, which was usually groomed perfectly, was curly and unruly, and it made me want to run my fingers through it desperately. He was writing on a yellow legal pad, but briefly flashed me a smile. "Sit," he said. "I just need to finish a note here, and then I'll be right with you."

I loved watching his long fingers move the pen around the pad. Everything about him was graceful and beautiful. If only I could be part of his life, part of it in a meaningful way, not as a client. I knew what people thought about such things; I knew that he was afraid, afraid of what people would think of him. He might lose his license, of course. How would we live? I couldn't think about that. I'd lived on nothing for a long time, ever since—

"Alright." He moved to his usual chair. He was wearing jeans, which made me catch my breath. Men in casual attire slayed me. I wondered if he knew that. "How are you today, Anna?"

My wig itched. I pulled at it, just a tug. "I feel pretty well today. You look fantastic."

He blushed. I didn't know how I was supposed to keep from jumping on him. "It's Saturday. I didn't think you'd mind if I did a bit of office casual." He flipped the pages on the legal pad and tapped it with his pen. "I wanted to see you today to have a very frank discussion about what happened."

A smile tugged at the corner of my mouth. "You mean when I attacked you?"

"It wasn't an attack, exactly." He shook his head, pursing his lips in a disapproving, yet amused, way. "I understand why you did it. It's very simple, and certainly nothing to be ashamed about." I said nothing, just watched him. "It's called transference. Usually that's when you take a traumatic event or relationship from your childhood, and transfer that relationship to someone in your present—"

"That's not what this is."

He took a breath, as if he expected me to say that. "I know that you don't see it that way."

"And you do?"

He sighed and fixed his eyes on me. He said nothing, just studied my face, which made me self-conscious. "I think you're marvelous. You're intelligent, witty, creative. You've dealt with your situation in a very unusual way, although it's totally understandable. I...I think I marvel at the person you will be when you've moved past this. And I want to help you. Not because I'm in love with you, but because it's what I'm meant to do."

"So, it's fate then, is it?" I shifted on the couch, pulling my legs up under me, moving toward him slightly. "You feel like you're destined to fix me?"

"No, no," he said, waving his hand dismissively. "You don't need fixing. You need help navigating what happened to you, as anyone would."

I couldn't talk about it. I *wouldn't*. He had tried, in so many ways, to get me to tell him, but I couldn't. He knew it, too. I was afraid that if I did talk, he would run away, as he should. Because what I had done—it was inexcusable, and he knew that. But unless he heard me say it, heard it from my own lips, he could pretend that he was helping me, or trying to get me to help myself. He already knew all the details, of course he did. But his prize was my confession, and I refused to give it to him.

"Come with me." He was standing at the door, gesturing toward me to follow him.

"Why?"

"We're going outside."

"I'm not a huge fan of outside," I reminded him.

He didn't answer. He just walked away, and I followed. He jogged down the stairs, and I tried to keep up, but with his long legs, he made it to the parking garage before I did, and he waited, tapping his foot impatiently. He wordlessly made his way to his car, opened the passenger door, and crossed around to the driver's side.

"Where are we going?" I asked, bewildered. This was how he put distance between us? An out-of-office excursion? I climbed into the car, though, marveling at how clean it was, how it smelled of polished leather and silk sweaters. "Are we not speaking? I thought that's what therapy was for."

"Sometimes words are just not adequate," he said as he pulled out of the garage and into traffic. He punched a radio setting, and classical music filled the space between us.

"I'd really love to know where we're going. Are you kidnapping me? Are we running off to Las Vegas?"

He chuckled, but kept his eyes on the road, easing onto the freeway.

I watched his profile as he drove. I felt like a teenager, giddy, running away with my boyfriend against the wishes of my parents. A smile tugged at my lips, and he caught it out of the corner of his eye. "You're smiling."

"I love an adventure."

"Oh, you do?" He laughed. "That's not something I would've said about you."

"Why not?"

He glanced at me, still laughing, but saw that I didn't get the joke, and the smile faded. "Oh. You're just...you have a few..."

"Quirks? Idiosyncrasies? Fucked-up notions?"

"I don't think I'd put it quite that way."

"Well, of course you wouldn't. You're British. You don't say 'fuck', I'm sure."

He frowned. "The British invented the word 'fuck', if you must know. Or maybe it was the Germans. I don't know. Either way, it was around long before America. So, you lot do not have a corner on that market."

"Good to know." We rode on in silence for about twenty minutes, and I was drifting off to the notes of Rachmaninoff, almost dozing in a peaceful, blissed-out wave of contentment. I felt more alive than I'd felt for—awhile.

His voice broke the trance of the music. "We're almost there. I hope you won't be angry." A nervous flutter shot through my stomach.

"Why would I be angry?"

He said nothing, just kept driving, exiting the freeway into an area I didn't know. As my anxiety started to rise, I looked for signs, signals, anything that would give me some knowledge about what he had in store. I started to pick at the scabs on my arms.

"Don't pick." He shook his head. "That's such destructive behavior. You know, it doesn't really help."

"It helps me." A blossom of blood sprang up from a scab on my wrist, and I licked the ruby wound. Suddenly my wig felt unbearably hot, itchy, uncomfortable, but I would be damned if I was going to take it off in front of him.

I scoured the landscape for any sign of what was to come, which by this time I knew was not something pleasant, not something I had hoped for. "Listen, you need to tell me where we're going. Otherwise, it's technically kidnapping."

"It's not technically kidnapping, Anna. You agreed to go with me."

"Not really. I had no idea where we were going."

"But you got in the car willingly." He seemed to be scanning the side of the road, looking for something. "I'm not going to take you to a seedy motel and have my way with you."

"Well, damn, that's what I was counting on," I said before I could stop the words from spilling out. He blushed, kept his eyes on the road.

After a few moments of awkward silence, he sighed. "Here it is."

I looked up at a freshly painted sign hanging between two dark-blue, wooden posts. *Friedrich Lake Recreation Area.*

Then I threw up all over the leather upholstery.

. . . .

I hear the water from the shower dripping, rhythmic, as Mellow hums in the bathroom. She's finished her shower, and I'm sitting in exactly the same position I was in when she went in.

The bathroom door creaks open, and a rolling wall of steam floods

the hall. "That was awesome," she says, toweling her hair. She's completely naked.

"You should put something on," I say, looking away. "Somebody
might see you."

She walks past, drops the towel at my feet, and sits on the bed.
"Who's going to see me except you? The drapes are pulled totally closed.
In fact," she says, jumping up, "I think I will flash the neighbors." She
pulls the ancient curtains open, leaving nothing but a sheer ivory panel
with two cigarette burns between her and the other denizens of the
Nighty-Night Inn.

"You really don't have any shame, do you?" Studying the map,
I'm recalculating the route we need to take, and how much we need
to drive to even approximate my original itinerary. It's looking like we
almost might not make it, unless we stop having so many side trips and
distractions. Looking at the 14-year-old girl in the window, I realize
that distractions are now most likely part of the permanent itinerary.

"Rhiannon used to say that shame was a useless emotion." She
grabs a t-shirt from her bag and throws it on. It's Mickey Mouse as
Steamboat Willie. Old school. "I agree with her on that, at least. Pretty
much everything else she said and did was totally fucked up. Thinking
back, she actually should have had some shame. Maybe it would have
made her a better mother."

Shame. Blame. Game. Too many words that sound the same.

"Speaking of," Mellow continues. She pulls my suitcase toward her,
snaps it open, and starts lifting things, looking for something.

"That belongs to me," I say quietly, eyes focusing on my crisscross
of red and blue lines on the map. "You're crossing a boundary."

She hums again, disregarding my comment. The idea of this girl
touching all of my things brings me to an immediate boil. I turn to
slap her hands away, but...there she is, holding the box. The box of
Unwanteds. "This." She cradles the box in her arms, like a baby. "This
is what I'm talking about. The shame. Do you want to talk about it?"

I try to grab the box, but she's faster than I am. She's at the window before I even get up. "Put that back," I whisper, biting harsh words behind my teeth. The Mickey peeking over the top of the box mocks me with a wink and a can-do attitude. Light filters through the gauze, giving her an angelic glow that belies the devil that's suddenly materialized.

"Listen, I'm only trying to help." She cavalierly pops the top off the box and flings the lid across the room. As I lunge for her, she races to the bathroom, shuts the door, and locks it.

"Give that back," I yell, pounding on the old wooden door. I could probably punch through it. Both fists. *Pound, pound, pound.*

"Jesus, don't flip out." A tinge of fear in her voice. So now I'm scaring little girls. Excellent.

"Sorry." *Breathe. Breathe.* "I'm sorry. I didn't mean to scare you. It's just—that box is very important to me."

"Obviously." She chuckles nervously. The door rattles a bit, sounding as if she's inching her way down, her back to the surface, until I imagine her sitting cross-legged on the cold tile floor, the box in her lap.

Silence. I kneel down next to the door, my ear pressed against the wood, listening for the rustle of newspaper clippings and the crackle of old photographs. I barely hear her breathing, rhythmic, regular. "Please," I whisper. "Please. Give it back."

No reply. I lean my back against the door, draw my knees up to my chin, and pull off the wig, which now seems incredibly hot and beside the point. What does she see? What do those things look like to her? A story, to be sure, but aren't we all stories in the end? I could tell her it's not about me, but that would be laughable, and this isn't funny. I could ask her to forget what she's seen, to move on as if we traveled back a few moments in time, to before she opened that box.

An impulse to cry lodges itself in my throat. No. *No.* We don't do that anymore. We can't. But there is no "we", not now. Not ever again. And she made me forget that, just for a little. Should I be grateful, or should I be grieving?

"Anna?" A strangled whisper from the other side. "Are you out there?"

"Yes."

"I'm coming out now." Scrambling of body rising from the floor, then the jiggling of the loose doorknob, and the bottom of the door nudges against the small of my back. "Can you move away so I can open the door?"

No reason to rise above the floor, so I pull myself to the perpendicular wall and lean against that for a while, leaving the wig in a sweaty heap.

From my vantage point on the floor, she looks like a prepubescent goddess, haloed in light from the tiny bathroom's frosted glass window. She holds the box reverently, with both hands. She kneels beside me. Her wet hair drips tiny tears onto the floor.

"This is you?" A newspaper clipping, now dried out, edges crumbling, a bit like me. I nod.

She scans the article, sees the picture, the picture of me and my husband, the photo of my smiling girl. I can barely look. My heart hammers, pounding against the wall of my chest in protest. After so many years of keeping it quiet, it demands to be heard.

I close my eyes and I can see the place, smell the green growing things, the living scent of water. We loved each other so much then, and I felt like a golden bubble surrounded us, kept us safe from everything, kept us apart from the world. Lying on a faded green-purple quilt, my husband's arm under my head (as it always seemed to be, a comfort), sun dappling our faces as our daughter splashed and dared the fish to nibble her toes. A perfect day.

"He had wanted a child for so long, and we'd given up. And then— he was so happy when I showed him the pregnancy test. So happy. He was kind of a goof, you know, and when we talked about names—he wanted something unusual, like Dragonfly, and I wanted Marcie, so we compromised—and so she was Darcy."

Mellow covers my shaking hand with her own. I look up and her eyes, crinkled with concern, peer into me, trying to find some explanation for what she's read. But there is no reason, no rhyme, no justice, no logic.

She places the clipping back in the box, pats it as if putting a child to bed. She gives me a crooked grin, then hands the box to me. "I'm really sorry," she says, her husky voice cracking. "It wasn't your fault." Leaning over hesitantly, she brushes her dry lips against my cheek, kisses it tenderly. A storm lying dormant in the center of my body rockets up, rises, hurricanes into my head and resonates earthquakes into all my limbs. A tiny bird of a whimper escapes my lips, and with that, a flock of sobs pours out, unending. As I lie prostrate on that hotel floor, the strange, damp girl shelters me with her body, pats my hair, and says, "There, there."

. . .

"I can't." I told him this many times. He wouldn't listen.

"You have to," he whispered in my ear, from the open passenger door. The stink of vomit filled my nose and made me want to heave again, but I had nothing left. Nothing.

"This is abusive," I said, words strangled.

This caught him off guard. He took a step back, blinked in the sunlight, then ran his hand through his hair, a sign that he was unsure. A chink in the armor.

"You need to take me back. Now." I swiveled so my legs were planted on the gravel path, trying to avoid the pool of bile. Inside, I was trembling. Inside, I was screaming, and I knew he was right. I knew this was the only way, but I did not want to go.

He knelt down, knee in gravel, and clasped my hand. "You're cold," he observed. He held my limp, damp hand between his palms and warmed it. "I am here. You are safe."

"I'm not safe," I hissed. "No one is ever safe." Tears? Tears had been banished, but they trailed down my cheeks, terminating in small, regular drips that were immediately absorbed by the gravel.

"Please, let me help you." His eyes were full of pain, longing, need.

I gazed into those eyes, I swam in those oceans, circled the dark centers and let myself be carried away. I leaped into his arms, sobbing.

His body tensed; he was startled. Then his muscles eased, and his arms knitted themselves into an embrace, like twisting branches of a tree in a fairy tale that grow around a damsel in distress and hold her fast. Such bullshit, these fairy tale images. No one ever held anyone fast, and no one was ever saved.

He released me enough to gently grab my arm and walked me to a granite boulder near the gate where I leaned in so I wouldn't collapse. He leaned next to me and there we were, two people looking at a cloudless blue sky for a heartbeat, two heartbeats, three.

"Tell me," he whispered. He worked his arm behind my head, a buffer between me and the hard surface of the rock.

"We came here as often as we could," I began.

. . .

"He bullied you into talking about it." Mellow stares at me, eye to eye, bringing me back from the memory.

"No, I *needed* to talk about it."

She shakes her head. "No. You weren't ready. He pushed you. Jesus, you puked in his car. That might have been a pretty obvious signal if his massive ego wasn't in the way." She shakes the box of clippings and artifacts about my life, and fine motes of dust float up into the stale air. "You kept all these things here, in this box, so you'd have them. When you were ready. When *you* were ready."

"He was trying to protect me—"

"The only thing you needed protection from was him," she spits, and stands up, towers over me, a vengeful young goddess.

"That's not true," I answer, but even as the words leave my mouth, I'm not sure.

. . .

"I want to help you," he said, caressing my forehead with the hand that was not under my head. "I want you to purge this memory and move on."

"I can't purge this memory," I said, almost laughing. "It's who I am. It's why I am."

"Then remake yourself. Reinvent. It's what Americans do best." He turns sideways so he is facing me. "You can love again. You can forget this ever happened."

My body felt numb in the places he'd touched me, and the numbness radiated down into my limbs, and crawled inside my brain, and fought with itself and with everything inside of me. A distant buzz of danger hovered at the edge of my consciousness, but I ignored it.

He kissed me, then. Gently. Not forcefully, but he didn't need to force.

. . .

"He's a fucking predator." Mellow slams a pillow into the bed, repeatedly. "I can't believe you don't see this. You're smart. You're capable. I know you've read a shit-ton of books. Why would you not see this?" I'm curled up on the floor, upright, back to the mattress, clutching the Box.

"He's not a—he didn't do anything I didn't want him to do. It's all so mixed up now…I'm not sure what I've made up and what really happened. Maybe he didn't do that. Maybe he never said that—I'm not sure. I'm sure he'd never act inappropriately."

"You're sure?" She careens furiously around the room, making an inhuman noise of frustration and fury before she squats down next to me, eyes crazed, wide, nakedly honest. "You're sure. Are you, really? Because I don't know you all that well…but I do know that you're not delusional, and even though you pull your hair out and pick at yourself, you know the difference between reality and fantasy."

"I—"

She grabs the Box from me and sits. "Here. October, three years ago." She waves a fragile piece of newsprint. "*Local Girl Dies from Water-*

borne Pathogen." I say nothing. "This is what happened. This is what you couldn't face. An accident."

"It wasn't an accident." A tight ball in my stomach, something made of poison and hate and guilt, begins to pulse.

Mellow reads from the article. "*A local 12-year-old girl has died from an infection by a freshwater amoeba, according to local health authorities.*" She looks to me for explanation, but of course, I have none. "*The girl, who name is being withheld at the request of her parents, was swimming at the Friedrich Recreation Area earlier this month. The CDC confirms that the lake water was tested and the freshwater amoeba, Naegleria fowleri, was found. This rare amoeba causes primary amoebic meningoencephalitis (PAM). The area has been quarantined until further notice.*" She looks to me for explanation.

I stare blankly at her, feeling drugged. I don't want to remember any of it. "Just leave it."

"I can't just leave it," she says, waving the paper in front of my face. "You've been telling me these stories about this doctor, all the way here. The guy you're going to see—to what, stop his wedding? You should be glad he's out of your life."

"Don't say that," I whisper.

"Jesus. You're no different from Rhiannon. You're an addict."

This gets my attention, slaps me out of my daze. "I'm not an addict."

"You are!" She sifts through the newspaper clippings like dirty snow. "You keep these, you keep punishing yourself. You want to hurt. He can hurt you more than anybody else, I guess, so you want to find him...so he can hurt you some more? If that happened to your best friend, what would you say?"

I am mute.

She slaps me on my arm, hard. "You'd tell your friend to get the fuck over it and forget about this asshole."

"He's not an asshole—"

"Don't defend him!" The high pitch of her voice rings in my ears. "You tell me, right now. Did he have sex with you?"

"I'm not talking about that. Not with you."

"Oh, because I'm too young? Too naive? I've seen stuff you've never even imagined, I bet. Living with Rhiannon was not exactly a sheltered existence." She sinks to the floor beside me, deflated, spent. We breathe together, and our respiration becoming rhythmic, synchronized.

. . .

I could hear him breathing beside me, I could feel it. Our bodies were touching at several points, connecting like stars in a constellation, invisible threads tracing shapes that only we could see. The kiss still lingered.

"I shouldn't have done that," he whispered in the voice of a boy caught stealing candy.

"I'm glad you did." I rolled over onto my side so I could look at him. His eyes were bright, excited, but his brows furrowed as if he were dismayed, and his lips were pursed too tightly. "I'm sorry about your car. About throwing up in your car."

He didn't seem to hear me but stared straight into the sky. "You're simply too rare for me to allow you to live in this pain. I know it's unconventional, but—" he swallowed hard. "I think you've shut down the part of yourself that lived through this horror. But that is also the part of you that makes you unique, and wonderful."

"You think I'm unique and wonderful?" I felt a pleasant flush work its way up from my midsection to my cheeks.

"Well, of course you are." He sat up and pulled me up with him. "At first, I saw you as...a challenge, I suppose. Your situation was so complex, and just so compelling. As we peeled the layers away, it became more and more intriguing. The depths to which you've gone to bury this trauma, and how you've coped, your—" he gestured toward my wig, my arms. "The intense physical trauma you've put yourself through, the isolation. It's absolutely fascinating."

Something buzzed at the back of my brain, some small, protesting voice. I forced it back into a cage with my other suppressed thoughts.

Instead, I concentrated on staring into his eyes, and studying the curve of his jaw and cheek bones, up close. I was so lucky to have someone as wonderful and rare as him to care what happened to me. I knew that.

16
PERIPHERAL VISION

I am not sure how long I sit on the floor, my eyes closed. I feel Mellow move away, hear the distant ding of a microwave, and then she's pressing a steaming paper cup into my hands. She's careful not to spill it—it's tea.

"All they had was Lipton's," she says apologetically. "No cream either. They do have sugar."

I shake my head and breathe in the steam. "Thank you."

"Tea makes everything better." She has a cup too. She sits on the floor next to me again. "I'm sorry I yelled at you."

"Did you?"

She sighs as only a teenaged girl can. "Are you senile? Yes, I yelled at you. You don't remember?"

I rub the bridge of my nose. "Sorry, no. I think I had a breakdown."

"Nope. I know what that looks like. You didn't have one."

Sipping the weak tea, I feel hollow, empty, like the biggest nesting doll without the small pieces inside.

"Tell me the rest," she says.

"What do you want to know?" I pull myself up so I'm on the edge of the bed rather than on the floor. The itchy shag carpeting may be full of germs. In fact, I'm sure of it. The bed is probably not much better. If I had a black light…well, I'd probably need to be sedated, honestly.

She hops up so she's sitting next to me. "Your daughter."

In the picture in my mind, Darcy is always twelve years old. Like the photos in the box, I keep that picture tucked, far, far away, out of reach, because looking at it feels like a wrenching rip from chin to belly. But I allow it, small, faded, to swim up from the recesses, resolve into clarity so I see that picture of her smiling on the rocks, sun-kissed, bandaged knee pulled up to her chin, long blond ponytail sticking out at odd angles from a green rubber band. She was always in such a hurry.

"What was she like?" Mellow whispers.

"Like you." Tears begin to push their way to the front, tears that have been stored in the same place as the mental photograph. "Funny, beautiful. Strange." So much pain comes in a wave at the memory that my stomach clenches. "She liked…comic books. She hated pink. She loved swimming."

Her head is on my shoulder now. "How long ago?"

"Three years, two months, five days. She was my hummingbird. That's what I called her."

"Why? Why did you call her that?"

"She never stayed still." I smile, remembering. "She ran from one thing to another, never stayed put. So active. Any water, she'd go right to it. We had a feeder in our yard, bright red, filled with sugar water, and on Saturdays, she'd sit on a stool—that's one of the few times she sat still, too—and she'd watch the hummingbirds dive into the feeding tubes, so fast it looked like they'd crash, but they never did."

"Did she love flowers too? Hummingbirds love that. Where we stayed once, there was a huge orange tree, and they just buzzed around those blossoms all the time."

"She did love flowers. She did. Especially anything that had a strong scent—jasmine, honeysuckle, lilac. She tried to grow lilacs, but they never really bloomed, because it's California and they just didn't. Not cold enough. One Christmas, though, she got up before it was light—

she was eight—and she came into our room, and she grabbed my hand while I was sleeping—because—there were all these violets sprouting all over our backyard. Small English violets, nobody had planted. She said the hummingbirds planted them, for her. I guess maybe they did. We never could explain how they were there."

Mellow stays quiet, and I'm away in a world of my own, letting images and snatches of songs and scents of flowers wash over me. I realize I've missed those things, that by hiding all the bad I was also hiding all the good. She says, "Let's go for a walk."

Sunset. Even this somewhat desolate place looks beautiful when kissed with color. I glance at this girl, this misplaced person, and wonder why. Why she found me, why her mother left, why my daughter died, why all of these circumstances collided and brought us here. I've left my wig in the room—something that is very hard for me to do, but I desperately wanted to feel the air on my scalp, and since I'm not alone, perhaps no one will decide I'm an escaped mental patient or a poster child for alopecia. Another person gives you a sense of belonging, even if the person is a stranger, and someone who vanishes into casinos, and smokes.

"I'm so sorry," she says finally. We've walked for nearly half an hour, and darkness starts to dust the corners of the field and road. A vast plain spreads before us and it looks like it goes on forever, eventually meeting an edge where you could fall and never come back. I wanted to find that edge and jump over it. Now, I'm not as sure.

"I am too. Sorry."

She walks a step ahead of me, kicking small blue stones with the toe of her shoe. "Weren't you married? The article said 'parents', so she had a father…"

"Of course, she had a father. Everyone does." My throat constricts, just a bit.

"Not everyone. Some people are test tube babies. You could have had a sperm donor."

"I did not have a sperm donor."

She chuckles and watches her shoes pick a path through the gravel.

"Right. So…" She stops and turns to me, an apologetic look on her face. "Who was he? Who was Darcy's dad?"

My heart beats too fast. Dizziness swims into my head, doing backstrokes, jumping off waterfalls. I crumple to the ground. She's right there.

Gently she rubs my back, like a mother would to comfort a child. "You can tell me. I read about it, from your shoe box."

"Then you already know," I say, choking.

She leans to whisper in my ear. "Tell me."

. . .

"Tell me," he said in my ear, close, so close. His breath, sweet peppermint, tickled and I wanted nothing more than to melt into him.

"You already know everything, don't you?" I searched his eyes for the answer. He blinked and looked away.

"I want you to tell me." He brushes my naked scalp with his graceful hand. "I want you to tell me, in your words, in your experience." He kissed the tip of my nose. "I want to share it with you."

The buzz again at the back of my brain, the distant radar ping of danger. I ignored it. This is what I wanted, this is exactly what I hoped for. "It's so awful. I don't want to share it."

He grabbed my damp hand and kissed it. "Please."

Why did it matter? It had happened, it was over. What difference did I make if I said it, out loud, to him? He wanted this knowledge. I could give it to him. We could be closer. "We used to come here."

"Yes," he leaned closer.

"We—my family—we came here. For picnics."

He nodded, stared at me, pupils dark and round, deep, I could easily fall in—

"And my—my daughter—"

"Her name?"

It caught in my throat, a rough-edged stone. I turned my head away. He grabbed my chin, forced me to look at him again—not forced, no, he didn't force. He was strong. He would help me. He—

"What was her name? I want you to say it." He pressed his cheek to mine, and a musky scent, jasmine-honey-leather-tea, filled my brain with thoughts—

"Darcy. Her name was Darcy."

"Ah." His breathing was heavy, and he realized it, so pulled away. He blinked, glanced up at the blue sky. "Darcy. Lovely." He closed his eyes, contemplating my answer as my gut twisted in protest. Why did it matter? It didn't matter. I didn't need to keep it to myself.

"And your husband." He nuzzled my neck this time, and ignited feelings in me that I thought had died. Electricity, blue and sizzling, raced in impossible speeds through my limbs, my lips, my nether region.

"Tom," I sighed, the name like an exhale of surrender.

He's touching me now, caressing my face, his hand traveling to my bare arm. "What happened to Tom?" He reaches my thigh. He squeezes, hard. "What happened to him?"

"He died too," I whispered, miserable.

I had given him what he wanted.

. . .

Mellow sits on a boulder, knees to chin, rocking slightly, teeth set in a grimace of anger. "Prick," she intones. "Prick, prick, prick."

My face feels so swollen I fear I might not be able to breathe, as if the red, puffy flesh might expand like bread dough into my throat. The girl grabs a fist-sized rock and throws it with titanic force toward the horizon.

"You *do* see what he did, right?" Her eyes blaze with revenge.

I wipe my nose on my sleeve and cannot look at her. She stands on the rock, arms—no, wings—outstretched, and she yells, so loud, so resonant. Her frustrated scream echoes off cactus plants and iguanas and cows and fences. It vibrates upward, exploding clouds in its path, seeking stars that have misbehaved.

"Sorry. I just had to get that off my chest." She hops down from her rock altar. "Okay, I get that this whole experience damaged you. I mean, Jesus. Your daughter dies from some crazy water infection, and then your husband—" I flinch at the word.

As quick as the wind shifts direction, she's sad. She's sniffling, blinking, eyes spilling tears into the dust. "He died."

I nod, unable to speak.

"He—he killed himself."

I nod, again, feel my chest crushed under the weight of this fact, pulling inward, an imploding star sucking everything good into its black, cold center.

I was never enough. Without Darcy, I was not enough, and I knew that, and he knew it. He couldn't stand that, and neither could I, but neither of us could leave the other and move on. At least, not in this world. Tom left. He followed her, and I would have, but I was too afraid. I was afraid to find out that it was all snuffed out, all gone, that there was just nothing after all.

"So, I was the most cowardly," I tell Mellow. "I couldn't go forward, couldn't stay. I just gave up and ran away."

She shakes her head. "You're here. That was the bravest thing to do. Tom? Your husband? He left *you* alone. That was chickenshit."

"Tom left so I could forget what had happened." Even as I said it, it didn't sound true.

"Bullshit. He left because he couldn't take it. He wasn't strong enough."

I slap her and she sits, stunned, petrified. "You couldn't possibly understand why he did it. I don't," I say, truthfully. "I can explain it in all kinds of ways, but none of them is right."

Blinking slowly, she gazes at the horizon, her mouth drawn tight. "That didn't even hurt," she says in the voice of a very small girl.

We go back to the motel, neither of us speaking. I am empty and sore, and I suppose she feels the same. Wordlessly, I take off my shoes and burrow under the bedding—all I want to do is sleep, even though the sun isn't down.

Mellow removes her shoes too, and although my eyes are closed, I feel her gently lift the bedspread and sheets by one small corner, and she eases herself into the bed next to me, moving in increments until I feel the heat of her limbs. My back is to her; she puts a comforting arm over me, and we fall asleep that way.

When I wake up, it's morning. The red glow of the cheap digital clock tells me it's 7:33. Mellow snores softly next to me, her arm heavy on my torso. I move it slowly so I don't wake her and pad in the dark to the bathroom.

The weak fluorescent light buzzes and flickers. In the mirror, I see a desperate woman with stubble for hair, grey skin, hollow-socket eyes. It's hard to remember what I used to look like—I never look at photos of myself from then. I've heard that since your cells die and renew themselves, technically you're a whole new person every—how many months? Years?

Water from the tap is lukewarm and smells of chlorine, but I splash it on my face anyway. I let a drop of water fall from the tip of my nose, and I get as close to the mirror as possible, so I can see it. The drop falls and splashes onto a tiny black spider that was crawling across the bone-white expanse of the sink.

One drop of water knocks that spider on its spider ass. It tumbles, legs akimbo, careening toward the yawning maw of the rusty drain. And down it goes. I can't save it. Just a spider, though. Not a daughter. Not a husband.

Tap tap tap. "Are you in there?"

"No," I answer.

"Well, if you weren't in there, how could you answer me?"

"I cannot argue with your flawless logic." I open the door. She gives me a crooked grin.

"I just wanted to be sure you were…okay," she says.

"You wanted to make sure I didn't off myself, huh?"

"No! No, that didn't even occur to me." Now she looks worried too. I know how to make people feel right at home. What a gift. "I woke up, and you were gone, so I thought—"

"You thought maybe I'd run out to play in traffic." I firmly twist the cold-water tap on the sink, hoping to spare future spiders from water-drop tidal waves. "Or guzzled motor oil out of the car of something."

"Is that a thing? The motor oil?"

"I have no idea." My stomach rumbles ridiculously. "Oddly, I guess I'm hungry. What about you?"

She nods, keeping her eyes on mine, checking for signs of impending doom. "Are we—do you want to get food somewhere?"

"I'm not eating that spider I just killed."

"You killed a spider? Was it big? Was it hairy?" She shudders. "I hate those huge, tarantula kind of spiders."

"I don't think we have any of those here, but I'll keep an eye open." I brush past her and flip on the switch, which bathes the main room in watery yellow light. The dome on the ceiling displays the corpses of many dead insects, their shadows making negative-image constellations on the glass.

A police siren wails, distant. Someone is getting bad news.

In separate corners of the room, backs to each other, we put on clothes silently. The Box sits, discarded, on the floor near the bed, its lid askew. "Where do you want to eat?" Mellow asks as she runs her fingers through her short hair.

"Doesn't matter. I want to walk, though." Door open, step out. Outside, the clean, new start of morning washes over me. Even in this place of dirt and cars and exhaust and exhaustion, you get to start over. I hadn't seen it when we came in, but there is a coffee shop attached to the office of the motel, with a blinking mint-green neon sign. I start walking toward it as Mellow hastily pulls on shoes, pulls our door shut, and stumbles after me.

"Where're you going?"

"That coffee shop." I gesture toward the sign.

"Hey, stop." Her voice is insistent, so I do. "Uh…are you…do you know…"

"Spit it out. What are you saying?"

She grimaces and points to my head. "You forgot something."

That's why it feels so cool, why I feel light and somehow taller. No wig. I touch the stubble on my scalp, rub it as if I'm making a wish. "That's okay."

"Oh," she says, relieved. She grins and grabs my arm, striding forward. "I'm glad. Your head is fun to rub when it's fuzzy." She runs her hand over my scalp, laughing.

We have an uneventful breakfast in the coffee shop, which is fairly empty and smells of old bacon. Mellow studies my face, but I don't feel much like talking, so I just munch on mountains of toast, licking melted butter from my fingers. The coffee is atrocious.

"Are you wondering what you say to me now?" I ask her after the waitress brings the check.

"I guess. I don't know what I should ask about and what I shouldn't ask about."

"Let's wait until we're driving and then you can ask me anything you want." I stand up, grease-stained check in hand.

"Wait. We're not still going, are we?"

"Why wouldn't we go? That's the plan." The woman at the cash register whose wrinkled skin hangs off her cheekbones pushes old-fashioned keys and the drawer pops open. I hand her the check and twenty dollars I found tucked in my suitcase, and she wordlessly counts change. "Here you go, honey." She hands me two golden Sacajawea dollars and a dime. "Them are dollars. I know they look like casino tokens, huh, but they're real U.S. dollars." Her watery blues eyes dart to my scalp. "Hope you're feeling better."

"I'm not sick."

"Oh." She blushes, afraid she had offended me. "Alright, then, you and your daughter have a good day."

"I'm not her daughter," Mellow says, shrugging and making a *whatcha gonna do* face.

"Uh huh." The woman squints at me, studying my face for signs of criminality. This part of the country sees its share of deviant travelers, I suppose, people looking to disappear into the open spaces and anonymous coffee shops. "Well, you all drive safe, then."

I pocket one of the two golden talismans and hand the other one to Mellow. "For luck," I say. She nods, slips her coin into her bra, and links arms with me as we walk back to the room.

As we're packing our meager things, she asks again. "No, seriously, why are we still going?"

"It's only another day's drive, really." I stop folding and sit on the bed, staring into nothing, for one heartbeat, two heartbeats. "I don't really know, but I know I have to go. You don't have to, though."

She blinks, stares at me as if I've lost my mind. "What else would I do?"

I have no answer.

"You're not trying to ditch me, are you?" Her voice is small, incredulous.

"No! Of course not."

"Why would you leave me here, then? I need to see how it all comes out. I need to know the end of the story! But whatever...leave the shoeless kid by the side of the road..."

"You *do* have shoes," I mention helpfully.

"That's not the point!"

"No, I know. I'm just saying that you do have options—"

"You don't need to make an excuse. I'm happy to get out of your—"

"Get out of my hair?"

There's a vacuum in the room for a heartbeat, and then snorting giggles that start small at first, but erupt into a crying fit of laughter.

17
REFERENCE POINTS

There is no further discussion of leaving her behind. We pack up, drive out of the dusty motel lot, and head down the road after consulting the map. We load up on snacks and fuel from a convenience store a couple miles up the road. I get a sideways stare from the wispy blond clerk, who assumes, I guess, that I'm a fragile cancer patient. When Mellow plunks a six-pack of Diet Coke on the counter, he frowns as he rings it up.

"That stuff's really bad for you," he comments. "I mean, in your condition."

Mellow watches me, to see what I'll do. "Oh, it's actually part of my treatment," I say breezily. He stares at me with buggy eyes. "They're using it for chemotherapy now. It kills cancer." Mellow snorts but pretends to cough into her hand.

A day's drive. I would see him in a day. The crumpled invitation, now frayed at the edges, is still nestled in my pants pocket.

"You said I could ask you anything." Her feet are bare, propped up on the dashboard. I've stopped trying to get her to put them down.

I peer into the sun, looking for signs. "I guess so."

"Oh, so now you're not sure?"

"It's fine. Ask me whatever you want."

Crunching on some unnatural orange snack food she says, "Okay. So, I want to know what you're going to say to Doctor Douche."

"Doctor Denture. Edward." I had run through the scenario in my mind enough times, but now…I'm not as sure as I was.

"I mean, so, we go to the wedding, right? And you do what? Present your invitation and say, 'So, it's me, your crazy bald ex-patient, with a homeless drifter girl, and pass the canapés'?"

"You know what canapés are?"

"I read. How else could I have put up with my mother?"

I lick my lips, stalling, because, truthfully, I am not at all sure what I'm going to do.

She abruptly pulls her feet back, tucks them under her legs and turns to face me, straining against her seat belt. "Aren't you just a little bit angry at what he did to you?"

"What did he do to me?"

"Seriously?"

"It's probably not wise to be driving and talking about this."

"Then pull over." She scans the horizon for a spot. "There. Turn out. Pull over."

"I want to keep driving."

"You just said you shouldn't drive and talk about this." I say nothing. "So? I see what you're doing. Pull over, or I'll pull the car over myself!" She grabs the steering wheel, causing me to swerve off the road and into the dusty gravel indent in the road.

"Why did you do that?" I yell.

"I want to know what the plan is before we get there!"

I turn off the car, roll down the window, and stare straight ahead, into the trunk of a scarred manzanita tree.

"The truth is, I don't know what I'm going to do," I say finally. "I haven't thought about actually seeing him, or getting there, or what I'll say."

She shakes her head. "Unbelievable. You plan this whole trip and don't even have an action plan?"

"Did you have an action plan when you started hitchhiking?" I snap.

"No, of course not, because hitchhiking by definition means you don't have a plan."

"I don't agree. I think that you could easily plan to hitchhike and strategize where you're going—"

She puts a hand over my mouth! "Okay. Stop. There are two choices. Two." I glare at her. "You go and watch him from afar. Or you confront him."

I swat her hand quickly away, disgusted by the contact of fingers to lips. A faraway bird makes a noise like an organic jackhammer. I can't stop hearing it. I have no answer for her. She's right and I know it, but I have no answer. Suddenly, the car seems so unbearably hot that I have to get out of it.

A warm wind on my scalp reminds me that I am sans wig. I certainly can't see him in this condition, can I? This place is so dry and so barren. My skin itches as if every drop of moisture has been sucked from it.

The road stretches out to a blank horizon, little dust devils swirling over the pavement. This is what my life has come to. An empty road, a meaningless quest, and the memory of what I can never retrieve. A fool's errand, I guess. A distraction.

"I'm sorry." Mellow stands next to me, brushing hair from her eyes.

"For what?"

"For all the bad things that have happened to you."

Bad things. Bad things *happening*, as if they are living, breathing entities on their own that conspire to destroy your life. And the idea that there is some supreme being throwing these lightning bolts, willy-nilly, to Earth, smiting whatever random sad-sack happens to be in the way? That's insane.

"Why are we here?" I ask her.

She blinks, confused. "Uh...to go get your boyfriend?"

I glare at her with contempt. "Not my boyfriend."

"Your...lover? Your soulmate? Fuckbuddy?"

"That's disgusting." I scratch a suddenly demanding itch on my scalp. "Do you think God hates us?"

"Wow. How did we get there?"

"If there is a God, and this deity supposedly loves us, why would these bad things *happen*?"

"Back to what I asked before, and you said I could ask you anything, remember," she says with the precision of a beltway lawyer.

"He didn't *do* anything to me."

"He essentially raped you—"

"We never had sex."

"He *emotionally* raped you."

"Not the same."

"Then tell me. Tell me what happened."

A silence descends, heavy with questions I don't like and answers I don't want to give. "He wanted to help me," I begin, but she exhales like a whale breeching the surface of the ocean, spraying spit everywhere.

"Do you listen to your own shit? It's amazing! You are a master of deception. Seriously. I thought Rhiannon was good at lying to herself. You have her beat by miles."

"I'm not lying to myself," I start, but she shushes me.

"Let *me* tell *you* what happened. If I'm wrong, you can correct me. Okay?" I nod slowly. I somehow do not think I'm going to like her rendition, and it will be wildly inaccurate. But at least she'll feel like she's said her piece. With young people, that's usually all they really want.

"He took you to the place where all the stuff happened. He knew you'd be vulnerable. He preyed on your need for connection, and on your vulnerability, and by seducing you, he made you give up the details of the accident, and what happened after. How am I doing so far?"

It feels like an earthquake is beginning inside me, like a moving plate inside the earth's crust, shifting imperceptibly. I know this movement, of even a fingernail's width, will result in a cataclysm. But as with an earthquake, all you can do it watch it happen, hang on, and hope nothing heavy falls and kills you.

"So?" she repeats. "How am I doing?"

"Not bad," I answer. So, I told her. I told her the story as it happened. All of it.

. . .

"Tom," I exhaled. "His name was Tom."

He caressed my cheek, leaned over me to block the sun. "You're not alone anymore, Anna. You're not."

Gazing into his eyes, I could have believed that, almost. But some small, strong cobalt-blue ball of pure will burned in my soul, and it was the part of me that knew what was true. I could not extinguish it, even if it would have made me more comfortable. It existed on its own terms, like a separate living being, and I could neither kill it nor silence it if it chose to speak.

Edward stroked my face, my bare arm, and smiled benevolently down at me, a God from the sky. "What happened to Tom?"

I didn't want to say it. Saying it made it more real, although it had become real enough. I wanted to keep it a secret, because I could pretend that I'd made it up somehow.

"Anna, it can only help you to say it out loud." He lightly pressed his lips to mine, and my body vibrated with desire and disgust. The cobalt-blue kernel of truth vibrated indignantly, threatening to explode in an atomic fission.

I sat up, despite my body's traitorous desire to stay down. "It isn't something I like to talk about."

"Well, of course not. Why would you?" He brushed a strand of wig hair from my forehead. "But look what keeping it inside has done to you—you see an outward manifestation of it in your hair, your skin. The story is literally clawing its way out of your body."

I studied the scars and pits on my forearms, thought about my prickly scalp. "I see what you mean."

"So, tell me. Let me share this burden. Let me lighten it."

He put a strong arm around my shoulders and hugged me to his chest. The scent of his shirt, his skin, it all conspired to evaporate my will.

I gave up. I leaned into him, willfully, pulled my legs up so as to make my body a small, tense ball, and I let him absorb me. I did not look at him as I spoke.

"We had gone swimming. We went there a lot. Nobody had ever warned us about—well, it wasn't a problem, I guess, until we went there, on that specific day. It's funny how one moment of one day can change your entire life, isn't it?" I felt him nodding, squeezing me as if to keep all the threads of the tales contained.

"My daughter—"

"Darcy."

I licked my lips. "Yes. Darcy." Her name stabbed at me, a dagger to the heart. "Darcy was a fish. She loved to swim." I smiled despite the story. "She begged me to get her a mermaid tail, so she could live in the water."

He said nothing but waited for the story.

"That day, we had come out here on the spur of the moment. Hadn't planned, really. We just all had a day off and decided to come swimming because it was unusually hot for May. I packed a lunch. I remember I worried about the food...wondered if it would spoil and we'd get food poisoning. That was a stupid thing to worry about, as it turns out. Very stupid."

"You weren't stupid," he whispered in my ear. "It was an accident."

"She went in swimming, and Tom and I sat on the blanket, watching, smiling. I remember this, so clearly—thinking that I should make a mental note, take a mental picture of this perfect day, because one day I would need it. I'd remember that it was beautiful, and that it was what life was about. So many people don't pay attention to the little daily moments that are really the gold in all the gravel. You mostly don't realize until it's too late. But I knew."

"And then?"

I wanted to stop. I didn't. "Then, we left. Got home, cleaned up,

Tom was going to grill in the yard. Darcy said she didn't feel well, but I thought it was too much sun. I told her to go to bed." Darcy, lying in her bed, not waking up, Sleeping Beauty after the spinning wheel. Pale but feverish, and we knew nothing.

"She had a waterborne infection." He continued for me. "She died from it, didn't she?"

I nodded, jaw clamped tight.

"Your only child?"

I nodded again, and tears spilled onto the dusty rock.

"And your husband—he blamed you?"

"No." I wiped at my eyes.

He gently held my chin, tilted my face toward his so I had to look into his eyes. "What happened to him?"

I stared into his eyes, not blinking, falling into something like a trance. I could dive into them and make it all go away. I could melt away the person I was and just comingle my atoms with his and become part of him, I imagined. Nothing would be true because I would cease to exist.

"Tell me," he whispered, his hand cradling my face.

"He killed himself." A crack in the center of my soul ruptured. "He couldn't stand it, life, not without her." My voice, barely audible, cracked and strained with the burden of the words.

He must have already known this, but he acted surprised, devastated. Tears welled at the corners of his eyes. "I'm so, so sorry, dear Anna," he murmured.

. . .

"And?" Mellow edges closer to me, so her face nearly touches mine. The car is uncomfortably hot, even with the windows rolled down, so I open the door and swing my legs around. The dirt-gravel is dusty and raises tiny tornados where my feet touch it.

Her door squeaks open also, and she marches around to my side.

"That's not the end of the story." She squats in the dust so her eyes are square with mine. "He was sorry. And that was it? I don't believe it." She sits and crosses her legs in a yoga pose, unmindful of the dirt cloud that has risen behind her like a desert halo.

"No, that wasn't all." The rest—I didn't want to admit it because it made me culpable in the crime, in the betrayal, the dishonoring of my entire family.

"So. Tell the rest."

"No. That was all that mattered."

"Liar!" She slaps my knee, her face red and enraged. "You're just like Rhiannon. Just the same. You seem like you're not, but underneath, you're both just liars who use stuff to forget."

"I'm nothing like her." I gaze into her angry face. "I'm sorry you're working out your mommy issues on me, but that's not fair. This has nothing—"

"Not fair? You know what's not fair? Growing up without a responsible adult anywhere nearby, never having a place to live, that's all unfair. She took drugs, you pick at your skin. And—" she seems to be running out of vitriol, "—you're trying to fix this all wrong. You're living some fantasy that you'll somehow go and pull a *Graduate* and stop this wedding."

"You couldn't possibly have seen *The Graduate.*"

"I have seen it, and that is beside the point."

I feel old. I feel used up. I rub absently at the bumps on my fore-arms, overwhelmed with the need to pick the raised spots, to make them bleed. I don't like to do it in front of other people, but I am unable to stop myself. There is a huge scab over a previous picking site, so I scratch at it, gently at first, and then more aggressively, until it comes loose. I pop it in my mouth.

"Did you just eat a scab?" She sounds horrified, as if I've killed a baby.

I don't comment. It's pretty obvious that's what I've done.

"You know that makes you, technically, a cannibal, right?"

"I don't think it counts if it's your own body. I think you have to eat someone else in your own species."

"I see you've done your research."

It feels good to laugh at it, to do it in front of someone. I'm not sure I've ever done that before. I find another, one on my left elbow where I scraped myself on a rock, a jagged, elongated scar that is now hardened and dark scarlet. I pick, pick, pick, until it comes loose from its cradle, and I examine it, then gently put it on my tongue, roll it around, learn its contours and salty-iron taste.

"That reminds me of Catholic school."

"Hmm?" I reach for a bottle of water, which is ridiculously warm, and wash down the remnants.

"Like, you know, communion, right? This is my body, this is my blood."

"You were raised Catholic?"

"No, Rhiannon dated a priest for a while. We went to church and it was repetitive, so I picked up some of the shtick. They were going for a more magical, metaphorical body of Christ, though, you know. They didn't actually eat scabs. I think they did drink wine, so if we have any—"

"This is a nervous habit, not a sacrament."

"Ha. Nervous habit. Like a nun."

"Jesus."

"Nowhere to be seen. Sorry. We're on our own, Sister Scabby."

I close my eyes and listen to the sounds in this dry and desolate place. Wind whips around rocks and plants as if it's chasing something or someone. A dog barks, but so far away. Trees bend but don't break, adapting to the wind, no matter which direction it blows.

Mellow flicks my cheek with her finger. "Alright, scab licker, let's go. If you're trying to spring a leak and drain your pool, it's not going to work. Your body just seals it up again, and you move on. So, let's get this show on the road so we can finish this godforsaken girl scout trip and do something more interesting."

She stands, circles the car, and hops into the passenger seat. As we exit the indent in the road, she starts to hum a song from the 1970s that she couldn't possibly know.

She doesn't press me for more details as we drive. My mind, though, spins in circles and comes back on itself like a snake biting its own tail. The closer we get to our destination, the more I question why I'm going at all. I should probably scrap the whole idea and drive home. I tell Mellow as much about two hours in.

"After you've come all this way? You have to go. You have to see how the story will end."

"I know how it will end," I say, not taking my eyes off the monotonous ribbon of asphalt. "I'll be embarrassed, he'll be embarrassed, I'll leave. We might get cake."

"Pull over. I have to pee."

I glance at her and frown. "Outside?"

"How do you think people peed before we had toilets? It's totally natural."

I dutifully maneuver the car to the roadside and kill the engine. Nothing but birdsong and the trees waving languidly. It seems a bit cooler, and the prickly hairs on my head rise up to meet the breeze. Mellow puts on her shoes and trots over behind a tree.

"How close are we?" she calls.

I open the map. "I think it's about another hour. Almost there."

"The wedding's tomorrow?"

I don't answer. The wedding is *tomorrow*. Tomorrow, Edward will have a wife, a bride, someone to spend his life with. How have I considered ruining this for him? He's done nothing but try to help me.

"I hear your brain spinning around," Mellow hollers from behind the tree. "Do you have any Kleenex or a roll of toilet paper?"

I grab a loose roll from the back seat and take it to her. "What do you mean, you hear my brain?"

"You're thinking of a way out."

"Out of what?"

"Out of confronting Doctor Douche."

"Please don't call him that."

She hops up from the ground, grasping the roll of toilet paper, her pants pulled up but unzipped. "I hope there wasn't any poison ivy down there. That's like the last thing I need. An itch that's not even a romantic itch."

"I'm not going to comment."

We get back into the car and she chucks the toilet paper into the back seat. "Please put it where it goes," I ask.

"Where does it go? Is there a designated toilet paper repository?"

I reach back and adjust it, setting it neatly between the shoulder bag, the gallon jug of water, the backpack full of vitamins and snacks, and Annabella's wig box. "There is a system. That's how I'm able to find things quickly."

"Control freak!" She yells, sticking her feet out the window and waving them to the trees as we drive by.

Seriously, though. I need a plan. My scalp itches when I even think about what I'm going to do or say when we reach the town.

Mellow has the map stretched in haphazard folds across her lap. "Here's where we are, I think," she says, squinting to find the freeway sign. "And this is where we're going." She stabs a spot on the map vindictively. "You have the address?"

"Of course. It's in my pocket."

"There's a sign up there." We approach it. Fort Collins: 30 miles.

"That's where we're going!" she squeals. My stomach starts to roil, and I seriously consider wrecking the car.

18
PRACTICE TEST

Thirty miles to Fort Collins.

On a dark night, the human eye can see a candle flame flickering 30 miles away. You can still have a long-distance relationship if you live 30 miles away from the person you love. The Nansen Ice Shelf in Antarctica is 30 miles long, but will soon break off because of global warming, and we'll probably all die.

"What in holy fuck are you doing?" Mellow's voice is reaching a pitch that can only be heard by dogs with extremely good hearing. "We've been sitting here for, like, 20 minutes! What are you looking up? I have the map!"

"I'm not sure." I stare out the window. "I'm just not sure."

"Of what?"

"If I want to go."

She shrieks in frustration. "You are insane. Of course we're going. Do you want me to drive? I can drive."

"Do have a license?" *Pick, pick, pick.*

"No. You have to have a car to have a license. Poor people don't have cars."

I cannot argue with that point. "So, you can't drive?"

"Of course I can drive. A monkey can drive."

I exit the car and walk around to the passenger side, motioning her to move over.

"Seriously?" she squeals. "You'll let me drive?"

"I'm not really in a fit state to navigate a motor vehicle." *Pick, pick, pick.*

She writhes and twists herself over the console so she's in the driver's position, adjusting the mirror and the seat and grabbing a pillow from the backseat to sit on. "I'm not that tall," she says, by way of explanation.

As for me, I am sweating profusely and finding it hard to breathe. If I have a heart attack here, outside of Fort Collins, would he find out? Would I make the papers? Does anyone read the papers anymore?

I close the creaky door and strap on my seatbelt. She looks so young behind the steering wheel, but she turns the key as if she's done it every day of her life. The car moves smoothly forward and onto the deserted road.

"I think we should switch now," Mellow says, about 20 minutes later. "We're getting close to the town. Are you calm enough to drive now?"

"I was fine before. I just wanted you to feel useful." She snorts. We both know that's not true.

"I'll pull over into this gas station. Do we need gas?" She glances at the fuel gauge, which still reads half full. Without waiting for a response, she glides the car onto the station's patchy asphalt.

"I may just stop here and never go back, so probably not," I blurt out.

"Seriously?" She puts the car in park and the engine coughs and slowly submits to being turned off, protesting as if it's a jittery patient succumbing to anesthesia. "Why would you stay in Colorado? And wouldn't you have to return the car if you borrowed it? You'd be a car thief then. I don't think you'd do well in prison."

She pauses for a second before continuing. "What's the plan, then?"

"Plan?"

"Are we going to check into a motel or something? Or just park outside the wedding venue and wait? Or rent a helicopter and parachute in? A plan. We need one."

I gulp and stare out the passenger window, hoping to find an answer in the brush. No signs are forthcoming. "I had a plan when I started," I murmur. "I don't think I thought it out very well."

"Duh." The leather seat squishes as she turns toward me. "Are you crying?"

I find that I am. I wipe at the tears furiously, as if they are wet traitors.

"Hey," she says gently, putting a hand on my arm. "You helped me, I'll help you. Let's go do this."

"I'm so stupid. This man wants nothing to do with me. That's so clear now. I have been delusional. I have no reason to be here."

"Except that he invited you." She leans forward and whispers, "So, why did he do that if he didn't want you to be there?"

"To...show me that he's moved on?"

"He could do that after the wedding—send you a postcard from Vegas or wherever people like that go for honeymoons. And then there would be zero drama. It would be a done deal."

"You're right." I see hope and determination in her face, something I've lacked for so long, except for this ridiculous pilgrimage. "You are right. There must be a reason he told me before it happened."

She grins widely, as if she's guessed the $64-dollar question. Of course, she'd have no idea what that means if I said it to her. A lot of people might not know what it means, including British doctors, which proves that I should probably be alone. I should not be inflicting my dated sense of humor on unsuspecting teenagers or Brits.

"So. We go." She exits the car, runs around to my side, and flings open my door. "C'mon! Get to driving!"

It does take exactly twenty minutes to reach the outskirts of Fort Collins, home to Colorado State University and an outstanding public school system, according to a brochure Mellow took from the last motel. She throws me tidbits about the town to calm my nerves.

"If you are seeking the Colorado lifestyle and a community in which you can reinvent and reinvigorate yourself, then Fort Collins is your city," she chirps. "Wow, this sounds perfect. Hey, isn't pot legal here now? I wonder if Colorado State University's mascot is a bong. Go fighting bongs!"

"That would be a challenging mascot costume." Rolling into town, we start to see shops, small storefronts designed to look like quaint, original places, but they're probably chains. That's been a trend, I think, mass-produced things and people designed to look original and quaint. At least I'd never be like that. Stubbly scalp will likely never trend.

"Okay. So, you said you made reservations at this motel, right?"

"Which motel?"

She flips through pages in my notebook. "Uh...Merical Inn. On Pembroke Street."

"Miracle? Did you say Miracle Inn?"

"No. *Merical.* Like 'merica, with an 'l' at the end." She squints at the streets we pass, and when she sees the turn, she tells me.

The inn is barely functional. The woman at the front desk, who could be the overblown twin Tweedledum to my friend Petra, appears to be dozing when we barge in.

She mumbles. A bit of drool strings down to the counter. I try not to bolt out of the place. Mellow grips my arm with steel fingers. "We have a reservation," she says in her best grown-up voice.

"We have a room reserved," I croak, realizing my wig is still in the car. "Anna Beck."

"Mmm?" Rouged lips furrowed with tiny lines pucker as if I've said a bad word. "Name?"

"Anna Beck."

She blinks slowly, owl-like, and opens a huge leather-bound book, uses one long, fuchsia nail to run down a ledger line. "Wow," Mellow says, peering at the book. "You don't use a computer?"

"Too many 'lectrical impulses," the woman wheezes. False eyelashes cling like drunken caterpillars to her lids. "I see it." She blinks again and stares at me. Is there a secret word? A handshake?

"So...can we check in?" I ask.

She seems to be considering it carefully, maybe because of my scalp. I point to it. "Cancer," I say, trying to sound as pitiful as possible. Mellow elbows me and turns a giggle into a coughing fit.

"Does she have it too?" Mrs. Blinky turns her gaze to the girl.

"No, she just has a swallowing disorder." This causes Mellow to cough even more.

Blinky shakes her head slowly and a frown forms on her brow like a glacier advancing. "We don't let people do drugs here."

"Of course not." Wallet, credit card, sympathetic smile. "We're just passing through. Only one night."

Her fuchsia pincers grab my card. As she painstakingly enters the numbers by hand, I wonder, *What will tomorrow bring? Wedding day. And what follows after?*

The clerk hands me a key attached to foot-long segment from a worn broomstick. "Room 16. Just pull your car into space 16, and it's right there. First floor."

Mellow frowns at this unusual keychain. "Did you have to kill a witch to get her broomstick?"

The woman behind the desk inhales forcefully, as if she's about to lecture us on using the word "witch" in polite company, but I cut her off. "Thank you. We'll find it." I drag Mellow by the arm and out the door, with much protesting on her part.

Room 16 is far from elegant, although it appears to be clean. As I place my wig and wig head on the dresser, it occurs to me that I haven't worn the hair for almost two days. Not at all. I reach up quickly to feel my scalp. The hairs are growing, small but stubbly, like new growth in a fallow cornfield.

"Yo, where are we going? Where's the big shindig?"

"Shindig." I snort at her use of such an old word. "I don't think there will be any shindigging at this wedding. It's going to be pretty formal." I sit next to her on the bed and take out my folder of printed pages, now bent and damp from travel. "Here. It's called the Broadmore. It's a whole resort. Outdoor weddings, very formal."

Mellow flips the pages, gazes wide-eyed at the beautiful color photographs. "So, somebody's got some money. What does the invite say about where it is exactly?"

The invitation, now crumpled, dirty, stained, only relays the time and location generally, not which particular room the wedding will be held in. "I guess we'll have to look for a sign or something when we get there. It's at one in the afternoon. That gives us time to get up, eat something, and try to figure out what to wear."

"What to wear?" Mellow blinks and curls her lip into an incredulous cartoon expression. "As previously stated, I got nothing."

"I brought two dresses, in case I hated one." In a hidden pocket in my suitcase, I pull out the garment bag that had been rolled and practically hermetically sealed to protect my secondhand elegance borrowed from some niece of Petra's who gained fifty pounds from an inconsiderate baby.

Like a child at Christmas, Mellow impatiently unrolls, unzips, fingers fumbling, to extricate the prize. As she sees the fabric, her expression of joy fades to one of dismay. "Uh…did you get these out of a Catholic school dumpster?" She shakes out one of the dresses, a cream satin number with poofy shoulder epaulets. "This one looks like somebody just stuck a couple of those shower scrubby things on the shoulders. I think it's made of polyester too. So that should be great in the heat."

She twirls it around on the hanger, so the cream lace overlay swishes a bit over the simple A-line of the skirt and bodice. A surprised-looking peach-pink rosette explodes from the bosom. "That makes it look like there's a stray nipple that is trying to escape."

I can't help but laugh at that, because she's right, that's kind of what it looks like. "Well, you'll be the belle of the ball, then."

"Oh, I'm not wearing it." She tosses the nipple dress onto the bed.

"Yeah, well, you might want to once you see the other one." Her eyes widen as she unzips (with more trepidation than Christmas enthusiasm) the second dress. It's chartreuse with an empire waist, made of georgette fabric with a forest-green satin under dress.

"The color is...unusual." She pulls it out of its cocoon, an over-sized praying mantis. "You might be able to blind everyone and knock the dude out and kidnap him."

I take the chartreuse dress and hold it up to my neck, checking the mirror on the dresser. A pale woman with dead cornfield hair and dry, dry lips stares back. I smooth the under dress, adjust the lace bolero jacket that is attached to it (also chartreuse) and smile as fetchingly as I can. "Would you rather wear this one?"

"Uh," she grimaces as her reflection appears in the mirror next to mine. "I guess I'll take my chances with the nipple dress. Can we cut off that third nipple, maybe?"

"Surgery? I don't know if the patient will survive. I'll look at it. Let's try these on first, to see what we need to do."

"Shoes!"

I've started to strip off my shirt so I can pull the great green goddess dress over my head. "Shoes?"

"Were you planning to wear your scrubby Crocs with this dress?"

"I do not wear Crocs. These are orthopedic sandals."

Mellow growls in aggravation. "Whatever. They're not dress shoes. Did you bring dress shoes?"

"Of course." I dig into the suitcase once again and pull out a pair of black patent flats, ballet slippers really, and a pair of cream Isotoners.

"Old lady slippers. Crap. So I won't even get to wear heels to this thing."

"I didn't know I'd be taking anyone with me. I hope you're a size 7." I place both pairs of shoes on the ground at the foot of the bed.

"I'm not, but those are stretchy." She picks up the nipple dress and shimmies into it. It's not bad on her. She shoves me over so she can look in the mirror, and preens like a model getting ready for a photo shoot.

"I look ah-maze-ing," she crows. "What time is the deal tomorrow?"

"One. One in the afternoon. Same as when you asked me last time."

"Sooooorrrrrry." She pulls the dress off and tosses it onto the bed.

"What do we do till D-day, then?"

"I don't know." I pull my dress over my head too, much more carefully. Care. It comes with age, I suppose, or with experience. The young don't have care, don't care to know, don't know enough to care. What a beautiful thing that we never appreciate when we're at that stage.

"I think you should tell me a story." She flops onto the bed, crosses her legs, and beams at me expectantly.

"Do you?" I sit more slowly on the edge of the bed, feeling the contours of its chintzy surface before committing myself to perching on it. Care. Have to be careful. "What kind of story?"

Her smile fades, only slightly, and she says, "Tell me about your daughter."

I lie back on the bed, stare at the ceiling, think about the asbestos harbored in the popcorn material. So much danger everywhere. "My daughter."

She lies down too, so we're parallel, our legs hanging off the side of the bed. "Just tell me all about her, so I feel like I know her."

As the light outside starts to fade, we lie there in our fancy dresses, and I tell her.

"She was born during a rainstorm, and those are rare in California, so I thought it was a sign of luck. My husband was there, saw her first when she was born, and he said, 'She looks like you!' which hurt my feelings, I remember, because she was so wrinkled and red and crying.

"We named her Darcy. She was like a treasure, something that I never imagined I could have, a piece of my soul. We both felt like that, Tom and I. Tom was my husband, and he was fragile, but I didn't know it then.

"She was a good baby, you know, she didn't cry much, and she slept through the night very early on, so I wasn't as exhausted as a lot of new mothers. It was hard, of course, because babies are hard, even good babies. Tom was working a lot, so it was just me and Darcy, in something like a waking dream...we'd go for a few hours, sleep, eat, sleep some more. It didn't seem real. It seemed like life had somehow paused. I had worked almost until the day she was born—just part time at a bookstore, but it helped—so when I quit to be with her, Tom had to do more, and I think…it was just hard for him, but he never told me. But he loved her so much. So much.

"She grew and turned into this curious, odd little person. I loved her for that. She was not like anyone else. She wasn't really like me, and she wasn't like Tom. From very early, she was just her own person. Her first word wasn't mama or dada or anything like that—it was wawa, water—she loved it. She played in it any chance she could get, loved baths, sprinklers, pools, lakes. She was a fish. A mermaid.

"We—Tom and I—we started to drift. At first, it was just things being hectic, and then that became the usual. We talked less and less, he was busier. I think he tried to find reasons to work late. It was my fault. I was so obsessed with Darcy, wanting to drink in every single minute of her life, etching it into my mind so I'd never forget it. I kept thinking, all the time, 'You never know how long you have', so I sacrificed. I gave up my job, didn't go back. I stopped writing. Yes, I used to write! And I guess I stopped being married.

"It's like the lobster in the pot, you know? How you put it in cool water and eventually the water heats up, boils, but the lobster doesn't notice because it's so gradual. Except for us, the water turned cold. It felt like we were bobbing in an ocean, and waves just kept pushing us further apart. We never talked about it. I think he tried, once, but I was very defensive, and I told him our child had to come first. She always did. And to be honest, I loved her more. I did. How could I not? She was a piece of me, and everything I wanted to be I saw reflected in her."

It feels good to tell it. Mellow had grabbed my hand as I told the story, and now I feel her grip, loose yet present, caressing the back of my hand and then the bumps on my forearm where I'd picked. "So, you weren't really happy even before," she whispers.

Was I? I'm not sure. I think I must have been, but it evaporated like rain falling from the sky and disappearing before it hits the ground. "I'm not sure if anyone is ever really happy," I say. "And thinking you are or that you could be is delusional."

She clears her throat. "It's not. You can be happy. I am."

I turn so I'm looking at her profile. "You're happy?"

She turns her head so our eyes meet. "Yes." She beams at me. "I am now. Because of you."

When I open my eyes again, the room is dark. Mellow is snoring lightly, an arm thrown over her head, the nipple dress all askew. The digital clock reads 11:17 p.m., and an amber streetlight winks at me through the blinds. I noiselessly ease off the bed, head to the bathroom, and quietly close the door.

Thankfully, the light in the bathroom is fairly dim. My face is lined with the contours of the bedspread, intersecting at odd angles across my cheek and forehead. I strip off the green dress, hang it on the towel rack and wash my face, allowing the cold water to wash the sweat and salt from my skin. White stubble is growing on my head. Actually growing, noticeably. I feel myself smile at the tiny, hopeful sprouts. I might dye it electric blue when it all grows in.

Tomorrow will be the end or the beginning. Momentous. A moment, like a stone monolith towering over a river of rushing memories. An occasion which calls for the giving of gifts. I know exactly, *exactly*, what to give him.

I turn off the bathroom light so I don't wake Mellow. It takes a few moments to locate it, but I lay hands on the Box of Unwanteds, caress the smooth cardboard sides of it as if it were a holy relic. Remove the lid, move the box closer to the sliver of light muscling its way through the heavy blinds. My fingers touch newspaper snippets, the faded photographs, the notes, the cards from well-wishers and the dog-eared informational handouts from clinically detached physician's assistants. *Sorry for your loss.* As if I'd misplaced an umbrella or forgotten a phone number.

I find what I'm seeking. A photo of Darcy, smiling, tanned, waving to me from a wooden bench framed by sweet, white jasmine blossoms. I captured a hummingbird in that photo by accident, hovering just above her head. It was there, I snapped the photo, it was gone when I blinked.

I will keep this.

I snug the lid back onto the box. Wrapping paper? No chance of finding that. I silently rummage through the chest of drawers, hoping for some inspiration, and I find it: Con-Tac paper drawer liners, strewn with faded pink roses. One is loose; I free it from its boring drawer duty and shape it around the box. No tape, so I snatch a gauzy green head scarf from my case and wrap it around the box, tying a stubby bow to finish the job. I set the gift in the sliver of light.

After getting ready for bed, I pad through the room quietly, like a cat, trying not to wake Mellow. I watch this improbable person, this girl who careened accidentally into my life...she is happy, because of me.

For the first time in what seems like forever, I sleep without dreaming.

19
FOLLOWING DISTANCE

"Let's go!"

I wake to Mellow bouncing on my bed, shaking her wet head like a dog.

"The wedding is in three hours. Let's go!" She bounces even more violently.

"I'm getting motion sick. Please stop."

"We need to get ready." She pulls the covers off my naked body, and I grab them back. "It's not like I haven't seen boobs before," she mutters as she runs to the bathroom. She's humming some tune that I think I know.

"What is that song?" I have to talk loudly over the sound of her humming and brushing her teeth.

"*I will survive…*" she sings from the bathroom. It makes me smile.

When she's finished, she runs back out to me. "Are you ready?"

"Well, no, I just woke up."

"C'mon!" She yanks my arm and shoves me toward the bathroom.

I primp as best I can. The green dress looks strange in this light, but it will have to do. The hastily wrapped gift with the makeshift bow fits my overall look, I suppose.

"What's in there?" She points to the box.

"A wedding gift."

"When did you have time to get him a present, and, by the way, why is it ghetto wrapped like that?"

I hold it up and frown. "I think it'll do."

"Like, it's a step up from brown paper bag wrapping, or newspaper." She grabs it, shakes it to her ear, hands it back. "It's definitely not a new car."

"No," I laugh. Smoothing the skirt on my dress, I look her in the eye. "I think I'm ready."

Mellow frowns and stares at me. "Huh?"

"What's wrong?" I ask.

She purses her lips and points to my head.

"Oh." My hand goes to my stubbly head, rubs the little sprouting hairs. "Yeah. I'm just going to go with it."

She smiles broadly, nods, and keeps singing as we head to the car in our semi-fancy dresses, wearing our beat-down shoes. I'm sure we look quite the pair.

I hand her the mutilated invitation, the paper with the directions to the Broadmore, and the gift, and we start our journey.

Mellow seems to sense that I want to be in my head, mentally preparing for battle. We drive in silence, with only the lulling sound of the tires on the road and the occasional whoosh of a truck passing on the left.

One more memory of Edward rises to the top of my consciousness. It was the day he told me he was leaving town.

. . .

"It's really not that significant to your recovery," he said, sitting behind his protective desk in the oxblood chair. He didn't look at me as he spoke, calmly, as if he were reciting a recipe.

I said nothing.

As he scribbled on his legal pad (what was he doing? Sudoku? Doodling?) he kept talking. "I've written down referrals to several excellent therapists in the area, any one of whom would be able to continue your care without interruption." He looked up at me. "They're all...women."

I nodded and continued to stare at him, as if my laser gaze might crack his porcelain exterior and send the wellspring of his great love for me flowing from his finely tailored jacket.

"I really wish you'd say something," he stammered.

"What should I say?"

He shifted uncomfortably in his chair and stared at the ceiling as if looking for divine intervention. "Alright. I'm sorry. Is that what you want?"

"No." I stood and took a step closer to his desk, which made him flinch slightly. "You know what I want. Honesty."

"I don't know how to be honest with you. That's why I can't be your therapist."

"You can't be my therapist because we were intimate."

"We were *not*." His face blushed deep red, and he would not look at me. "That was a...lapse in judgment. On my part, absolutely. I don't blame you in the slightest."

I stepped even closer, and he scooched his chair back so he was leaning against the bookcase behind him. "You don't *blame* me?"

"Stay right there. Do not come any closer." His hand was on the phone. I retreated, sat down. He relaxed and ran his fingers through his hair. How many women knew he did that when he was nervous? Did his bride know that?

He sighed and put his head down on his desk. "I've muffed it from the get-go," he mumbled.

"No," I answered. "No, you've saved me, don't you see? I didn't think I could ever love anyone, not ever. Not after what happened with Darcy and Tom. But now I know I can. I can love someone. I love you."

He sat up, covered his face with his hands. "That's just it, Anna. You can't love me. I'm your doctor. It's not allowed, and in fact, I could be arrested for all of it, my practice ruined, my life ruined. I know you don't want that for me, do you?"

"Of course not. But we have to be honest. You do love me."

He met my gaze and said, "I may. But I can't."

Just like that, a wall slammed shut between us, a circuit severed, a door closed tight. His face was blank as he finished discussing the transition of my care to some other doctor (whom I would never see), and he finally smiled wanly, and passed the paper over to me, across the desk. I touched his hand when he gave it to me.

His jaw clenched tight, his lips trembled just a bit. A mournful, dark tornado swept up from my solar plexus and obliterated all the good feelings. I walked out, exhausted, empty, ready to die.

. . .

"Next turn," Mellow says, fanning herself with the directions. The nipple dress is polyester, so she's sweating little crescent moons all over it, under the arms, at the breasts. Mine is synthetic too. We both look like we've been in a dunking booth.

A small, tasteful sign directing us to Broadmore House affirms her directions.

My heart beats so fast I think it might stop, but I keep driving, pull into the large, perfectly groomed grounds of Broadmore House. It's a sprawling cream-colored resort, one of those that's made to look old but isn't really. Graceful pillars and tasteful antique-gold and sage-green trim remind me of a stately plantation home.

Mellow watches me intently. "So? What's the plan?"

I park the car away from the Rolls-Royces and Bentleys. "Where are they? Where is it happening?" I say as I grab the wrapped box and my bag.

She consults the invitation. "On the Bellacourt Lawn. Let's go look at the sign thing." She points to a pedestaled venue map framed in antique gold to make it look like a piece of art. Out of the car, the air is warmer, oppressive. "According to this, the Bellacourt Lawn is that way." She points to the left, past the main building, the one with the pillars.

As we pass the house, faint strains of music waft up from behind it. Rachmaninoff, "Rhapsody on a Theme of Paganini." Did I tell him I loved that song? I can't remember. It was from a shlocky movie about two people who loved each other even though they were from different periods in time, and one had time traveled in some way or another. One was like a ghost from the past, or the future. Christopher Reeve, before he became broken, was the male lead.

"Come on," Mellow hisses, tugging at my arm. The stubble on my head is beginning to sweat, and my hands are slick too. I'm afraid I'm perspiring onto the gift. Does that make it even more personal?

She drags me behind the main house, toward the music. Down a cobbled path, through some sapling trees casting welcome shade, and then we come out on the top of a hill overlooking a wide, flat lawn, manicured, perfectly green like the felt on a pool table.

Below, a small, tasteful crowd is seated in white plastic folding chairs in neat little rows. An arbor covered in white roses sets the stage, and a generic minister of some indeterminate faith holds a black book that I presume to be the bible or instructions on how to ruin a life. Perhaps that's the same thing? Ah, no distracting yourself with political commentary, my dear. You're here, and it's now.

"Is that him?" Mellow whispers even though there is no way any of the people below could hear us.

I nod wordlessly. There he is, a small wedding-cake figurine in a tuxedo with a crimson vest, wearing a black top hat. The music stops.

The ridiculous Wedding March begins. How unimaginative. From behind the crowd, a cream-puff meringue of a dress floats toward the rose-bedecked arch. Two little cherubs hold the train of the ostentatious dress, and I'm quite surprised she hadn't commanded them to fly with little mechanical wings. It's all so perfect.

The song continues and she floats slowly, slowly toward the front of the audience, milking every millisecond of her queenly parade. My eyes are fixed on him, really, the broadness of his back, how hot it must be in the tuxedo and top hat, wondering if he's thinking of me.

"Are we going to rush the ceremony?" Mellow asks gleefully, tugging at the rosette that threatens to wilt at her breast.

"No, of course not."

She grabs my shoulders and turns me so I face her. "What? You're just here to…watch? What good is that?"

"I'm a witness. I want him to know I'm here, that's all."

"Yeah, but he doesn't know you're here."

A shiver runs through my body, from head to toe; I turn, and he's facing the bride, watching her approach on the runway. But his gaze wavers, and suddenly, he's looking at our little hill, looking at us, above his bride's head, and he *sees* me, I know he does.

In movies, when two lovers meet after a traumatic trial of endurance, the rest of the world blurs into soft focus, leaving only the two of them, connected by their gaze. Everything else falls away for them, leaving them with just the truth of their love, and the reality of their relationship. That is all that matters, all that ever has mattered.

Mellow continues to prattle on, but I do not hear her words. My eyes are fixed on him, and time slows down, the bride becomes mired in molasses, and the invisible line between us lengthens, shortens, becomes solid, then invisible again.

He raises a hand, slightly, so no one would notice, just to the height of his shoulder, then plucks at his boutonnière to cover the movement. He sees me. He knows it is me.

My heart beats, drum-like, pounding in my ears. The bride arrives at her final destination next to him, and he is still glancing, surreptitiously, over at my hill. Mellow, silently following this unspoken drama, sighs next to me. "I think he sees you."

The wedding goes on, but I still feel that he watches me watching him. Is that just fantasy? Probably. The ceremony appears to be wrapping up—just long enough to make it legal, not so long as to make it boring—and a pre-recorded string quartet belches Pachelbel's

"Canon" onto the lawn.

"Come on," I whisper to Mellow as I grab her arm.

"Where are we going?" We're both still whispering.

"Reception."

Like two badly dressed Soviet-era spies we sneak about, glancing for counteragents who might spoil our mission. We do not encounter anyone so we make for the parking lot, hoping for some directional signs. "Maybe we should ask somebody?" Mellow squeaks. "Anyway, you saw him get married. Can't we just go?"

"I have to give this to him." I shake the rose-patterned box.

"I know what's in there. Are you sure you want to give that up? To them?"

"It's for *him*. Not *them*." We're back where we started, near the parking lot, on a brick path lined with tastefully groomed plants. A reed-thin man in a gray suit approaches and Mellow's inclination is to bolt, but I am through with that.

"Excuse me—" I scan his tasteful Mission-printed name tag. Todd Preston, Facilities Liaison. "Mr. Preston." The expression on his face goes from surprise to suspicion to fear in the blink of an eye. Clearly, we are out of place.

"May I help you?" the way he says it, you can tell: he's really saying, *Why the hell are you two ragamuffin bitches throwing shade on my well-groomed plants?*

"Yes." I try to sound as cultured and confident as possible. "We're here for a wedding. Dr. Denture. I believe the ceremony just wrapped up...we were a bit late. Can you point us to the reception area?"

He frowns at my raggedy gift and our stained dresses. "Let me just check on that. One moment." He walks a few feet away, keeping his eye on us at all times as if we might disappear. He pulls a cell phone from his pocket.

"He thinks we can't hear him," Mellow whispers, hardly moving her mouth.

"Jennifer? Todd. We have two...uh...guests who appear to be misplaced. Can you have Matteo come down with his golf cart?"

"Matteo," Mellow whispers again, imbuing the name with menace. "Hey, we have in invitation." She waves the soggy, ragged remnants of it at him, and he wrinkles his nose in distaste.

Todd keeps his eyes on us but smiles from the nose down. "If you could just stay right here for a minute or two, I have someone coming to help—"

"No need." I brush right by him, and sense Mellow's intense surprise and glee. "We'll find it." She two-steps behind me quickly, unprepared for the sudden movement.

"If you—could you please wait—" Todd is dumbfounded, confused. How could someone like me disregard someone like him? It was so clearly *wrong*.

Some preternatural homing instinct and the strains of tasteful jazz lead me to the reception hall. Todd tries to follow us without appearing to run.

Inside, the room is filling up with the well-heeled wedding guests. From their expressions, we don't quite fit the demographic. As I approach the gift table with my box firmly under my arm, bodies part for us like the Red Sea.

Mellow follows in my wake, staying close. I consider putting my box on the table, but it will be so noticeable amidst the Tiffany boxes and Saks giftwrapping that I elect to hang on to it. "What are we doing?" Mellow whispers in my ear as I turn to face the room full of vaguely horrified rich people.

"I have to give this to him in person."

People try not to look at us by pretending to be casually involved in conversation, but they keep glancing over to see if we're still there, as if we are simply plebeian hallucinations that will disappear in a poof, leaving their lovely scene uncluttered. I slowly drift away from the gift table, toward the tasteful cheese and fruit spread. In the middle of the massive silver trays of food a lovely ice swan arches gracefully with outstretched, frozen wings.

"Now what?" Mellow stands a bit too close for comfort, but I can't blame her. I can feel the waves of resentment coming off the guests. Todd is trying to make his way across the room to us, treading cautiously across the parquet floor as if he has no real destination in mind. You can't spook a herd of upper crust gazelles, or they panic and ruin the buffet.

"We need to keep moving," Mellow hisses at me, tugging my arm, so I follow. She scoots around behind the ice swan so Todd does not have a direct line of sight to us. I'm still clutching the rose-patterned, sweaty shoe box, trying not to touch anyone as I move, like a massive human version of the board game of Operation.

Suddenly, the focus of the room shifts, and polite applause begins. My breath catches in my throat because, through the melty swan wing, I see the newlyweds enter the room.

"That dude is coming to kick us out," Mellow whispers as she puts two hands on my shoulders and forces me under the white linen tablecloth.

So now we're sitting under the massive ice swan table, cross-legged on the carpet. Someone has scrawled FUCK WEDDINGS on the Masonite underside of the table. I nod in agreement. "I assume you've done this before?" I ask.

She nods. "We used to crash a lot of weddings. Free food, and they have a hard time kicking people out unless they get trashed, which my mother usually did if it was an open bar."

Through the space at the bottom of the tablecloth we see expensive shoes walking here and there, most turned toward the entrance to the room. Apparently, we've dodged Todd's dogged efforts to scoop us out like pond scum. A male voice says, "Mr. and Mrs. Edward Denture!" More polite applause. So, he's here. In the room.

I am frozen like the melting swan, clutching the box full of my memories.

"Please, everyone." His deep baritone makes me shiver. "Enjoy the food, the drinks. Thank you for coming." The chatter rises again, so I know they must be mingling, shaking hands with all of their well-dressed guests.

"Check and see where he is," I whisper. Mellow dutifully crawls on her belly so she can see through the gap.

"I can only really see the knees down, but I think the Todd guy may have left. Dr. Douche…he's walking around, talking. He's really tall. I didn't picture him that tall."

I belly-scooch over next to her to get a glimpse. It is, indeed, Edward.

From under the table, it's kind of like watching a movie of someone else's life. It's painfully obvious I do not belong here, but it's too late to go back now. And I have a mission.

"What are you going to do?" Mellow whispers.

I could stay under this table until the room clears, I guess. Just wait it out. Let it go. I could make a huge scene, grab his pants leg, tug at him until they take me away, sedated. Or I could do something else. I turn to Mellow. "Stay here." I reach over and kiss her on the forehead. Her eyes are bright when I draw back away from her.

"You just gave me a forehead kiss!" she whispers excitedly.

I smile. "Yes."

"I've always wanted someone to do that." She bowls me over like an ecstatic puppy, hugging me so tightly it's tough to breathe. But I don't mind.

"Stay here," I tell her again. She nods, eyes shining.

Clutching the gift, I find an area relatively clear of shoes in the gap under the tablecloth and do my best to act like a regular person who just happens to be climbing out from under a buffet table.

I smooth out my dress, run a hand over the stubble on my scalp… that might attract some attention, I suppose. In fact, the people in my immediate vicinity back up a step or two and look away. I wonder if I ever did that when I was normal?

Framed by a long window, the verdant lakefront behind him, he chats amiably with a dowager in a pink pillbox hat. I pretend that I'm invisible as I walk through the room, keep my breathing low and light, focus only on him, his figure against the greenery. My pulse pounds in my ears, louder as I get closer to him.

As if he senses me, he turns his head just slightly, and his eyes go wide. He expertly extricates himself from the pillbox lady, who smiles, nods, walks away. A tense smile is frozen on his face. He doesn't move, so I approach him.

"Hello." I offer him the box. "Congratulations."

He stares at me, blinks rapidly as if trying to reconcile my presence in this room. "Anna."

"Edward." He checks out my stubbly head. "Yeah, I ditched the wig."

"It's...nice." He glances nervously over my shoulder, I presume looking for Mrs. Dr. Denture. "I honestly didn't expect you to make the trip."

"Then why did you invite me?"

He blinks, refocuses on me. "I—I thought it would be...healing."

"You didn't think I'd come, though."

He grins briefly, nervously, only with his mouth. "No, honestly. I didn't. But I'm quite honored." He looks down at the box. "What's this?"

"Open it."

He clumsily peels the rose-patterned drawer liner from the shoe box. The smile freezes, relaxes, and he reverently picks the first photo off the top of the pile and examines it. It's from when she was very small, riding on a tricycle. "Is this—"

"Darcy? Yes."

Do I detect a slight tremble in the fingers? He rubs a thumb over the surface of the photo, then gently places it back in the box. "I can't accept this." He won't look at me.

"Why not?" Mellow is at my elbow now. Edward arches his eyebrows and studies the pair of us.

"And you are...?"

She sticks her hand out. "Mellow."

"Ah." He shakes her hand limply, then returns his gaze to me. "So how did you get here? You certainly didn't fly, did you?"

"I drove. But that's not really important."

"Oh, but it is," he says, glancing over my shoulder again. "Come with me."

He leads us through a small door that looks like part of the paneling and shuts it softly behind us. The quiet room smells of expensive furniture polish and musty antiques.

"Now." He beams at me, shyly. "How did you get here? Who is this girl? Why are you giving the box to me?"

Mellow steps forward. "You pretty much ruined her life, you know."

"I hardly think I—"

"But you did." She takes a menacing step toward him, which is somewhat less menacing because of the nipple dress. "She told me all about what you did to her. I don't know a lot, and I've been living on the road for practically my whole life, but I know one thing—you don't play with peoples' minds. Especially when they're hurt. So…"

He leans against a mahogany desk, as if she's threatening him, which is ridiculous since he's about two feet taller. His eyes are on me, though. "I never meant to do anything but help you, Anna."

"I know that." I gently put an arm around Mellow's shoulder and pull her back. "Thank you," I say to her. "You've helped me much more than I thought anyone could."

"Thank you—" he grins, blushing.

"No, I mean her." I gaze, unblinking, into his eyes, and realize that this will probably be the last time I see him. "It was random chance that brought us together, but I was on the road because of you, Edward. What you did wasn't right, but it wasn't wrong either, really. You wanted me to move on, and I did, I moved on and toward you. But you weren't the solution. You were the vehicle."

He's beaming at me, his smile wider. "But that's fantastic. All I wanted was for you to face your past. That's really all."

"Then why did you invite her to your wedding?" Mellow asks, anger coloring her voice. I arch my scant eyebrows and stare at him.

"I…It wasn't…I never meant for you to come here," he said, gesturing with his hands. "I know this isn't your world. You're not comfortable here. I just thought…it would make it easier for you. If you knew I was getting married."

"But you never...you didn't feel..." I can't even articulate it. "What about the times when you kissed me?"

He blushes violently and stares at the Aubusson rug. "That was a mistake. My mistake."

"Yeah, but why did you do it in the first place?" Mellow hisses, stepping even closer to him. "You knew she was fragile. Why would you do that?"

This man, this man I thought I loved and who loved me, is cowed by the fierceness of this little girl. His lips drawn in a tight line, he shakes his head and says, almost imperceptibly, "I thought it would help her. I really did."

"But you didn't really love her?" Mellow whispers in his ear, close enough to touch.

He cannot answer.

And that was all I needed.

20
END OF THE ROAD

Windows rolled down, we cruise toward a melted orange ice cream sunset, Mellow letting her hand surf on the wind.

"Do you feel better now?" she asks.

"I do." The road winds ahead, and although I can't see where it goes exactly, I don't feel afraid of it anymore. I know that I am worthy of love, and that not everything is my fault.

"Are you going to grow out your hair then?"

I rub the stubble. "Not sure. I might keep it short. I like the freedom of it."

My wig, attached to the car's antenna, waves in the breeze, a trophy.

"What now, then?"

"I don't know. Should I drop you off somewhere? Do you have some aunts or uncles who aren't drug-addled morons?"

"I have aunts and uncles somewhere, but I don't know where that is, and it's really likely that they *are*, in fact, drug-addled morons." She props her feet on the dash and attempts to paint her toenails at 65 mph.

"So, then, I guess we should look for your mother?"

In answer, she just makes a contorted goofy face at me.

"So, you're coming with me? To California?"

"Why not? What else do I have to do?" She messes up one of her pinky toes, smearing it with crimson. "Dammit. At least it's a little toe. Nobody can ever even see those anyway."

"But look. I'm not set up for a child—"

"I'm not a child."

I look over at her. "No. I guess you're not."

"I can help you. I can be your, like, Girl Friday, or whatever, your sidekick. I can clean your apartment."

"You can go to school." I put down the sun visor to block the waning orange light.

"Oh, Jesus, really? School?"

"I'm not living with a high school dropout."

She grins, and I can feel it even if I can't see it. "So, that means I'm living with you?"

I can't help but grin at her excitement. "It won't be easy. And somehow, I'd need to figure out how we do it, legally. I have no idea, honestly. I'd have to get a job, I guess, and we'd need a bigger place." The enormity of it hits me, but I decide to embrace it and give in to it. And to not be afraid. "But I guess the big question really is: knowing what you know and seeing what you've seen, do you *want* to live with me?"

"More than anything!" She leaps on me as I'm trying to drive, hugs me, and we nearly go off the road. I pull over to the shoulder so I don't kill us both, which would be an unhappy ending to a mostly unhappy story, and no one wants that.

Feeling this sweaty, messy girl clutching my back as if I'm a raft in a churning sea, I'm filled with apprehension, but also an unspeakable joy. And I realize I'm holding on to her as hard as she's holding on to me. I hug her, properly, and realize that sometimes, when you can't get what you want, you get what you need instead.

ACKNOWLEDGMENTS

I have many people to thank for helping bring *Anna Incognito* to the printed page.

My Publishizer campaign is what made this possible. Thanks to Guy Vincent and Lee Constantine for coming up with a great model for matching authors and publishers.

My backers (who pre-ordered the book) include super backers Don Victor, Bob Vryheid, Steve Montgomery, Tershia D'elgin, Virgil Mann, Jon Schwaiger, Linda Boyed, Nathan Bassetti, and Shaun Davis.

And I have to thank my family: Chris Klich, Noel Klich, Austin Klich, my pups, and also Don Loper and Beth Gunter for proofreading. Thanks to Nina Spahn at Mascot for meticulous edits.

Additional backers were Alexandra Hart, Amie Wilson, Angela "Kay"Loftis, Angela Jones, Ann Preble, Anneke Doty, Barbara Wilson, Barrie Summy, Becky Armour, Billie Fogle, Bill Andrews, Brooke Kesinger, Bruce Levine, Camille Vernon, Candice Hepworth, Carla Nell, Carolyn Teschler, Carrie Williams, Cass Fey, Catherine Tschilitsch, Chansamone O'Meara, Cheance Adair, Chelsea Ramet, Chelsea Betancourt, Christina Newton, Christine Rose, Clarissa Meckstroth, Connie Henry, Dan Tricarico, Darla Peterson, David Cardenas, Deirdre Oakley, Delia Knight, Denise Cabrera, Don Loper, Donna Feoranzo, Duane Daniels, Elizabeth DeMars, Erin Lewis, Geneva Wallace, Gil Quintana, Holiday Adair, Janal Urich, Jean Bergeson, Jeff and Pam Stevens, Jennifer Randall-Valdes, Jennifer Wilson, Jerry Burkey, Jill Harris, Jill Coffey, Jincy Kornhauser, Joel Miller, John Gilmore, John Freeman,, Jonathan Hammond, Julie Brossy, John and Julie Harland, Julissa Cota, Jyl Kaneshiro, Kaly McKenna, Karen Hammond, Karen Orosco, Katie Leonard, Kim Covert, Kit Stowell, Kurt Kalbfleisch, Kym Pappas, Lane Shefter Bishop, Lisa Stewart, Loree Trim, Lucy Palmer, Madelyn Moydell, Maggie Willingham, Marilynn Zeljeznjak, Marissa Henry, Martha Sullivan, Martin Dean, Mary Jarsma, Mary Kresena, Megan Barahura, Michael Johnson, Michelle Beauchamp, Monika Lee, Olga Flores, Paige Shapiro, Paige Dillard, Pam Howard, Patricia Castillo, Randall Dobbins, Rhiannon McAfee, Robert Scally, Robin Brockman, Samantha Clark, Sarah Baker, Scott Havey, Shelley Lekven, Stephanie Macceca, Stormie Graham, Sue Holcombe, Susan Arthur, Susan Murray, Susan Duerksen, Suzanne Sannwald, Tali Nadav, Tammy Steeves, Tim Flint, Tokeli Baker, and Yvonne Rini.